He froze, staring at the mirror.

He turned his head to the right and then to the left. The face in the mirror moved when he moved. It definitely belonged to him.

But it was the face of a stranger.

A wave of dizziness hit him hard and he grabbed at the sink, lowering his head and closing his eyes until the worst of it passed.

How did he get here? Almighty God, he couldn't even remember his name.

Suddenly feeling something in his shoe, he went into a corner of the room and started to pull off one of his boots. And then he quickly pulled it back on again.

He was carrying a side arm. A .22 caliber.

In his boot.

Dear Reader,

Once again, Silhouette Intimate Moments brings you an irresistible lineup of books, perfect for curling up with on a winter's day. Start with Sharon Sala's *A Place To Call Home,* featuring a tough city cop who gets away to the Wyoming high country looking for some peace and quiet. Instead he finds a woman in mortal danger and realizes he has to help her—because, without her, his heart will never be whole.

For all you TALL, DARK AND DANGEROUS fans, Suzanne Brockmann is back with *Identity: Unknown.* Navy SEAL Mitchell Shaw has no memory of who—or what—he is when he shows up at the Lazy 8 Ranch. And ranch manager Becca Keyes can't help him answer those questions, though she certainly raises another: How can he have a future without her in it? Judith Duncan is back with *Marriage of Agreement,* a green-card marriage story filled with wonderful characters and all the genuine emotion any romance reader could want. In *His Last Best Hope,* veteran author Susan Sizemore tells a suspenseful tale in which nothing is quite what it seems but everything turns out just the way you want. With her very first book, New Zealander Fiona Brand caught readers' attention. *Heart of Midnight* brings back Gray Lombard and reunites him with the only woman strong enough to be his partner for life. Finally, welcome Yours Truly author Karen Templeton to the line. *Anything for His Children* is an opposites-attract story featuring three irresistible kids who manage to teach both the hero and the heroine something about the nature of love.

Enjoy every one of these terrific novels, and then come back next month for six more of the best and most exciting romances around.

Yours,

Leslie J. Wainger
Executive Senior Editor

Please address questions and book requests to:
Silhouette Reader Service
U.S.: 3010 Walden Ave., P.O. Box 1325, Buffalo, NY 14269
Canadian: P.O. Box 609, Fort Erie, Ont. L2A 5X3

IDENTITY: UNKNOWN

SUZANNE BROCKMANN

Published by Silhouette Books

America's Publisher of Contemporary Romance

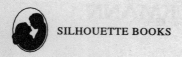 **SILHOUETTE BOOKS**

ISBN 0-373-07974-5

IDENTITY: UNKNOWN

Visit us at www.romance.net

Printed in U.S.A.

Books by Suzanne Brockmann

Silhouette Intimate Moments

Hero Under Cover #575
Not Without Risk #647
A Man To Die For #681
*Prince Joe #720
*Forever Blue #742
*Frisco's Kid #759
Love with the Proper Stranger #831
*Everyday, Average Jones #872
*Harvard's Education #884
*It Came Upon a Midnight Clear #896
*The Admiral's Bride #962
†Undercover Princess #968
*Identity: Unknown #974

*Tall, Dark and Dangerous
†Royally Wed

SUZANNE BROCKMANN

lives just west of Boston in a house always filled with her friends—actors and musicians and storytellers and artists and teachers. When not writing award-winning romances about U.S. Navy SEALs, among others, she sings in an a cappella group called SERIOUS FUN, manages the professional acting careers of her two children, volunteers at the Appalachian Benefit Coffeehouse and always answers letters from readers. Send her a SASE along with your letter to P.O. Box 5092, Wayland, MA 01778.

For Lee Brockmann

Chapter 1

"**H**ey, hey, hey there, Mission Man! How ya doin', baby? Rise and shine! *That's* my man—open those eyes. It's *def*initely the a.m. and in the a.m. here at the First Church Shelter, we go from horizontal to vertical."

Pain. His entire world had turned into a trinity of pain, bright lights and an incredibly persistent voice. He tried to turn away, tried to burrow down into the hard mattress of the cot, but hands shook him—gently at first, then harder.

"Yo, Mish. I know it's early, man, but we've got to get these beds cleaned up and put away. We're serving up a nice warm breakfast along with an A.A. meeting in just a few minutes. Why don't you give it a try? Sit and listen, even if your stomach can't handle the chow."

A.A. Alcoholics Anonymous. Could it possibly be a hangover that was making him feel as if he'd been hit by a tank? He tried to identify the sour taste in his mouth but couldn't. It was only bitter. He opened his eyes again, and again his head felt split in two. But this time he clenched his teeth, forcing his eyes to focus on a smiling, cheerful, weather-beaten African-American face.

"I knew you could do it, Mish." The voice belonged to the face. "How you doin', man? Remember me? Remember your good friend Jarell? That's right, I tucked you into this bed last night. Come on, let's get you up and headed toward the men's room. You could use a serious washing up, my man."

"Where am I?" His own voice was low, rough and oddly unfamiliar to his ears.

"The First Church Homeless Shelter, on First Avenue."

The pain was relentless, but now it was mixed with confusion as he slowly, achingly sat up. "First Avenue...?"

"Hmm," the man named Jarell made a face. "Looks like you had yourself a bigger binge than I thought. You're in Wyatt City, friend. In New Mexico. Ring any bells?"

He started to shake his head, but the hellish pain intensified. He held himself very still instead, supporting his forehead with his hands. "No." He spoke very softly, hoping Jarell would do the same. "How did I get here?"

"A couple of Good Sams brought you in last night." Jarell hadn't gotten the hint, and continued as loud as ever. "Said they found you taking a little nap with your nose in a puddle, a few blocks over in the alley. I checked your pockets for your wallet, but it was gone. Seems you'd already been rolled. I'm surprised they didn't take those pretty cowboy boots of yours. From the looks of things, though, they *did* take the time to kick you while you were down."

He brought his hand to the side of his head. His hair

was filthy, and it felt crusty, as if it were caked with blood and muck.

"Come on and wash up, Mission Man. We'll get you back on track. Today's a brand-new day, and here at the shelter, the past does *not* equal the future. From here on in, you can start your life anew. Whatever's come before can just be swept away." Jarell laughed, a rich, joyful sound. "Hey, you've been here more than six hours, Mish. You can get your six-hour chip. You know that saying, One Day at a Time? Well, here on First Avenue, we say one *hour* at a time."

He let Jarell help him to his feet. The world spun, and he closed his eyes for a moment.

"You got those feet working yet, Mish? That's my man. One foot in front of the other. Bathroom's dead ahead. Can you make it on your own?"

"Yes." He wasn't sure that he could, but he would have said nearly anything to get away from Jarell's too-loud, too-cheerful, too-friendly voice. Right now the only friend he wanted near him was the blessed, healing silence of unconsciousness.

"You come on out after you get cleaned up," the old man called after him. "I'll help you get some food for both your belly and your soul."

He left Jarell's echoing laughter behind and pushed the men's-room door open with a shaking hand. All of the sinks were occupied, so he leaned against the cool tile of the wall, waiting for a turn to wash.

The large room was filled with men, but none of them spoke. They moved quietly, gingerly, apologetically, careful not to meet anyone's eyes. They were careful not to trespass into one another's personal space even with a glance.

He caught a glimpse of himself in the mirror. He was

just another one of them—disheveled and unkempt, hair uncombed, clothes ragged and dirty. He had the bonus of a darkening patch of blood on his dirt-stained T-shirt, the bright red turning as dingy as the rest of him as it dried.

A sink opened up, and he moved toward it, picking up a bar of plain white soap to scrub the grime from his hands and upper arms before he tackled his face. What he truly needed was a shower. Or a hosing down. His head still throbbed, and he moved it carefully, leaning toward the mirror, trying to catch a look at the gash above his right ear.

The wound was mostly covered by his dark shaggy hair and…

He froze, staring at the face in front of him. He turned his head to the right and then to the left. The face in the mirror moved when he moved. It definitely belonged to him.

But it was the face of a stranger.

It was a lean face, with high cheekbones. It had a strong chin that badly needed a shave, except for a barren spot marked by a jagged white scar. A thin-lipped mouth cut a grim line, and two feverish-looking eyes that weren't quite brown and weren't quite green stared back at him. Tiny squint lines surrounded the edges of those eyes, as if this face had spent a good share of its time in the hot sun.

He filled his hands with water, splashing it up and onto his face. When he looked into the mirror again, the same stranger looked back at him. He hadn't managed to wash that face away and reveal…what? A more familiar visage?

He closed his eyes, trying to recall features that would've been more recognizable.

He came up blank.

A wave of dizziness hit him hard and he grabbed at the sink, lowering his head and closing his eyes until the worst of it passed.

How did he get here? Wyatt City, New Mexico. It was a small city, a town really, in the southern part of the state. It wasn't his home...was it? He must've been here working on...working on...

He couldn't remember.

Maybe he was still drunk. He'd heard about people who'd had so much to drink they went into a blackout. Maybe that was what this was. Maybe all he'd have to do was sleep this off and everything he was having trouble remembering would come back to him.

Except he couldn't remember drinking.

His head hurt like the devil. Heaven knew all he wanted to do was curl up in a ball and sleep until the pounding in his brain stopped.

He leaned down into the sink and tried to rinse the cut on the side of his head. The lukewarm water stung, but he closed his eyes and persisted until he was sure it was clean. Long hair dripping, he blotted himself dry with some paper towels, gritting his teeth as the rough paper scraped against his abraded skin.

It was too late to get stitches. The wound had already started to scab. He was going to have a scar from this one, but maybe some butterfly bandages would help. He'd need his first-aid kit and... And... He stared at himself in the mirror. First-aid kit. He wasn't a doctor. How could he be a doctor? And yet...

The men's-room door opened with a bang, and he spun around, reaching beneath his jacket for... Reaching for...

Dizzy, he staggered back against the sink. He wasn't wearing a jacket, just this sorry T-shirt. And sweet Lord help him, but he had to remember not to move fast or he'd end up falling on his face.

"The Ladies' Auxiliary is having a clothing drive," one of the shelter workers announced in a too-loud voice that made many of the men in the room cringe. "We've got a box of clean T-shirts, and another one full of blue jeans. Please take only what you need and save some for the next guy."

He looked up into the mirror at the stained and grimy T-shirt he wore. It had been white at one time—probably just last night, although he still couldn't remember back that far. He pulled it up and over his head, gingerly avoiding the wound above his right ear.

"Dirty laundry goes into this basket over here," the shelter worker trumpeted. "If it's labeled, you'll get it back. If it's torn, throw it out and take two." The worker looked up at him. "What size do you need?"

"Medium." It was something of a relief to finally know the answer to a question.

"You in need of jeans?"

He looked down. The black pants he was wearing were badly torn. "I could use some, yeah. Thirty-two waist, thirty-four inseam, if you've got 'em." He knew *that,* too.

"You're the one Jarell called the Mission Man," the shelter worker remarked as he searched through the box. "He's a good guy—Jarell. A little too religious for my taste, but that wouldn't bother you, would it? He's always giving everyone nicknames. Mission Man. Mish. What kind of name is Mish anyway?"

His name. It was…*his* name? It was, but it wasn't. He shook his head, trying to clear it, trying to remember his *name.*

Dammit, he couldn't even remember his *name.*

"Here's a pair what's got a thirty-three-inch waist,"

the shelter worker told him. ''That's the best I can do for you, Mish.''

Mish. He took the jeans, briefly closing his eyes so that the room would stop spinning around him, calming himself. So what if he couldn't remember his name? It would come back to him. With a good night's sleep, it would *all* come back to him.

He told himself that again and again, using it like a mantra. He was going to be fine. Everything was going to be fine. All he needed was a chance to close his eyes.

He went into the corner of the room, out of the line of traffic around the sinks and stalls, and started to pull off one of his boots.

He quickly pulled it back on again.

He was carrying a side arm. A .22-caliber.

In his boot.

It was slightly larger than palm-sized, black and deadly looking. There was something else in his boot, too. He could feel it now, pressing against his ankle.

He took his jeans into one of the stalls, locking the door behind him. Slipping off the boot, he looked inside. The .22 was still there, along with an enormous fold of cash— all big bills. There was nothing smaller than a hundred in the thick rubber-banded wad.

He flipped through it quickly. He was carrying more than five thousand dollars in his boot.

There was something else there, too. A piece of paper. There was writing on it, but his vision swam, blurring the letters.

He took off the other boot, but there was nothing in that one. He searched the pockets of his pants, but came up empty there, too.

He stripped off his pants and pulled on the clean jeans, careful to brace himself against the metal wall the entire time. His world was tilting, and he was in constant danger of losing his balance.

He slipped his boots back on, somehow knowing how to position the weapon so that it wouldn't bother him. How could he know that, know what size jeans he wore, yet not know his own name? He put most of the money and the piece of paper back in his boot as well, leaving several hundred dollars in the front pocket of his jeans.

He came face-to-face with his reflection in the mirror when he opened the door of the stall.

Even dressed in clean clothes, even washed up, long, dark hair slicked back with water, even pale and gray from the pain that still pounded through his battered body, he looked like a man most folks would take a wide detour around. His chin had a heavy growth of stubble, accentuating his already sun-darkened complexion. His black T-shirt had been washed more than once and had shrunk slightly. It hugged his upper body, outlining the muscles of his chest and arms. He looked like a fighter, hard and lean.

Whatever he really did for a living, he *still* couldn't remember. But considering that .22 he had hidden in his boot, he could probably cross kindergarten teacher off the list of possibilities.

Rolling up his torn pants, he tucked them under his arms. He pushed open the men's-room door and skirted the room where breakfast and temperance were being served. Instead, he headed directly for the door that led to the street.

On his way out, as he passed the shelter's donation box, he dropped a hundred-dollar bill inside.

"Mr. Whitlow! Wait!"
Rebecca Keyes headed for Silver at a dead run, swing-

ing herself up into the saddle and digging her boots into the big gelding's sides. Silver surged forward, in hot pursuit of the gleaming white limousine that was pulling down the dude ranch's dirt driveway.

"Mr. Whitlow!" She put two fingers in her mouth and whistled piercingly, and finally the vehicle slowed.

Silver blew out a loud burst of air as she reined him in next to the almost absurdly stretched-out body of the car. With a faint mechanical whine, the window came down and Justin Whitlow's ruddy face appeared. He didn't look happy.

"I'm sorry, sir," Becca said breathlessly from her perch atop Silver. "Hazel told me you were leaving, that you were going to be gone a *month* and I... I wish you had informed me earlier, sir. We have several things to discuss that can't wait an entire month."

"If this is more of your wages garbage—"

"No, sir—"

"Thank God."

"—because it's *not* garbage. It's a very real problem we're having here at the Lazy Eight. We're not paying the ranch hands enough money, so they're not sticking around. Did you know we've just lost Rafe McKinnon, Mr. Whitlow?"

Whitlow stuck a cigarette between his lips, squinting up at her as he lit it. "Hire someone new."

"That's what I've been doing with staff turnovers," she said with barely concealed frustration. "Hiring someone new. And someone else new. And..." She drew in a deep breath and tried her best to sound reasonable. "If we'd simply paid someone solid and responsible like Rafe another two or three dollars an hour—"

"Then he would've asked for another raise next year."

"Which he would have deserved. Frankly, Mr. Whitlow, I don't know where I'm going to find another stable hand like Rafe. He was a good man. He was reliable and intelligent and—''

"He was obviously overqualified. I wish him luck at his next endeavor. We don't need to hire rocket scientists, for God's sake. And how reliable do you need a man to be, to shovel—''

"Mucking out the stalls is only a small part of the job description," Becca countered hotly. She took a deep breath, forcing herself to calm down again. She'd never won a shouting match with her boss, and she wasn't likely to start winning that way now. "Mr. Whitlow, I don't know how you expect the Lazy Eight to gain the reputation of being a high-class dude ranch if you insist on paying your staff slave wages."

"Slave wages for slave labor," Whitlow commented.

"My point exactly," Becca said, but he just blew cigarette smoke out the window.

"Don't forget about that opera thing in Santa Fe next week," he commanded as, with a soft buzz, his window began to shut. "I'm counting on you to be there. And for heaven's sake, dress like a woman. None of those pant-suits that you wore last time."

"Mr. Whitlow—''

But the window closed tightly. She had been dismissed. Silver sidled to the right as the limo pulled away and Becca swore pungently.

Slave wages for slave labor, indeed. Except Whitlow had it wrong. He believed he was paying his staff low wages for low-priority, bottom-of-the-barrel, physical-labor jobs. But the truth was, without those jobs done and done well, the entire ranch suffered. And if the owner insisted on paying low, the quality of work he'd get in return would also be low. Or the workers would leave—

like Rafe McKinnon had, and Tom Morgan last week, and Bob Sharp earlier in the month.

It seemed all Becca did these days was office work. Far too often, she found herself sitting inside, behind her desk, doing phone interviews to fill all-too-frequently-vacated staff positions.

She'd taken this job at the Lazy Eight Ranch because it was an opportunity to use her management skills *and* put in most of her hours out-of-doors.

She loved riding, loved the hot New Mexico sun, loved the way the storm clouds raced across the plains, loved the reds and browns and muted greens of the mountains. She loved the Lazy Eight Ranch.

But working for Justin Whitlow was the pits. And who said a woman couldn't look feminine in a pair of pants, anyway? What did he expect her to wear to schmooze with *his* friends and business associates? Something extremely low-cut, with sequins? As if she could even afford such a thing on her pitiful salary.

Yes, she loved it here, but if things didn't change, it was only a matter of time before *she* walked, too.

The night was moonless, but he lay quietly on his stomach, taking the time for his eyes to get fully used to the dark again, and in particular the dark here, just inside of the high-security fence.

He breathed with the sounds of the night—crickets and bullfrogs and the trees whispering overhead in the gentle wind.

He could see the house on the hill, and he silently crept closer on his knees and elbows, staying low, staying invisible.

He stopped, smelling the cigarette before he saw the

red glow of light. The man was alone. Far enough away from the house.

He silently lifted his rifle, double-checking it before he sighted along the sniper's scope. He brought the night-vision setting up a notch so he could really look at the target. And the man with the cigarette *was* the target. Not the gardener out for a late-night stroll. Not the chef hunting for the perfect variety of wild mushrooms. No, he recognized this man's face from the photos he'd seen. He gently squeezed the trigger and...

Boom.

The muffled sound of the gunshot still managed to pierce his eardrums, set his teeth on edge, stab through his brain.

Eyes wide open, he sat up, instantly aware that he'd been dreaming. The only noise in the dimly lit room was his ragged breathing.

But the room was unfamiliar, and he felt a new wave of panic. Where in hell was he now?

Wherever it was, it was a far cry from the church shelter he'd woken up in yesterday morning.

His gaze swept across the impersonal furnishings, the cheesy oil paintings on the wall, and it came to him. Motel room. Yes, he'd checked in to this place yesterday morning, after leaving the shelter. His head had been pounding, and he'd wanted only to fall into bed and sleep.

He'd paid in cash and signed the registration M. Man.

Heavy curtains were pulled across the windows, letting in only a tiny sliver of bright morning light. Hands still shaking from his dream, he pushed the covers off, aware that the sheets were soaked with his own sweat. His head still felt tender, but no longer as if the slightest movement would make him want to scream.

He could remember, almost word for word, the brief

conversation he'd had with the man at the motel's front desk. He remembered the aromatic smell of coffee in the motel lobby. He remembered the clerk's name—Ron—worn on a badge on his chest. He remembered how endlessly long it had taken Ron to find the key to room 246. He remembered pulling himself up the stairs, one step at a time, driven by the knowledge that soothing darkness and a soft bed were within reach.

He could remember that dream he'd just had, too, and he didn't want to think about what it might mean.

He stood up, aware that the movement jarred him only slightly, and crossed to the air conditioner, turning it to a higher setting. The fan motor kicked in with a louder hum, and coolness hit him in a wave of canned air.

Slowly, deliberately, he sat back down on the edge of the bed.

He could remember the shelter. He could see Jarell's smiling face, hear the sound of his cheerful voice. *Hey, Mission Man. Hey, Mish!*

He closed his eyes and relaxed his shoulders, waiting for memories of being brought into the shelter, waiting for memories of what had happened that night.

But there was nothing there.

There was only…emptiness. Nothingness. As if before he'd been brought to the First Avenue Shelter, he hadn't existed.

He could feel a new sheen of perspiration covering his body despite the cooler setting of the air conditioner. He'd slept off whatever had ailed him—whether it was the result of alcohol or some other controlled substance or simply the blow he'd received to his head. In fact, he'd slept solidly for more than twenty-four hours.

So why the hell couldn't he remember his own damned name?

Hey, Mission Man. Hey, Mish!

He stood up, staggering slightly in his haste to get to the mirror that covered the wall in front of a double set of sinks. He flipped on the light and...

He remembered the face that looked back at him. He remembered it—but only from the bathroom mirror at the shelter. Before that, there was...

Nothing.

"Mish." He spoke aloud the nickname Jarell had given him. The word sent a small ripple of recognition through him again, as it had yesterday morning. But what kind of name was Mish? Was it possible that he remembered— very faintly—Jarell calling him that when he was first brought into the shelter?

Mish. He gazed into the unfamiliar swirl of green and brown that were his own eyes. What kind of name was Mish? Well, right now, it was the only name he'd got.

Mish splashed cold water on his face, then cupped his hand under the faucet and drank deeply.

What was he supposed to do now? Go to the police?

No, that was out of the question. He couldn't do that. He wouldn't be able to explain the .22 and that huge wad of money he was carrying in his boot. He knew—he didn't know how he knew, but he did—that he couldn't tell the police, couldn't tell *any*one anything. He couldn't let anyone know why he was here.

Not that he could have, even if he'd wanted to. *He* didn't know why he was here.

So what was he supposed to do?

Check himself into a hospital? He turned his head, gingerly parting his hair to look at the gash on his head. Without yesterday's fog of pain clouding his eyes, he knew with a chilling certainty that the wound on his head had been the result of a bullet's glancing blow. He'd been shot, nearly killed.

No, he couldn't go to a hospital, either—they'd be forced to report his injury to the police.

He dried his face and hands on a small white towel and went back into the main part of the motel room. His boots were on the floor near the bed, where he'd left them last night. He picked up the right one, dumping its contents onto the rumpled sheets. He turned on the light and sat down, picking up the .22.

It fit perfectly, familiarly into his hand. He couldn't remember his own name, but somehow he knew he'd be able to use this weapon with deadly accuracy if the need ever arose. This weapon, and any other, as well. He remembered his dream, and he set it back down on the bed.

He pulled the rubber band off the fold of money, and the piece of white paper that was fastened along with it slipped free. It was fax paper; the slippery, shiny kind that was hard to read. He picked it up and angled it toward the light.

"Lazy Eight Ranch," he read. Again, the name was totally unfamiliar to him. There was an address and directions to some kind of spread up in the northern part of the state. From what he could tell from the directions, it was about four hours outside of Santa Fe. The words were all typed, except for a note scrawled across the bottom in big round handwriting. "Looking forward to meeting you." It was signed, "Rebecca Keyes."

Mish opened the bedside-table drawer, looking for a telephone book. But the only thing inside was a Gideons Bible. He picked up the phone and dialed the front desk.

"Yeah, is there a train station or a bus depot in town?" he asked when the desk clerk came on the line.

"Greyhound's just down the street."

"Can you give me the phone number?"

He silently repeated the number the clerk gave him, hung up, then dialed the phone.

He was going to Santa Fe.

Chapter 2

Becca was out front, helping Belinda and Dwayne welcome a van load of guests, when she first spotted him.

He would have been very easy to miss—the solitary figure of a man walking slowly along the road. Yet even from this distance, she could tell that he was different. He didn't have the nonchalant swagger of the cowboys that worked the nearby ranches. He didn't carry the bags and sacks of crafts and jewelry that many of the local Native Americans took into Santa Fe to sell. He had only one small bag, efficiently tucked under one arm.

He turned into the Lazy Eight's long drive, as somehow Becca had known he would.

As he drew closer, she could see he wasn't wearing the Western gear that was the standard outfit of the Southwest. He had on the blue jeans, but he wore a new-looking T-shirt instead of a long-sleeved Western-cut button-down shirt. His arms were deeply tanned, as if he spent quite a bit of time outside.

His black boots weren't the kind a real cowboy would wear, and he wore a baseball cap instead of a Stetson on his head.

From a distance, he'd looked tall and imposing. Up close, he merely looked imposing. It was odd, really. He had to be at least an inch or so shorter than six feet, and he was slender, almost slight. Yet there was a power about him, a quiet strength that seemed to radiate from him.

It may have been in the set of his shoulders or the angle of his chin. Or it may have been something in his dark eyes that made her want to step back a bit and keep her distance. His gaze swept across the drive, over the van and the luggage and the guests, over the ranch house, over the corral where Silver was waiting impatiently for another chance to stretch his legs, over Belinda and Dwayne, over *her*. With one quick flick of his eyes, he seemed to take her in, to memorize, appraise, and then dismiss.

Becca tried to look away, but she couldn't.

He was impossibly, harshly handsome—provided, of course, that a woman went for the dark and dangerous type. His face was slightly weathered, with high cheekbones that even Johnny Depp would've been jealous of. His lips were gracefully shaped, if perhaps a shade too thin, too grimly set. His dark hair was longer than she'd first thought, worn fastened back at the nape of his neck. His face was smooth-shaven, but he had a scar on his chin that added to his aura of danger. And those eyes...

Becca watched as he approached Belinda. He spoke softly—too softly for Becca to hear his words—as he drew a piece of paper from his pocket.

Belinda turned and pointed directly at Becca. He turned, too, and once again those eyes were on her, coolly appraising.

He started toward her.

Becca came down the ranch office steps, meeting him halfway, pushing her beatup Stetson further back on her short brown curls. "Can I help you?"

"You're Rebecca Keyes." His voice was soft and accentless. His words weren't a question, but she answered him anyway.

"That's right." His eyes weren't dark brown as she'd first thought. They were hazel—an almost otherworldly mix of green and brown and yellow and blue. She was staring. She knew she was staring, but she couldn't seem to stop.

"You sent me this fax?"

This time it *was* a question. Becca forced her gaze away from his face and looked down at the paper he held in his hands. It was indeed fax paper. She recognized the standard directions to the ranch, caught sight of the messy scribble of her handwriting at the bottom. "You must be Casey Parker."

He repeated the name slowly. "Casey Parker."

He didn't look the way he'd sounded during their telephone interview. She'd pictured a larger, older, beefier man. But no matter. She needed a hired hand, and all of his references had checked out.

"Do you have any ID?" Becca asked. She smiled to soften her words and explained. "It has more to do with filling out employee tax forms than verifying that you're who you say you are."

He shook his head. "I'm sorry, I don't. My wallet was stolen night before last. I got into some kind of fight and…"

As if to prove his story, he took off his hat and she could see a long scrape above his right temple, disappearing into his wavy dark hair. He had a bruise on his cheekbone, too. She hadn't noticed it at first—it was barely discernible underneath the suntanned darkness of his skin.

"I hope you don't make a habit of getting into fights."

He smiled. It was just a slight upward curve of his lips, yet it managed to soften his harsh features. "I hope not, too."

"You're a week early," Becca told him, hoping her briskness would counteract the effect his quiet smile and strange words had had on her, "but that's good, because another hand quit on me yesterday."

He was silent, just standing there watching her with those eyes that seemed to see everything. For a moment, she was almost convinced he could see back in time, to yesterday morning's disastrous conversation with Justin Whitlow, and back even further to Rafe McKinnon's quiet resignation. For a moment, she was almost convinced he could see her anger and her frustration and her defeat.

"You *do* still want the job...?" she asked, suddenly afraid that he didn't like what he saw. After all, bad things always came in threes.

He turned, squinting slightly at the blinding blueness of the summer sky. His gaze swept across the valley, and Becca was certain that unlike most people, this man saw, really *saw* the stark New Mexico countryside. She was sure that with his intense hazel eyes, he could see the terrible, almost painful beauty of the land.

"You own this place?" he asked in his quiet voice.

"I wish." The words came out automatically and all too heartfelt. As his eyes flicked in her direction, she felt exposed—as if, with those two little words, she'd given too much of herself away.

But he just nodded, his lips curving very slightly in the beginnings of a smile.

"Who *does* own it?" he asked. "I like to know the name of the man I'm working for."

"The owner's name is Justin Whitlow," Becca told him. "He's the one who pays your wages. But I'm the boss. You'll be working for *me*."

He nodded again, turning back to gaze out at the vista, but not before she saw a glimmer of amusement in his dark eyes. "I don't have a problem with that," he said quietly.

"Some men do."

"I'm not some men." He looked back at her again, and Becca knew without a doubt that his words were true. This quiet, slender man with the watchful hazel eyes wasn't just "some men."

But exactly what kind of man he was, she didn't know for sure.

"Hey, babe, long time no see." Lt. Lucky O'Donlon of U.S. Navy SEAL Team Ten's Alpha Squad pulled Veronica Catalanotto into his arms and kissed her hello as he came into the kitchen of his captain's house.

"Luke. Hi. Did Frankie let you in?" Ronnie's smile was warm and she seemed genuinely glad to see him. And since she was one of the top ten most beautiful, nicest, smartest women he'd ever met, that welcoming smile was going to be good for quite a number of fantasy miles. But then she went and ruined it by smiling exactly the same way at Bobby and Wes, who had come in behind him. "How was your trip, boys?" she asked in her extremely classy British accent.

Captain Joe Catalanotto's wife always called the intensely dangerous and highly covert operations that Alpha Squad was sent out on "trips." As if they'd been away sightseeing or visiting museums.

Wes rolled his eyes. "Oh, man, Ron, we came really close to being cluster—"

Bobby's size extra-extra-large elbow went solidly into his swim buddy's side.

"Fine," Wes said quickly. "It was fine, Ronnie. As always. Thanks for asking, though."

Veronica wasn't fooled. Her smile had faded, making her eyes look enormous in her face. "Is everyone all right? I mean, of course I've already asked Joe, but I'm not sure he'd even tell me if someone *had* been hurt."

Ever since a year and a half ago, when the captain had nearly been killed by terrorists on what should have been a routine training mission, Veronica looked even more fragile than she had before when the squad went out on an op. She'd never found it easy to deal with the fact that her husband regularly left—sometimes without any warning—on highly dangerous missions. And now, after seeing Joe in a hospital bed, fighting for his life, it was even more difficult for her.

"Everyone's fine," Lucky said quietly, taking her hand. *"Really."* Hotshot Cowboy Jones had jammed his ankle coming in too hard from a HALO jump, but aside from that, they'd all made it back to California in one piece.

Veronica smiled, but it was a little too bright and a touch too brittle. "Well," she said. "Joe's expecting you. He's down on the beach."

"Thanks." Lucky squeezed her hand before he released it.

"Should I set extra plates for dinner?" Veronica asked evenly.

Lucky exchanged a look with Bobby. The captain had called them to this meeting on their pagers, sending them an urgent code. Whatever was up was important. Despite the fact that they'd only been home a day and a half, chances were they'd be going wheels-up again within the next few hours. And knowing the way Joe Catalanotto liked to lead from the front, it was more than likely he'd be shipping out with them. It seemed, however, that he hadn't mentioned anything about that to his wife.

"I don't think so, Ronnie," Bobby told her gently. "Probably not this time. It really smells great, though. Those cooking lessons are paying off, huh?"

"I was working all day," she told him ruefully. "Joe made the stew."

Damn. The captain's wife may have been beautiful, smart and sexy as hell, but the woman was a menace in the kitchen.

"Are you sure you can't stay?" she added. "There's plenty and it's quite good. There's no way Joe and Frankie and I can possibly eat all of it."

"Something's come up. I think the captain's planning to take us kids out on another field trip," Wes told her before either Bobby or Lucky could muzzle him. Mr. Insensitive and Completely Oblivious. "So, yeah, we're sure we can't stay."

"Well," Veronica said tightly. "Off for another month, are you? Thanks for letting me know, although that's something that would've been nice to hear from Joe."

Double damn. Lucky cringed. "Ron, honest, I don't know what's up. If he didn't mention anything to you, well, maybe we're *not* going anywhere."

Veronica visibly composed herself. And sighed as she looked up into their somewhat panicked faces. "Don't look at me like that," she chided them. "I'm stronger than you think. I knew what I was getting before I married him. I don't have to like it when Joe leaves—isn't that what you SEALs always say? I don't have to like it, I just have to do it. Just take care of him for me, all right?''

She was pretending to hang tough, but her lower lip trembled an infinitesimal amount, giving her away. "Go," she said. "He's waiting. And you can tell him he doesn't have to worry about breaking the terrible news to me anymore."

Lucky followed Bobby and Wes out the kitchen door but hesitated on the deck, looking in through the window to watch her set only two places at the kitchen table—for herself and Frankie, her toddler son—still trying not to cry.

Lucky knew by the time Joe came back to the house, she'd be perfectly composed and probably even smiling.

Veronica's acceptance of Joe's career was a rare thing. SEALs had a divorce rate that was off the scale, in part because many of their wives simply couldn't take the strain of being left behind again and again and again, waiting and worrying.

"I'm never getting married," Lucky murmured to Wes as they went down the steps that led to the beach.

"You and me, Luck," Wes agreed. "Unless Ronnie decides to leave the captain. Or am I already too late? Have you already started marking your territory in a big circle around her? No offense, Lieutenant, sir, but that kiss was just a little too friendly."

Lucky was stung. "I was just saying hello. I'd never—"

"You'd never what, O'Donlon?" All six feet and four dangerous inches of Joe Cat materialized from the mist that was blowing in off the Pacific. One second they were alone and the next he was breathing down their necks. How the hell could a man built like a professional football player *do* that?

"I'd never hit on your wife," Lucky told his captain bluntly. There was no point in trying to hide the truth from Joe Cat. Somehow he'd find out—if he didn't already know. That's why he was the captain. "I'd never, ever, *ever* hit on Ronnie." Lucky shot Wes a disbelieving look. "I can't believe you think I'd do something that low, Skelly. My feelings are seriously hurt—"

"What's happening, Captain?" Bobby interrupted.

Joe Cat motioned towards the ocean. "We need to walk," he told them. "We really should be talking in a secured room, but getting one would raise too many eyebrows, and that's the last thing I want to do."

Whatever this was, it was bigger than Lucky had imagined. He stopped giving Wes dirty looks and focused on what the captain was saying.

But Joe was silent until they were next to the breaking surf. The beach was deserted and misty, the setting sun hidden behind clouds.

"I've been doing some work for Admiral Robinson," Joe Cat finally told them, his voice low. "Acting as a liaison for one of his longhairs who's out on a black op for the admiral's Gray Group."

Longhair was the name given to any SEAL who might need to blend in with a dangerous and motley crowd of terrorists and mercenaries at any given moment. He had to go on top-secret, extremely covert "black" operations, where a man with a military haircut would stick out like a sore thumb. And once that man stuck out, he would be one very dead sore thumb.

So these covert op SEALs got tattoos. They pierced their ears. They didn't shave for weeks on end. They dressed in what would have been known as "grunge" in the early nineties. And they grew their hair very, very long.

Of course, when it came to longhairs, the captain should talk. He wore his own hair in a thick, dark braid down his back. When he shook his hair out, he looked like a pirate or maybe a really wild rock star—and absolutely nothing like a highly decorated, extremely well-respected captain in Uncle Sam's Navy.

"The admiral's off doing diplo-duty in a place where it's impossible to get a secured telephone line," Joe Cat told them curtly. "I can't even report to him that as of twenty-four hours ago, his SEAL missed his weekly check-in. And frankly, I'm concerned. Apparently this guy's better than a clock when it comes to check-ins. So I've got to go out to New Mexico to try and track him down, and I need a team to watch my six."

New *Mexico?* What the…?

The captain looked at Bob, then Wes, then Lucky. "I'm looking for volunteers here. This will be a black op as well—completely off the record, no paperwork, no acknowledgement of the situation by any of the top brass. If you choose to come along, you'll be paid, but not in the usual way. In fact, you'll have to take leave so your whereabouts can't be traced."

It sounded like some serious fun. "Count me in, Skipper," Lucky said, and Bobby and Wes were only nanoseconds behind him.

Their captain nodded. "Thanks," he said quietly.

"Who's the little lost SEAL we're tracking down?" Wes asked. "Anyone we know?"

"Yeah," Joe said. "You worked with him six months ago. Lt. Mitchell Shaw."

"Oh, man," Bobby said in his basso profundo, voicing exactly what Lucky was thinking. "He's gonna be hard to find if he doesn't want to be found, Cat. He's a chameleon—good with disguises. The admiral once told me that he nearly pulled the hair off a little old lady, thinking she was Mitch under cover.''

''What's a Gray Group operative doing in New Mexico?'' Lucky asked.

''This is top-secret information I'm about to give you,'' Joe told them seriously. ''It goes no further than the four of us, understood?''

''Yes, sir.''

Joe sighed, turning to squint out at the ocean for a moment. ''Remember that break-in at Arches?''

Last year, the security at Arches Military Testing Lab in Colorado had been breached and six canisters of Triple X had been stolen. Lucky, Bobby, Wes and Mitch Shaw had all been part of the team that located and destroyed the deadly nerve gas. Yeah, they remembered that break-in all too clearly.

''The Trip X nerve agent wasn't the only thing taken,'' Joe Cat continued grimly.

Wes ran his hand down his face. ''I don't think I want to hear this.''

''Plutonium,'' Joe said. ''Enough was taken to make a small nuclear weapon.''

A small nuke. Great.

''Shaw was working to track it down,'' Joe Cat continued. ''He was following a lead both he and Admiral Robinson thought was probably empty. That's why he was out there alone. The bulk of the Gray Group's manpower is working from the other end—finding the potential buyer seemed easier than finding the plutonium in the haystack. But now that Shaw's gone missing, I'm not sure what's going on.''

''New Mexico's a big state,'' Bobby commented.

He was right. And if Mitch was working a black op,

he wouldn't have broadcast his whereabouts to anyone. "How the hell are we gonna find him?"

"Shaw was carrying ten counterfeit hundred-dollar bills," Joe answered Lucky. "Admiral Robinson implemented a technique used by the spooks at the Agency— apparently his wife's a former agent. See, how it works is if some bad voodoo goes down and the agent—or SEAL in this case—is eliminated by the opposition, that funny money tends to go into circulation. It makes sense, right? An agent is hit and his or her body disappears. But if you're the guy who did the hit, you check pockets for weapons or cash. No point in sinking *that* in the quarry with your victim's earthly remains, right? So the money changes hands, so to speak. In the past, this method has occasionally been effective enough to track all the way to the killers. Once they start spending the money—as soon as it's ID'd as fake—it's like a big red flag gets dropped."

"Are you saying you think Lieutenant Shaw is dead, sir?" Wes swore sharply. "I liked the guy."

"I don't know what's up with Shaw," Joe told them. "But one—and only one—of his counterfeit hundred-dollar bills showed up in Wyatt City, New Mexico. In the donation box of the First Church Homeless Shelter, of all places."

"When do we leave?" Bobby asked.

"We've got a flight out to Las Cruces in three hours," Joe said. He smiled crookedly. "I, um, need a little time. I haven't exactly told Ronnie yet that I'm leaving."

"Well, sir, we, uh…" Wes braced himself. "*I* kind of took care of that for you, Cat."

Joe closed his eyes and swore.

"I'm really sorry, Captain," Wes said.

"Skipper, you know… Me and Ren and Stimpy here can handle this. You don't have to come along—it'd be overkill anyway,'' Lucky earnestly told the captain. ''We've worked with Mitch, we know what he looks like—at least when he's not in disguise. And like you said, the rest of the Gray Group's covering the other end. Give yourself—and Veronica—a break.'' He paused. ''And give me a chance to practice those leadership skills they worked so hard to teach me at the academy, sir. Let me take care of this.''

Joe looked up at the hillside above the beach, at the warm lights of his home cutting through the thickening fog.

He made up his mind. ''Go,'' he said. ''The paperwork giving you leave is already at the base. But I want sit-reps over a secured line every twelve hours.''

''Thanks, Captain.'' Lucky held out his hand.

Joe clasped it and shook. ''Find him. Fast.''

''Are you Casey?''

Casey. Casey Parker. If that *was* his name, why couldn't he remember it? ''Yeah, that's me.''

A ten-year-old kid had come into the barn. He stood in front of Mish now, his eyes magnified by a crooked pair of wire-framed glasses. ''I'm supposed to tell you to saddle up a pair of horses for me and Ashley. Ashley's my sister. She's a pain in the butt.''

Saddle up some horses...

''What's your name?'' he asked the boy.

''My real name's Reagan. Reagan Thomas Alden. But people call me Chip.''

Mish turned back to the stall he was shoveling out. ''Rumor has it, Chip, guests under age eighteen aren't allowed to ride out on their own.''

''Yes, but...I'm not signed up for a ride until after *four o'clock*. What am I supposed to do until then?''

"Read a book?" Mish suggested, getting back into the easy rhythm of his work.

"Hey!" Chip brightened. "*You* could ride out with me and Ash. There's this place, about a half a mile east of here where there's these big, creepy-looking rocks, kind of like some giant's fingers sticking out of the ground. I could show 'em to you."

"I don't think so."

"Come on, Casey. You're not doing anything important right now."

Mish kept right on shoveling. "The way I figure it, I've got one of the most important jobs here—making sure the horses you ride have a clean place to sleep at night."

"Yes, but...wouldn't you rather be riding?"

Mish answered honestly. "No." The truth was, he could remember nothing about horses. If he'd at one time known how to ride, that knowledge had slipped away with his memories of his name and his past. But somehow he doubted that. Somehow, he got the sense that horseback riding was a subject he'd never bothered to learn much about.

It was troublesome. If he *was* Casey Parker, then he'd lied to get this job. And if he *wasn't* Casey Parker, then who in heaven's name *was* he?

Casey Parker or not, he couldn't shake the feeling that he wasn't going to like finding out who he really was.

The handgun in his boot. The wad of money. The bullet wound. It all added up to the same grim conclusion: he was not on the side of the angels.

If his dream had held just one ounce of truth, he was a killer. He was someone who shot and killed other people for a living. And, if that was the case, he didn't want to remember who he was.

He—and the world—would be better off if he simply

stayed here for the rest of his days, shoveling manure and—

Mish lifted his head, listening intently to a low rumble. Was it thunder? Or an approaching truck?

"That sounds like Travis Brown," Chip told him. "Doing what Becca calls his first-rate imitation of a damn fool."

It was the sound of pounding hoofbeats—faint, but growing louder until it became a clatter of noise directly outside of the barn. It was accompanied by a high-pitched whinny of fear and pain from the horse. *That* sound was echoed almost identically—except this second scream came from a human throat. Mish dropped his shovel.

"That's Ashley!" Chip bolted for the door, but Mish swung himself over the wall of the stall and beat him there.

A riderless horse stood on its hind legs, pawing the air as a man dressed in fringed leggings and a leather vest lay sprawled behind him. A young girl crouched in the dust in front of the enraged horse, covering her head with her arms.

Mish didn't stop. He started toward the girl at a sprint.

He could see Rebecca Keyes running just as quickly toward them from the direction of the ranch office. Her hat fell into the dust, and she reached the horse's bridle just as Mish grabbed the girl and pulled her out of harm's way.

The horse's slashing hooves came within inches of Rebecca's face, but she didn't flinch.

Mish shoved the girl into Chip's arms and stood ready to come to Becca's aid. But she simply and slowly backed away, letting the animal have some space.

The horse's sides were torn, as if slashed with too-sharp

spurs. His mouth was frothing and flecked with blood. His dark body was slick with sweat and trembling.

The man who'd been thrown scrambled out of range of the beast's powerful back hooves. "Did you see that?" he said as he pulled himself to his feet. "That damned horse nearly killed me!"

"Quiet!" Becca didn't even look in the man's direction. All of her attention was focused on the horse. Although she didn't speak loudly, there was stern authority in her voice.

The rider wisely shut up.

As Mish watched, the horse returned to all fours. He twitched nervously, though, sidling and still trembling. Becca moved closer again, crooning softly to the frightened animal, her hands and body language nonthreatening.

She could have been a lion tamer. Mish felt his own tension start to drain from his shoulders and neck just from the sound of her soothing, hypnotic voice. As she gazed at the horse steadily, Mish could see none of the anger that he knew she must be feeling toward the abusive rider.

He knew that her eyes were an unremarkable shade of brown, but as she looked at the horse, they reflected a serenity that was almost angelic. And for a moment, as he gazed at her, Mish couldn't breathe.

Rebecca Keyes wasn't what most folks would consider to be beautiful. Oh, her face was pretty enough—cute, actually. It was maybe a touch too round, though, making her look younger than she really was. Or maybe she *was* just plain young, he didn't know for sure. Her nose was small and couldn't be described as anything other than childlike. It was dotted with freckles that added to that effect. Her mouth was generously wide, her lips gracefully shaped. The only makeup she wore was a light coat of gloss on those lips—and Mish suspected she wore it as protection from the harsh sun rather than for cosmetic effect.

But as she reached for that shuddering horse, soothing, peaceful comfort seemed to radiate from her every movement, her every word, her every glance, and Mish could not breathe.

He wanted her to turn to him, to look at him that way, to lay her gentle hands on him, to bring to *him* the peace he so desperately needed.

Instead, he watched as she touched the horse.

The animal snorted, nervously sidestepping, but Becca moved with him. "It's okay, baby," she murmured. "Everything's going to be okay... Shhh..." She ran her hands down the horse's neck. "Yeah, everything's all right now. Let's get you cleaned up." She looped the reins over the animal's head, leading him gently toward the barn. "Casey here will take care of you," she added, still talking in that sweet, soothing voice, "while I take care of the idiot who hurt you."

She looked up at Mish, reaching out to hand him the reins, and just like that, the warm calm in her eyes flickered and changed—replaced by sheer, cold, nearly murderous anger. She was going to "take care" of the rider, indeed.

But first she turned toward the young girl who'd nearly been run down in the driveway. "Are you all right, Ash?"

Ashley and Chip were standing alongside the barn, arms still around each other. The girl nodded, but she was clearly shaken.

"Chip, run to the office," Becca crisply ordered the little boy. "Have Hazel crank up the cellular phone and locate your parents.'' She turned back to Mish. ''Get that horse inside the barn.''

Mish gently tugged on the reins, leading the huge animal into the quiet coolness of the barn. He looked up into the beast's big brown eyes, and could see mistrust. He tried to gaze back confidently, but knew he was failing. Truth was, he didn't have a clue what to do.

He wrapped the reins around one of the bars on the nearest stall, keeping one ear tuned to what was going on outside of the barn.

''Mr. Brown, you have exactly fifteen minutes to pack your bags and get down here to the ranch office,'' he could hear Becca tell the man who'd been riding the horse, her tone leaving no room for any dissent.

There was a buckle that seemed to hold the saddle on and Mish tried to unfasten it, but the animal shifted away, snorting. He was no Dr. Doolittle, but he couldn't miss the horse's message. *Don't touch me.*

Outside, Brown sputtered. ''*I'm* the one who was thrown—''

''You've had your warnings,'' Becca cut him off, her voice tight with anger. ''You've been told again and again that you may *not* wear spurs with *any* of our horses. You've been told again and again not to yank the reins, to treat the horse the way *you'd* want to be treated if *you* had a bit in your mouth.''

Mish put his hand on the horse's neck. He just rested it there, steady and firm, trying to push all of his uncertainty far away, knowing the animal could sense it. He *could* do this. He'd seen enough Westerns. He had to get the saddle off, and the blanket underneath, then somehow cool the horse down.

''You've been told again and again that horses *must* be kept to a slow walk around the ranch buildings,'' Becca's voice continued. ''This time you might've badly injured Ashley Alden. And this time, I'm done giving you warnings. This time, I'm telling you to pack your bags and get off this ranch.''

''I want the sheriff! I want an ambulance—I hurt my back in that fall! I'm going to sue—''

Mish reached for the buckle again, this time his movements steady and sure. The horse twitched and blew air out of his nose, hard, but Mitch got the job done. He lifted off the saddle and set it on top of a rail. And then he couldn't resist sneaking a look out of the barn door. A crowd had gathered—guests and ranch hands silently watching.

Becca had Travis Brown backed against the split wood railings of the corral, her eyes shooting fire. When she spoke, her voice was soft but it carried in the stillness.

''Go ahead and call the sheriff, Hazel,'' she said to the gray-haired woman on the ranch office steps, her eyes never leaving Brown. ''It's entirely likely that Ted and Janice Alden will want to press charges against Mr. Brown for nearly killing their daughter. Reckless endangerment—isn't that what it's called?''

''You can't kick me out. I'm a shareholder.''

''You're an *idiot*,'' Becca said sharply. ''Get the *hell* off this ranch.''

He moved toward her, threateningly. ''You little bitch! When Justin Whitlow finds out about this—''

''Fifteen minutes, Brown.'' He towered over her, but Becca didn't back down. She stood her ground, chin raised, as if daring the man to raise a hand to her.

The man pushed past her, exaggerating his limp as he headed toward the guest cabins.

Becca turned, looking first at Hazel. ''Did you reach the Aldens?''

The plump older woman nodded. "They're on their way."

"Call the sheriff, too—in case they want to register a complaint."

"Already done."

Becca's gaze swept across the crowd and landed on Mish. He realized suddenly that he'd come all the way out of the barn, toward her, ready to jump in if Brown had tried to strike her.

"How's Stormchaser?" she asked, heading directly toward him. "The poor baby's going to have to go into therapy after this."

"He doesn't seem to want me to touch him," Mish admitted, following her back into the barn.

She gave him an odd look over her shoulder. "*She* doesn't know you. *She's* bound to be a little spooked."

She. The horse was female. He hadn't even thought to look. He'd simply assumed that since the animal was so big and powerful... Thou shalt not assume. He'd broken one of the biggest rules, and he'd given himself away.

Rules. Rules of *what?* God Almighty, it was back there, just out of his line of sight. All of the answers, dancing at the edge of his mental peripheral vision. He wanted to close his eyes, to somehow grab hold of the truth, of his identity. But Becca Keyes was talking to him.

"Why don't you get her cooled down," Becca said, obviously repeating herself as she gazed at him with her seemingly average brown eyes.

She was challenging him. Her words were a test—she wanted to know if he could do it.

But he couldn't.

Mish met her gaze levelly, honestly. "I'm afraid that's a little out of my league. But if you tell me exactly what needs to be done, I can—"

She'd already turned away from him. "Perfect," she was muttering. "Incredibly, amazingly, stupendously *perfect.*" She spun back to face him. "You're telling me you don't know how to cool down a horse, aren't you?"

"I'm a quick study," he said quietly. "And you're short of hands—"

"Short of brains, too, obviously." There was a flare of that hot-burning anger in her eyes, but the heat was weakened by her frustration and disappointment. "Dammit. *Dammit!*"

The disappointment was hard to take. He would have far preferred her anger. "I didn't intend to deceive you." He couldn't explain. How could he?

She just laughed as she took the saddle blanket from Stormchaser's back. "Right. Go and make sure Brown's packing his bags. He's in cabin number 12. Walk him back to the office, finish up the stalls, then stay out of my sight for the rest of evening. I can't handle this right now—we'll talk in the morning."

Mish may not have known a thing about horses, but he knew when a situation called for silence.

He turned and left the barn. He'd awakened again this morning with no past, no name, no sense of self. Yet somehow he now felt even emptier inside.

Chapter 3

It was after two o'clock in the morning, and someone was pounding on her apartment door.

Becca sat up, groping for her flashlight in the darkness and coming up empty. The pounding continued—a frantic tattoo accompanied by a high-pitched voice calling her name. She flung herself out of bed and nearly stumbled as she made her way to the light switch on the wall.

Grabbing her robe from the hook next to her closet, she moved toward the noise and opened the door.

Fourteen-year-old Ashley Alden stood on the other side of the screen, her face streaked with tears. "Chip's gone," she said.

Becca pulled the girl inside and shut the screen before the entire mosquito population of New Mexico came into the kitchen with her. "Gone where?"

"I don't know! I was in charge, and I fell asleep, and when Mom and Dad came home, Chip was *gone!* He took the blanket off his bed—I think he's playing cowboy and sleeping outside somewhere.'' Ashley was trying her best to hold back her tears, but a fresh flood brimmed in her eyes. "And now *they're* fighting, and a storm's coming and *some*one's got to go find Chip before he's struck by lightning!"

The girl was right. A storm *was* coming. Becca could hear the ominous rumble of thunder in the distance. Although dangerous, lightning was the least of their worries. If Chip had set up his bedroll in one of the arroyos, or on the gentle valley of the dry riverbed... It didn't have to be raining here for the arroyos and river suddenly to flood. It only had to be raining upstream.

She looked at the kitchen clock. Two-fifteen. No doubt the Aldens had stayed at the local roadhouse, drinking until the two o'clock last call. And if that was the case, they weren't going to be a whole hell of a lot of help in finding their son.

Thunder crackled again, closer this time.

Still, she was going to need all the bodies she could get.

"Go get your mom and dad," she commanded Ashley, already on the cordless phone to Hazel. "And wake up as many of the other guests as you can. We'll meet in front of the ranch office."

Ashley disappeared out the door.

Hazel sounded dazed as she answered her phone, but she rallied quickly.

Becca pulled a pair of jeans on over her nightshirt as she rattled out a stream of orders to her assistant. "Wake up Dwayne and Belinda—tell them to saddle up the horses. The search'll be easier on horseback." She yanked on her boots and jammed her hat on her head. "I'll wake the hands in the bunkhouse."

* * *

The bus ride was interminable, but as the driver pulled up to the checkpoint at the first of the fences, Mish didn't want it to end. He closed his eyes, not wanting to see the gate shutting behind them, locking him in. He kept his eyes closed. There was no point looking at the security. No point studying the watch towers and the fences. He was here. And he'd stay here until Jake got him out.

The bus jolted to a stop, but Mish didn't move until one of the guards approached and unlocked him. He had been wearing both arm and leg shackles.

Mish stood up, and the guard roughly pulled his arms behind him, cuffing his hands behind his back. He still wore a tether, a short length of chain that connected his two ankles. It was hard navigating the steps down from the bus, and he jumped the last two, landing lightly in the dusty prison yard.

Prison. He was in prison. He felt sick to his stomach as he looked up at the harsh gray buildings towering above him.

"Move it," one of the guards barked. "Inside. Let's go."

Mish started to sweat. Out here was bad enough, but at least out here he still had the sky, open and free above him. Inside would be only walls, only bars, only these chains that marked him as a very, *very* dangerous man.

The guard shoved him and he stumbled, but he forced himself not to react, to find serenity from deep inside, that same serenity that had saved him so many times before. He was here. He didn't have to like it. He just had to endure it. Jake was counting on him. Jake needed him to…to…

The answers were there—who Jake was, and what he needed Mish to do there in prison—but they were just beyond his grasp.

Everything shifted then, the way dreams often do. And then Mish was in an alley, thunder rolling as the first huge drops of rain began to fall. In an instant, he was soaked.

He pushed his wet hair back, out of his face, wishing he had a ponytail holder. Dim light gleamed on the barrel of his side arm and he ducked into the shadows, waiting for the footsteps to come closer. Closer...

"Casey! Come on, Casey, wake up!" Rough hands shook him, and Mish opened his eyes, instantly awake,

Rebecca Keyes leaned over him, her hair tousled from sleep.

He was shocked. What was she doing in his bed? Not that he didn't want her there, because he did. Badly. But he couldn't remember how she'd gotten there. And he couldn't imagine acting on his attraction for this woman. It would be flat-out wrong to become intimately involved with *any*one until he'd reintroduced himself to himself.

He couldn't imagine Becca allowing herself to be seduced, either. She'd been so frostily angry with him. How had that happened? He couldn't remember how he'd convinced her to warm up and sleep with him. And maybe worst of all, he couldn't even remember the sex. And that was shockingly alarming.

Was this more amnesia? It didn't make sense. He could remember going to bed—alone—and turning off the light. He could remember the way Becca had looked straight through him during dinner. He could remember waking up in the shelter, his head pounding. He could remember Jarell, the motel, the bus ride to...

Prison.

He'd dreamt about *prison*. Being cuffed and chained. Remembered someone named Jake...

She shook him again. "Snap to, dammit! I need you to help."

Reality crashed in. Mish was lying in a cot barely large enough to sleep one, let alone two. And Becca wasn't dressed for a night of one-on-one—unless her idea of one-on-one was a cattle-roping contest. She was wearing jeans and boots and a wide-brimmed cowboy hat on her head.

He sat up, the blanket sliding off of his bare chest, and Becca took a step back, as if afraid he wasn't wearing anything at all beneath those covers.

He was. Boxers. He also remembered keeping them on last night.

"Chip Alden's gone AWOL," she told him bluntly, "and we've got a storm moving in. I need all the man-power I can get—searching for the kid before the riverbed floods."

Mish nodded, clearly reading her silent message. She needed all the help she could get—even from a low-down, good-for-nothing, lying snake such as himself.

He swung his legs out of bed and pulled on his jeans and the T-shirt he'd worn yesterday, slipping into his boots as she turned and sprinted away. He followed her, quickly catching up. Thunder continued to rumble as the crowd of guests and employees gathering outside the ranch office glanced worriedly up at the dark sky.

Becca quickly split them into groups, sending them off in different directions, some on horseback, some on foot.

"Check the barn and public buildings," she ordered Mish before easily swinging herself up onto a horse and riding out.

He could hear the echoing voices of the search parties as they headed into the darkness, calling loudly, hoping to awaken the sleeping boy.

His was a throwaway job. He knew Becca didn't think they'd find Chip in the barn or the dining hall or even the arcade room. But someone had to look there, and he was that someone.

He went into the barn.

Stormchaser was the only horse left in the stables, and she cocked her ears curiously at him, as if amazed by all of the predawn activity.

It had been Stormchaser's stall that Mish had been cleaning when Chip had come into the barn just that afternoon, to try to con him into saddling up a pair of horses.

Mish froze, suddenly hearing an echo of Chip's prepubescent voice. *There's this place, about a half a mile east of here where there's these big, creepy-looking rocks, kind of like some giant's fingers sticking out of the ground....*

There was a relief map of the ranch on the barn wall, and Mish quickly measured the scale with his fingers, trying to find those rock formations Chip had mentioned. He knew how to read maps, and he easily found something six-tenths of a mile east-northeast that might've been those rocks. It was right next to a low-lying area—the dry riverbed.

Thunder cracked, closer this time, and the first plump drops of rain began to fall, hissing on the dry barn roof.

If Chip had set up camp in that riverbed...

Mish ran out toward the corral, but everyone was gone. He could hear their voices in the distance. Most of them had headed south.

He went back into the barn, where a huge flashlight hung by the door. But even using that, it would be impossible for him to achieve any real speed running more than a half a mile over the rough terrain.

He turned and looked Stormchaser directly in the eye.

She whinnied nervously as another bolt of lightning flashed, the boom of thunder close behind.

"Yeah, I don't like this weather, either," Mish said to the horse, opening the stall door, "but I know where this kid is, and I've got to get out there, so what do you say we make this a team effort?"

Stormchaser didn't disagree. Of course, she didn't exactly agree, either.

"I've never done this before in my life." Mish took a bridle down from the wall, speaking in a low, soft, soothing voice, the way he'd heard Becca talk to the horse. "But I spent most of yesterday watching the procedure, so let's just give it a try, okay?"

As Mish drew closer, the mare clenched her teeth.

"I think this bit thing is supposed to go *behind* your teeth, not in front of them," Mish told her, still in that low voice. "And I think I saw the other guys touch you back here a bit, and just kind of wait until you're maybe not paying quite so much attention and then...*slip* it in. There we go. Good horse. Atta girl. Way to go."

Stormchaser snorted, chomping disgruntledly on the bit.

"I can't imagine that feels very pleasant," Mish continued, slipping a saddle blanket onto her strong chestnut-colored back. "I can't imagine any of this is a whole lot of fun for you, especially after the way that idiot treated you this afternoon."

He took a saddle off the wall, gently placing it in the center of the blanket, and secured the belt around the horse's belly. As he'd seen the other ranch hands do, he waited until Stormchaser relaxed, and then tightened it several notches.

The stirrups seemed to be about the right length for his legs, so he looped the reins over the horse's head and led her out into the night, tucking the flashlight under one arm.

The rain was falling heavier now, and Stormchaser tried to back away, into the barn.

"No, you don't," he murmured to the horse, pointing her in the direction he wanted to go. "What kind of tough-as-nails Western cow horse are you, anyway?" He put his left foot into the stirrup and held onto the pommel. "I'm probably doing this all wrong and backwards, so I appreciate your patience," he said as he tried to imitate the move Becca had made, and swing himself into the saddle. He landed with a thud, nearly going over the other side. "Whoa!"

Stormchaser snorted, pricking up her ears as Mish took gentle hold of the reins. He had to remember that these things were attached to the horse's tender mouth.

Now, what was the opposite of whoa? "Giddyap!" he said.

Lightning flashed, thunder crashed, and Stormchaser bolted.

Becca couldn't believe her eyes. Lightning flashed again, and again she saw Stormchaser, running like a bat out of hell with Casey Parker lying low and flat along the mare's neck, riding like a seasoned rodeo cowboy. She felt a flash of annoyance—the guy had led her to believe he didn't know the least little thing about horses—including riding.

She moved to cut them off just as Casey reined Stormchaser in.

"I know where Chip is," he called out, seemingly unaware of the rain that was now falling steadily, streaming down his face.

He nudged Stormchaser's sides, and the horse took off again. Becca followed, pressing Silver hard to keep up.

She had her flashlight on, and in its bright beam, she could see that Casey wasn't riding like a professional cowboy—he was holding on for dear life.

"I talked to him this afternoon," the man shouted to her, "and he wanted to go out to this place where there were some rock formations."

Finger Rocks. God, that was right on the edge of the dry riverbed. Only, with all this rain, it wasn't going to stay dry for long—if it wasn't already flooded from the rain up in the mountains.

Becca gave Silver his head, letting him fly across the ground, praying they weren't too late. Please, God, let them find this little boy still alive....

She heard it before she saw it.

The river was running.

Lightning flared, and Finger Rocks appeared out of the darkness, looming crazily over them. The water in the riverbed was dark and frothy, and filled with bobbing logs and debris being washed downstream.

There was no sign of Chip.

Becca slid down off Silver, using her flashlight to illuminate the banks of the river.

Casey was still atop Stormchaser, and he pointed out into the rushing water. "There!"

She saw it, too.

She saw what might have been the top of a small head near a branch that had been snagged on an outcropping of rocks.

"Chip!" she shouted over the roar of the river and the bursts of thunder. "Chip!"

The head moved and became a small, pale face that reflected the light from her torch.

It was Chip. He was clinging for dear life to the end of a weathered old branch.

As Casey slid down off Stormchaser, Becca saw him take in the situation with a glance. The branch Chip was holding on to was wedged between two rocks at the river's edge, right before the water took a hard loop to the left and swept even faster down the hill. The white water down there told of rapids—rocks that could crush the life out of a ten-year-old flung against them with the water's raging force.

It was only a matter of time before the debris knocked Chip free from his perch and swept him downstream.

The tumble of rocks at the side of the river made it treacherous going. Casey slipped and slid over them, turning back to give Becca a hand.

She didn't need or want his help. "I'm fine," she shouted at him. "Keep going!"

Finally, they were both there.

"Hang on, kid," she heard Casey call to Chip. "We'll get you out of there!"

"I want my mom!" The little boy was weeping. "Please, I want my mom!"

"Just let us pull you out of there, and we'll find her right away," Casey told him, his voice reassuring. They *would* get the boy out of the river. And if he was feeling any doubt about it, he wasn't letting it show. He tugged at the thick end of the branch Chip was clinging to, but it wouldn't give. Becca set down her flashlight and helped. It didn't take long to realize that the damned thing wasn't going to budge. They weren't going to be able to free the branch to pull the kid out of there.

The rain was falling unmercifully now, streaming off the brim of her hat in a solid sheet.

"I'll have to climb out after him," she shouted to Casey.

He used one hand to wipe the water from his face, little good that it did. He shook his head. "No. I'll do it."

"Are you kidding? That branch won't hold your weight!"

"It might not hold yours."

"Hold onto my legs," Becca told him. "If the branch breaks, I'll hang onto it, and you can haul us both out of the water."

He didn't like it, but she didn't give him a chance to argue. She just started inching her way out along that branch.

She could feel his hands on her legs, his fingers hooking around the bottom edges of her jeans. She could see Chip's pale, frightened face as lightning flashed again.

The boy was edging toward her, even as she was moving closer to him.

She was so close. Another foot and a half, and—

It happened so fast.

A piece of wood barreling downstream caught Chip full in the chest, and with a shriek, his handhold on the branch was broken.

Becca heard herself scream as the boy, eyes wide with terror, fingers reaching for her, was swept underneath the water.

She felt herself hauled upward and nearly thrown onto the shore and sensed more than saw Casey scrambling back up and over the rocks. She grabbed for her flashlight, holding it high, illuminating the river, praying for a glimpse of Chip's brown hair, praying he'd manage to grab hold of another branch.

She saw him!

Dear God, no! The boy was being swept downriver. Another few seconds, and he'd hit those rapids.

But then she saw Casey, running along the river bank, heading directly for the place where the river turned. She saw him dive, a graceful, athletic movement.

And then he was out of range of her light, and she saw nothing more.

Mish knew without a doubt in the stretched-out seconds that he hung suspended over the raging water that he knew how to swim.

And he didn't just know how to do the dog paddle. He *knew* how to *swim*. As uncomfortable as he'd been while riding Stormchaser, here in the river he was completely in his element. He was at home in the water unlike anywhere else in the world.

He hit the river with a splash and it grabbed him, tugging, pulling, yanking him downstream. He went with it, using its power to push him up back toward the surface. Only when his head was above water again did he fight the current, searching for any sign of Chip.

He saw the debris coming—it looked like a solid chunk of a telephone pole—but he didn't have time to get completely out of the way. It hit him solidly in his left side, pushing him under and spinning him around, the white blaze of pain made worse by the water burning his lungs.

He kicked and stroked against the pain, surfacing with a rush, coughing out the water he'd inhaled and gasping in a blessed flood of air.

And the kid was swept right into his arms.

If he hadn't believed in the workings of some kind of higher power before, he did now.

Mish let the force of the water take him again, using

his strength as a swimmer merely to steer them toward the rocky shore.

And then he was crawling out, his side on fire, Chip still clinging to his neck, both of them sobbing for air. And Becca was there, helping pull the kid to even higher ground. She then reached for him.

Lightning flashed, and he saw that she'd lost her hat. Her dark curls were plastered to her head and beneath her jacket, her shirt was glued to her breasts. It wasn't a shirt, he realized. She was wearing a white nightgown. And absolutely nothing underneath. She had an incredibly gorgeous body, but it was her eyes he found himself wanting to see again. Brimming with the warmth of emotion and relief, her eyes were impossibly beautiful.

He could have sat there in the rain all night, just waiting for the lightning, so he could get another glimpse of her face.

But Becca scooped Chip into her arms and pushed herself to her feet. "Let's get back to the ranch."

Ted Alden, Chip's father, came out of their cabin. "The doctor says he's got a few broken ribs, but his lungs are clear and his blood pressure's strong. We'll monitor that through the rest of the night—make sure there've been no internal injuries we don't know about."

The rain had stopped, and the clouds were breaking up. Becca could see the first faint stars shining hazily in the sky. She nodded. "Do you need help? You look as if once you fall asleep, you're going to stay asleep for a day or two."

Alden ran his hands down his face. "No, we've got the alarm clock set. And Ashley's set hers, too. Just in case."

"Well, I'm here if you need me."

"Thanks."

Becca turned to go, but he stopped her.

"We've caused nothing but trouble this trip. Are you going to ask us to leave tomorrow?"

She had to laugh. "You mean, like the way I asked Travis Brown to leave?" She shook her head. "No, I'm trying not to make a habit of running paying guests off with a shotgun. It's bad for business."

"Thank that cowboy again for me," Alden said. "If the two of you hadn't been there, Chip might've..."

Chip *would* have died.

Becca knew what Ted Alden couldn't bring himself to say aloud. His son would have died. The hell with her—she'd had very little to do with saving the boy's life. The truth was, if it weren't for Casey Parker, they would be dragging that river right this very moment, searching for Chip's crushed and lifeless little body.

Becca swallowed a sudden rush of intense emotion. She had to blink hard to push back a surge of moisture in her eyes. "I'll thank him," she said quietly. "Kiss Chip good-night for me, all right?"

Alden nodded, easing the screen door shut behind him.

It must have been the fatigue bringing all these waves of emotion to the surface. Becca couldn't remember the last time she'd cried, yet here she was, ready to curl up into a soggy ball and weep like a baby.

Everything was all right. The boy was safe. But she couldn't keep herself from thinking about what might have been. She couldn't help remembering that look of pure fear on the little boy's face as he was swept out of her reach, *Why didn't you save me?* echoing in his eyes. If Chip had died, his face would have haunted her for the rest of her life.

If Chip had died...

What if Casey hadn't been there with his amazing abil-

ity to swim like some kind of sea animal? What if the
river had swept Chip past him? What if…?

Her insides churned and bile rose in her throat. She had
to sit down, right there on the edge of the muddy road,
and try her damnedest not to retch. She clung to her wet
jacket, wrapping it tightly around her, praying for the nausea to pass.

"Are you all right?" The voice came out of the darkness, soft and gentle.

"Yeah," she lied, not wanting to look up and into the
bottomless depths of Casey's eyes, not wanting him to see
that she was shaking. "I'm just… I'm…"

She felt him sit down next to her, felt his closeness and
warmth. He didn't say anything. He just sat there as she
tried to breathe, as she desperately tried to regain her equi-
librium and stop this damned shaking that was rattling her
very brain.

When he finally did start to speak, Becca thought she
might've been imagining it. His voice was so soft and
perfectly woven into the velvet tapestry of the predawn.

"You know, I don't think I've ever ridden a horse before," he told her. "At least not since I was a kid. I don't
know why I haven't tried it—it was great. Exhilarating.
Kind of like flying. But you already know that, right? I
can picture you as the kind of kid who was born astride
a horse." He paused, but only briefly. "When I was riding
Stormchaser, I remember thinking it was kind of like being on a motorcycle, except this thing I was riding had a
brain and a *soul*…"

Becca knew exactly what he was doing. He was gentling her, soothing her with the softness of his voice, the
way someone might talk to a frightened animal. The way
she'd spoken to Stormchaser just that morning. And as
Stormchaser had, she clung to the sound of that gentle

voice. It was the only thing solid and steady in a night that was spinning and shaking.

No, it wasn't the night that was shaking. *She* was shaking. And crying, she realized. Although there was nothing she could do to stop her tears. Nothing at all.

He was still talking, describing his ride, describing the way he'd put the bridle and saddle on Stormchaser. His words were unimportant and she stopped listening, focusing only on the rise and fall of his voice. And when he reached out and touched her, gently, lightly running one hand across her shoulders and down her back, she didn't pull away. She didn't want to pull away. Instead she leaned toward him, letting him enfold her in his arms.

He held her as she trembled, rocking her slightly back and forth, infusing her with his warmth, encircling her with his solid strength. "It's okay now," he murmured over and over. "Everything's okay."

It was working. She could feel her nausea begin to fade, felt herself relax into his strong arms.

And he *was* strong. His slenderness was only an illusion. His arms and chest were solid muscle. She hadn't missed that fact when she'd gone in to wake him up and found him half-naked in bed. He had no extra fat or weight on his body, none at all. Yet his arms were soft, too. Gentle.

He continued to stroke her back, then ran his fingers gently through her hair, murmuring words of reassurance. He held her close without being threatening, offering only comfort, falling into silence as her trembling finally stopped.

She let her head rest on his still-damp shoulder, let her eyes close, let all of the awful what-ifs float away.

Except for one. What if this man whose arms felt so good around her turned his head and kissed her?

Becca opened her eyes. That was a completely crazy thought. She pulled herself away from him, pushing herself to her feet.

She shivered slightly, cold without Casey's arms around her, as the first glimmer of dawn started to light the eastern sky.

He was still a shadow, sitting in the grayness. Becca backed away quickly, both afraid that he might break the silence, and afraid that he might not.

"There's no way I could ever pay you enough for what you did tonight," she said softly. Oh, she could think of one way she could certainly *try* to repay him, but she firmly pushed that wayward thought away.

"I didn't pull the kid out of the river for money," he said.

"Oh, no," she said, afraid she might've offended him. "I didn't mean that. I just meant... I wish there was some way I could thank you for what you did." Her voice shook slightly. "And for sitting here with me just now."

"Sometimes the hardest part of the battle comes after it's over," he said quietly, "when the adrenaline level drops and there's nothing left to do but think about what went down."

Becca lingered as the sky continuously grew lighter, knowing she should say good-night and put a healthy distance between herself and this man. She was drawn to his gentle voice and quiet smile more than she wanted to admit. And as for his arms...

"Were you in the army?" she asked, instead of taking her leave.

He was silent for several long moments, then he pushed himself to his feet in one easy, fluid motion. "Are you sure you want to start a conversation right now? You look as if you could use about twelve hours in bed."

With him? The thought popped into her head and she tried her hardest to pop it right back out again. What was wrong with her tonight? "You're right," she said. "I'm just... I'm still..."

He held out his hand. He had big hands, strong, capable-looking hands that were callused from hard work. Attractive hands that were attached to attractive arms.

"Come on," he said. "I'll walk you back to your cabin."

Becca shook her head. "I'm okay." She was afraid to touch him again. Even just his hand. "Thank you again, Casey."

He nodded, dropping his hand. "I have a nickname," he told her, "that I prefer to answer to. It's Mish. I know it's...unusual, but it's how I think of myself."

"Mish," she repeated. "Is it Russian?"

"No. It's short for..." He laughed almost self-consciously. "It's short for 'Mission Man.'"

Mission Man? "What does that mean?"

She saw another flash of his straight white teeth in the growing dawn. "I'm not sure I know myself. It's just a handle I was given by a...a friend."

Becca backed further away. "Well, thank you. Mish." She paused. "We should...probably set up a time to talk in the morning," she told him awkwardly.

"Whenever you like," he answered simply. "You know where to find me."

Chapter 4

L. Lucky O'Donlon sat alone in the back corner booth, in a deserted section of the Denny's on Water Street in Wyatt City, New Mexico, finishing his breakfast.

Water Street. Yeah, right. The entire street—the entire *town*—was dry as a bone. He'd woken up after a ten-minute combat nap this morning, yawned, and his lip had split. God, he missed the ocean.

He and his team had arrived in Las Cruces later than he'd anticipated. By the time they'd gotten their hands on an inconspicuous-looking car and driven all the way through the desert to Wyatt City, it had been well after midnight. Lucky had grimed himself up, said goodbye to Bob and Wes, gotten out of the car nearly a mile away from the First Church, and had walked over to the home-less shelter there.

As he now watched, Bobby and Wes sauntered out of the shiny new motel across the street from the Denny's, clearly in no huge hurry to meet him for their scheduled sit-rep. In fact, Wes stopped to light a cigarette in the parking lot, cupping his hands to shield his match from the wind.

Bobby nimbly plucked the cigarette from Wes's lips and tossed it to the gravel, grinding it out under his size-seventeen-and-a-half boots. And, as Lucky watched, they argued for the nine-thousandth time about Wes's inability to quit smoking.

Or rather Wes argued, and Bobby ignored him.

Bobby headed for the restaurant, and Wes followed, still arguing. They were showered and shaved and looking far fresher than Lucky. They were both wearing jeans and T-shirts, and Wes actually had a weather-beaten cowboy hat jammed onto his short brown hair.

Bobby, with his darkly handsome, Native American features, looked like he could be one of the locals in Wyatt City. Wes looked exactly like what he was—Popeye the Sailor man in a cowboy hat.

"I'm gonna quit," Wes was saying as they came into the restaurant and headed back toward Lucky's table. "I swear I am. I'm just not ready to quit right now."

Bobby finally spoke. "When we're out on an op and we're buddied up, I can smell the smoke on your breath from yards away. And if *I* can smell you, so can the opposition. You want to kill yourself by smoking, that's your business, Skelly. Just don't kill *me*."

For once in his life, Wes didn't have anything to say.

Bobby sat down next to Lucky, clearly preferring, like the lieutenant, to keep his back to the rear wall. Wes slid all the way over on the other side of the booth, sitting half-turned, his back against the mirrored side wall, so that he, too, could see the rest of the restaurant. Good habits died hard.

Too bad *bad* habits died hard, too. Bobby was dead

right about Wes's smoking. When they were out in a group, the scent of a cigarette smoked six hours earlier could conceivably put them all in jeopardy.

Bobby gazed at Lucky. "Whoa, you smell ripe. Sir."

"And you both look as if you had ample opportunity to shower after a great night's sleep."

"The room was very nice, thanks."

"Yeah, I'm looking forward to seeing it from a prone position with my eyes closed," Lucky told them. Unfortunately that wasn't going to be soon.

He hadn't gone to the church to sleep. He'd been there to check the place out thoroughly—to sneak and peek and find out as much about the shelter as he possibly could. He'd spent most of the night chatting up the volunteer workers, finding out how the system worked.

"The shelter's purely a church-run organization," he told Bob and Wes. "The only rules are no drugs, alcohol, weapons or women on the premises. And the men have to be out of both the building *and* the neighborhood before 8:00 a.m. because the facility's used as a preschool starting at 8:45."

"Anyone remember seeing Mitch?" Wes asked.

Lucky shook his head. "No. And they don't keep records of the men who use the shelter. But they *do* have records in the church office of the volunteers who work the different shifts. One of you is going to have to go into that office and charm a list out of the church ladies who work there. We've got to find out who was on duty the nights we think Mitch might've been there."

Wes pointed to Bobby. "He'll do that. Church ladies give me a rash."

Bobby shrugged. "I'll do it—if you quit smoking."

"Oh, God." Wes slumped forward so his head was on the table. "Fine," he said, his voice muffled by his arms.

''I'll quit smoking. You just keep any church ladies away from me.''

Bobby turned to Lucky. ''Luke, I've been thinking. If Mitch came into the shelter in disguise...''

''Yeah, I've been thinking that, too.'' Lucky signalled the waitress to freshen his cup of coffee. She poured cups for Bob and Wes, too, and told them she'd be back in a minute to take their order. He waited until she was gone to continue. ''If he doesn't want us to, we're probably not going to find him.''

''Provided he's still alive,'' Wes said darkly.

Lucky took a sip of his now-hot coffee, feeling it burn all the way to his stomach. ''How well did you guys get to know Mitch Shaw last year when we were working with Admiral Robinson?''

Bobby looked at Wes, and Wes looked at Bobby. Guys who had been swim buddies for years, the way these two had, could have entire conversations with a single glance.

''Not very well,'' Bobby admitted. ''He pretty much kept to himself.''

Wes looked at Bob again. ''Or hung out with Zoe Lange.''

''Zoe *Robinson,* now.'' Bobby sighed from the memory. ''I always kind of figured Mitch had a thing for her.''

''She have her baby yet?'' Wes asked. ''I never knew a pregnant woman could be so sexy until Zoe got knocked up.''

''She's not due for another few weeks,'' Lucky said, looking at Bobby and rolling his eyes in exasperation. Only Wes could refer to the pregnancy of a highly decorated and respected admiral's wife as ''knocked up.'' ''Can we stay on track here? Let's focus on Mitch Shaw. I didn't get to know Mitch very well either.''

''He was one spooky dude,'' Wes said.

"Jake Robinson trusts him," Bobby pointed out. He frowned slightly at Wes. "And don't talk about him in the past tense, please."

"Okay." Lucky pointed at Bobby. "You go make friends with the office staff at the church." He pointed at Wes. "You get on the computer and search out whatever personnel records and files you can about Mitchell Shaw. I want to know where he grew up, what his nickname was during BUD/S training, what medals he's won, his favorite vegetable, his favorite color. I want to know everything there is to know about this guy."

Bobby stood up. "I'll grab a donut on my way out." He pulled the motel room key out of his pocket and put it on the table in front of Lucky. "You'll be wanting that."

"I want it but I'm not going to use it. I'm going to go check out the neighborhood around the church shelter. See if anyone in the grocery shops remember seeing Mitch. And as soon as the bars open, I'll check them out, too."

"Forgive me for singing the same old refrain, but you look worse than you smell, Lieutenant," Bobby said. "Maybe you should crash for a few hours."

"We've got another check-in with the captain coming up in twelve hours," Lucky reminded them. "I'm not looking forward to giving him a repeat of this morning's sit-rep—that we're here but we're still clueless." Lucky slid out of the booth's bench seat and threw enough money onto the table to cover his breakfast. "I'll take a quick shower, but that's all I have time for. Let's meet back at the motel at 1300 hours."

"God, I wanted a real breakfast." Wes gazed longingly at the scrambled eggs and ham pictured on the menu, then pushed himself out of the booth.

"I'll buy you a super-deluxe breakfast special to go," Bobby said, "if you'll trade assignments with me."

"Searching computer records versus duking it out with the church ladies?" Wes shook his head. "I don't want breakfast *that* bad."

The Aldens were leaving.

Mish waved goodbye to Chip as the van pulled away, down the long driveway.

Last night's events had been too much for them. Their vacation was over, Ted Alden had told him as he'd thanked Mish again. Besides, they wanted to get Chip checked out by their personal physician back in New York.

"Are you completely insane?"

Mish turned to see Becca standing slightly behind him. She was holding a piece of paper in her hand and...

He turned away, recognizing it as the exorbitant check—a thank-you gift, the man had called it—Ted Alden had tried to press into his hand as he said goodbye.

"How could you refuse to accept this?" Becca asked, moving in front of him, holding the damned thing up.

There was no way he could explain that the thought of taking money for saving a kid's life made him squirm—especially since the nightmarish dreams that continued to haunt him made him wonder if maybe he'd earned that big wad of money he carried by *taking* people's lives.

"I didn't go into the river after Chip because I wanted a reward," he told her. "I did it because I liked the kid." He shook his head. No, that wasn't exactly true. "Look, I would've done it even if I *didn't* like the kid. I just...I did it, okay? I don't want Alden's money. He thanked me—that was enough."

Mish headed back toward the barn. There were stalls

to shovel out and other chores that needed doing. He'd gotten a late start today, *and* he was moving more slowly than usual, thanks to that piece of telephone pole that had smashed into him in the river. He didn't think his rib was broken, but it probably had been cracked. Either way, there wasn't much he could've done about it. He'd grabbed an Ace bandage from the first-aid kit in the barn, and he'd wrapped himself up—not that it really helped. It hurt, but that would fade in time.

Becca followed him, a sudden brisk breeze making her clutch her cowboy hat to her head. "Casey—*Mish.* God, this check is for a *hundred* thousand dollars! That kind of money is nothing to Ted Alden—he's got bushels of it back on Wall Street. But for someone like me or you… You can't just say 'no thanks' to an opportunity like this."

He stopped short, and she nearly ran into him. "Funny, I thought I already did."

She was completely bemused and almost entirely confused as well as she stood there gazing up at him, as if she were trying to see into his head. "I promised Ted I'd talk you into accepting this."

"You're going to have to break your promise, because I don't want it," Mish said again. He reached for it, intending to tear it up, but she pulled it away from him, safely out of reach, as if she *had* been able to read his mind.

"Don't you dare! I'm going to hold on to this for you while you think about accepting it. Take all the time you need."

Exasperated, he turned back to the barn. "I don't need time. I've already thought about it. You'll just have to send it back to him."

Again, she followed, all the way inside. "With this kind

of money, you wouldn't have to work here, shoveling horse manure for most of the day.''

He glanced back at her as he picked up his shovel and started doing just that, trying to ignore the flare of pain in his side. "Are you firing me?"

"No!" Her answer came quickly. "That's not why I said that. I *need* you to stay, I'm shorthanded already, but actually I'd…" She cleared her throat. "I'd like it if you stayed."

Mish didn't stop his work cleaning out the stall, but he couldn't keep himself from glancing up at her again.

She was wearing jeans and a long-sleeved shirt open and untucked over a T-shirt. It hid the soft curves he didn't need to see to know were there. She'd fit perfectly in his arms last night. Maybe a little *too* perfectly. As she gazed back at him, her eyes were dark brown, bottomless pits that he knew he could fall into and lose himself in far too easily.

She was looking at him as if he were some kind of hero. And he knew with a flash that his refusal to accept that money had only made her like him more. *Damn.*

"That is, if you want to stay," she added, embarrassment tingeing her cheeks with pink. "You know, just…for a while."

Mish forced himself to look away, forced himself not to think about the fact that he couldn't remember the last time he'd had sex. Of course he couldn't remember. Everything before Monday was a total blank. Yet still, somehow he knew—as he'd known the waist and inseam measurements of his jeans—that it had been a long time since he'd been with a woman. A very long time.

And he found this woman to be incredibly appealing.

She'd turned down his offer to walk her back to her cabin as the sun was starting to creep over the horizon early this morning. That had been a good call on her part—Mish didn't know what he'd been thinking at the time. She'd just been through an emotional wringer and surely had been vulnerable.

He himself had been running what-if scenarios all morning. It had been sheer luck that Chip had been swept directly into his arms in the river. Sheer luck the kid hadn't been killed. The line between what was and what might have been was a very thin one. Tragedy had been averted by mere inches. And afterward, Mish had been a little too close to an emotional edge himself, and he knew now what he'd only suspected last night.

It wouldn't have taken much for that friendly comfort he'd given Becca to turn into comfort of an entirely different kind. If he'd walked her home and she'd invited him in, he would've kissed her sweet mouth. And if he had kissed her...

He focused on the job at hand, attempting to banish the too-vivid thoughts of just where kissing Becca might've led. He couldn't let himself think that way. It wouldn't be fair to her. It wouldn't be right.

Mish couldn't tell her the truth, although, Lord, there were times when he longed to confide in her. But he couldn't. Just the thought of it filled him with an overpowering sense of unease. Somehow he knew he wasn't supposed to talk about any of this—why he was here. He couldn't risk revealing too much, couldn't give anything away. Why? He didn't remember. But the need for secrecy had obviously been ingrained in him. He couldn't tell her.

And he'd already deceived Becca once—by convincing her he was capable of this job as a ranch hand, during that phone interview he couldn't remember. There was no way he was going to deceive her again by becoming physically intimate with her. At least not until he knew for sure exactly who he was. And maybe not even after that.

This was not a woman who'd want to have anything to do with a criminal. And he was probably an ex-con at best, if his dreams of handcuffs and prison walls were based on any kind of truth.

Although, when she looked at him the way she'd been looking at him just a few seconds ago, it was easy to imagine his resolve to keep his distance flying right out the window. It was easy to imagine her melting willingly in his arms as he pulled her down with him, right here on the sweet-smelling, fresh hay he'd just spread on the floor of the stall and...

Lord have mercy. Yes, it had been far, far too long since he'd been intimate with a woman.

But Becca wanted him to be a hero, so he was going to do just that—by not letting himself get too close to her.

She looked down at the check she still held in her hands, her cheeks still slightly pink, as if she'd been able to follow his wayward thoughts. "I just can't imagine why you would want to work for slave wages, with somebody willing and ready to hand you this much money."

Mish shrugged as he set the shovel down. "Money's not everything." He picked up the handles of the nearly full wheelbarrow and pushed it out of the stall. He passed closely enough to Becca to catch a whiff of the same fresh perfume he'd breathed in last night when he'd wrapped her in his arms. Lord, but she smelled good. He moved away from her quickly, leaning closer to the overpowering contents of his wheelbarrow to exorcise her scent as he headed toward the back entrance of the barn.

"It may not be everything, but it's damn close," Becca countered, following him out. "If *I* had this kind of money—" She broke off. "Mish, please, you should at least *think* about accepting this check. This could be the break you need.''

He squinted against the bright morning sunshine as he pushed his pungent load out to a manure pile well back from the barn, his side smarting with every step he took. ''Your giving me this job was the break I need,'' he said. ''Of course, that assumes I need a break in the first place.''

''You walked in here with one change of clothes under your arm, no wallet and no ID,'' she pointed out. ''You accepted a job at an embarrassingly low hourly rate. This isn't the movies. I've pretty much rejected the idea that you're some kind of eccentric millionaire in disguise.''

He glanced back at her. ''Yeah? What if I am?''

Becca laughed, her eyes sparkling with amusement. She really had beautiful eyes. ''If you are, why the heck are we having this conversation while you lug a load of manure in this heat? Let's call for a break and reconvene for dinner at your favorite restaurant in Paris. Because as long as you can afford it, I've always wanted to fly on the Concorde.''

She was teasing, but there was some truth in her words. She wanted to have dinner with him. He could see it in her eyes. Mish dumped the wheelbarrow, feeling glad— and very stupid. He didn't *want* her to like him. He *couldn't* want her to like him. Yet he was happy that she did. ''Sorry, I seem to have misplaced my bankcard.''

''Aha,'' she said with another smile. ''Proof that even if you *are* a millionaire in disguise, you need a break.''

She had such a beautiful smile, it was impossible not to smile back at her. And as he did, Mish felt himself start to slip.

She more than merely liked him. He may not have been able to remember his own name, but he knew how to read a woman. And this woman was Interested, with a capital *I.* If he pulled her into his arms and lowered his head, she would lift her mouth to meet his. And while getting it on with her on the floor of the barn in the middle of the day was stretching the edges of the fantasy envelope, the idea of spending the night in her bed in the very near future was not so far-fetched.

But she wanted a hero, he reminded himself. So instead of moving closer, Mish took a step back.

"I *do* need a break," he told her, willing her not to move any closer. "And the fact that you're letting me stay despite knowing that I lied to you is—"

"But you didn't," she told him, moving closer despite his attempt to control her through telekinesis. She moved close enough for him to see the individual freckles that swept across her nose and cheeks. Close enough to see the flecks of green and gold mixed in with the darker brown of her eyes. "Not really. I looked in your personnel file, at the notes I made when we spoke on the phone. You definitely omitted some information, but I didn't ask, so it wasn't a lie. You told me you were mainly a handyman and that you'd worked on ranches before. I made the mistake of assuming you'd be able to handle the horses, too."

Personnel file. There was a personnel file with his name on it, somewhere in Becca's office. It was entirely possible that file would contain his last known address and phone number. He had to have some clothes, some belongings *some*where, didn't he? If he could find those, he might start to remember who and what he was.

"I wasn't completely honest with you, either," Becca continued. "I didn't mention the fact that your starting salary isn't going to increase any time in the near future. The owner of the Lazy Eight doesn't believe in raises."

"The money you're paying me is good enough for now." Mish pushed the wheelbarrow back toward the barn. He was far from done with the stalls, yet it was nearly time for lunch. He was simply going to have to grit his teeth against the pain and pick up his pace.

Becca's pager went off and she looked down at it, turning it off. "Shoot, I've got to go take this call." She started toward the office, walking backwards. "What do you say you let me treat you to a drink after dinner tonight? As a sort of a thank-you? There's a roadhouse about twelve miles down the road—it's not too far away. They have a really great band on Thursday nights."

She'd asked him out.

Mish had thought he was safe as long as he kept his distance and didn't do something crazy like invite her to have dinner or a drink with him. But he should've known that Rebecca Keyes wasn't the kind of woman who'd sit back and wait for something she wanted.

"Um," he said, but she didn't give him a chance to figure out how he could turn her down without hurting her feelings.

"I've got to run," she told him with another of those killer smiles that made his insides tangle. "I'll talk to you later."

And she was gone, leaving Mish with an entirely new set of what-if questions.

What if he let himself go out with her? She only wanted to have a drink. It wasn't as if she'd invited him over to her place to spend the night, was it?

So what if he went? He'd have a chance to sit across the table from her in some dimly lit bar. He'd have a chance to gaze into her eyes as they talked.

As she asked him questions about himself.

Where he came from. Where he'd worked before this.

Questions about his family. His childhood. His hobbies. Former girlfriends. *Present* girlfriends.

Lord God, what if he was married? What if he had a wife and children somewhere, but he simply couldn't remember them?

Of course, it was entirely likely that if he *had* been married, his wife had left him while he was in *prison.*

Mish shook his head as he began shoveling out the next stall in the barn, almost welcoming the punishing pain in his side.

Yeah, he was one hell of a hero.

Chapter 5

Mish cleared his throat. "Excuse me. Is Becca here?"

Hazel, the gray-haired woman who worked part-time in the Lazy Eight's office, looked up from her computer and smiled at him. "Oh, hi, Casey. Yeah, she's in the back. You want me to call her for you?"

"No," he said. Somewhere in this office was a personnel file with his name on it. Was it in the file cabinet underneath the far window, or the one next to the computer? "Thanks, but if she's busy, it's not necessary."

"She's not busy. *Becca!*" Hazel called, then turned back to Mish. "A package came for you today," she told him.

That drew his attention away from the file cabinets. A package. For *him?*

"It says Hold For Arrival," she continued, pushing her chair back and pulling herself to her feet, "but since you arrived early, I can just give it to you now, can't I?"

Hazel pulled a small brown padded mailing envelope

from a set of mail cubbyholes and slid it across the counter to Mish.

A *package*.

There didn't feel as if there could be much inside as he picked it up and turned it over. There was no return address, not even on the back. "Casey Parker" and the address at the ranch was written in a large, faintly childish hand. The handwriting—messy block letters—was completely unfamiliar to Mish. But then again, just a few days ago, his own face had been unfamiliar.

The post-office cancellation stamp on the package read "Las Cruces." That was the closest large town to Wyatt City, where he'd woken up in a homeless shelter. Coincidental? Maybe.

Maybe not.

"Hey, Mish, hi. Did you get mail?" Becca came out from the back, her eyes and smile warm, clearly glad to see him.

"Yeah, I, uh, did." Mish nodded to Hazel. "Thank you."

"Anything good?" Becca leaned over the counter, smiling up at him.

"Nah." He shrugged as he tucked the package under his arm. "Just, you know, tax information from my accountant—about my stock portfolio."

She laughed. "Oh, of course."

Mish's heart rate had accelerated at the thought of what he might find inside that innocuous brown envelope, but he'd wait for the semi-privacy of the bunkhouse to open it. He couldn't imagine what might be in there that he'd need to keep private, but then again, he hadn't suspected he'd find a huge wad of money and a .22-caliber handgun in his boot, either.

"It's going to be slow around here tonight," Becca told

him, her chin in her hands, her eyes warm as she looked up at him. "If you'd like, we could leave as early as six, grab some dinner while we're out...?"

At least he'd *thought* it was the package that had made his pulse kick into double time. But maybe it had been the sight of Becca's smile.

It would be so easy to tell her *yes*. It was what he wanted to do, *and* it would keep him from disappointing and possibly even embarrassing her. Rejection was never fun, even when it was done as gently as possible, with the best of intentions.

He glanced over at Hazel who was working on the computer again.

"Actually..." He lowered his voice, and Becca leaned closer to hear what he had to say, close enough for him to catch a whiff of her subtle, sweet scent. But it wasn't perfume, he realized. That was her hair he could smell—her shampoo. And that made so much more sense than perfume. Becca didn't seem like the type of woman who would get dressed in worn-out jeans and a T-shirt, apply only sunblock to her face, and then spritz herself with designer perfume for a hard, hot day of work on a ranch.

"Actually what?" Her voice was husky, and he realized he'd been staring at her for many long seconds, just breathing in her sweetness.

Their two heads were close together. Almost close enough to kiss. Thank heavens the counter was between them or he might well have pulled her into his arms, both Hazel and his good intentions be damned.

Even if he hadn't already completely lost his train of thought, he would have done so as Becca's gaze dropped to his mouth. She quickly jerked her gaze back up, but she'd given herself away. Her body language may have been inadvertent, but it was unmistakable. She wanted him to kiss her.

And he wanted...

He wanted to bury himself in the serenity of her beautiful eyes. He wanted to hide from whomever and whatever he'd been in his probably lurid past. He wanted...

"It's funny, isn't it?" she said softly. "When an attraction is as strong as this." She laughed in disbelief. "I mean, where did it come from? Why does it feel so *right?* Mike Harris—he was a cowboy who worked here up until a few weeks ago—he asked me out maybe five different times. He was good-looking, too, like you, but..." She shook her head. "We had a lot in common, but there was no chemistry. I thought it was the bad timing—I was trying to figure out whether to keep working here or to start sending out résumés, but that hasn't changed. I'm *still* trying to figure out what to do with my life. The timing's *still* lousy. And yet..." She forced a nervous smile, as clearly as shaken by his proximity as he was by hers. "Here I am, asking you to dinner. Go figure, huh?"

Mish found his voice. "The timing's bad for me, too, Becca. *Really* bad."

Becca glanced at Hazel, who seemed completely absorbed by the information on her computer screen. "I have four million things I need to take care of before I'm done for the evening. What do you say we pick up this conversation in a few hours and—"

Mish forced himself to straighten up, to back away. "I think it would be better if I just stayed here at the ranch tonight."

He looked down at the floor so he wouldn't have to see her face. She straightened up, too.

"Oh," she said quietly. "The timing's *that* bad, huh?"

"Yeah. I'm sorry." He truly was. He knew it was time

for him to take his sorry ass and make a quick exit, but
instead, he made the mistake of looking up. And when he
saw the mixture of embarrassment, disappointment and
chagrin in Becca's eyes, he couldn't seem to make himself
go anywhere. Instead he opened his mouth again. "I'm
also... I could really stand to get to sleep early tonight,"
he told her. "I got a little banged up in the river and..."

Wrong. That was the dead wrong thing to say, and he
knew it as soon as the words were out of his mouth.
Someone like Becca wouldn't respond to news that he'd
been hurt by casually waving and saying "Oh, too bad.
Hope you feel better—see you in the morning."

"It's nothing, really," he added hastily. "Just, you
know, a cracked rib."

"Just?" Becca looked at him as if he'd just announced
his intention to cross the Pacific Ocean in a leaky canoe.
"Oh, my God, Mish, why didn't you tell me last night
you were hurt? You didn't say anything at all!"

"I'm fine," he said, silently cursing himself even while
a completely twisted part of him enjoyed her wide-eyed
concern. "A piece of wood—nothing big—hit me while
I was in the water. Like I said, it's only a—"

"Cracked rib," she finished for him, her gracefully
shaped lips tight with disbelief. "I know what a cracked
rib feels like, my friend, and I'm sorry, it's not an *only.*"
She opened the hinged part of the counter that allowed
access to both the front and the back of the room with a
bang. "Get in the truck, I'm taking you to the hospital."

"No!" He *couldn't* go to the hospital. If one of the
doctors or nurses looked a little too closely at the healing
wound on his head...

She looked surprised at his vehemence—even Hazel
glanced up. Mish forced himself to smile. "You know

that all they'll do is wrap it, and I've already done that." *Let's be grown-ups about this,* he told her with his tone.

But Becca was upset. "How do you know it's not broken? I've heard of people with broken ribs actually puncturing their lungs—"

"It's not broken." Mish raised his voice to speak over her. "I know it's not broken because I've had medical training."

He was as surprised by his words as she was. *Medical training.* He hadn't been thinking, and the words had just spilled out. Dear Lord, was it possible he really was a doctor? Or was he just an accomplished liar?

Whichever it was, he'd managed to distract her from her mission of getting him into the truck and to the hospital.

"Look, I'm just a little bruised," he told her, pushing for a win while he was ahead. "Nothing a good night's sleep won't go a long way toward healing."

Becca still didn't look convinced. "I wish you'd told me about it last night."

"I should have," he agreed. "You're right. I just... I knew it wasn't that big a deal. You had enough to think about, and..." He had to put his hands in the back pockets of his jeans to keep himself from reaching out to touch her reassuringly. "Don't make me go to the hospital, Bec. I'm too tired to handle their red tape and...and to sit in the waiting room for hours, and..." He shook his head. "Come on. Please?"

She exhaled a burst of air, as if giving in to a tough decision. "Let me see it."

He blinked at her in surprise. "Let you...?"

"You heard me," she said brusquely, motioning toward the open counter and the door behind it. "Step into the back room if you're modest. Do it right here if you're not. Take off your shirt and let me see.''

She wasn't kidding.

''It looks worse than it is,'' he told her. ''It's pretty badly bruised—doing the ugly rainbow thing, you know. Yellow and green and purple?''

''Now it's *badly* bruised? I thought it was just a 'little' bruise.''

''Well, yeah, it is. I meant compared to other bruises I've had. You know. I mean, I've had worse.'' Lord help him, he was babbling.

Becca crossed her arms. ''Then what's the big deal, Parker?''

The big deal was that he'd managed to wrestle his T-shirt on this morning, but taking it off—especially now, after he'd tightened up a whole lot during the day—was going to be next to impossible. Or screamingly painful. Or both.

''I don't think I can get my T-shirt off,'' he admitted. ''I'm okay, you understand? I just have a little bit of…of discomfort when I lift my arms above my shoulders.''

It was the understatement of the century, and Becca knew it, too.

She shook her head in exasperation. ''You should've worn a shirt that buttons in the front.''

''Yeah, well, the butler must've sent them all to the dry cleaner.'' He was able to make a joke, but he was ashamed to admit he didn't have a shirt that buttoned down the front. He felt his face heat with embarrassment. What kind of man didn't have more than a few T-shirts, four pairs of boxer shorts, and two pairs of jeans to his name? He'd hoped he'd regain his memory and find his closet, but clearly that wasn't going to happen any time soon. And whoever had sent him this package clearly hadn't included his wardrobe.

He had to go into town, spend some more of that money he'd found in his boot. He just hoped it was his to spend.

Becca put her hand on his arm. Her fingers felt cool against his skin. "I'm sorry," she said quietly, squeezing him slightly before she pulled her hand away. "I didn't mean to sound—"

"No," he interrupted her, wishing he'd covered her hand with his, glad that he hadn't. "It's all right."

"I have a few shirts you can borrow. Castoffs from old boyfriends," she explained with a rueful smile. She raised her voice, turning toward the back of the room. "Hazel, excuse me. Do you still have that big pair of scissors in your desk?"

Hazel opened her top drawer. "Miracle of miracles, I actually do."

"May I borrow it, please?"

"Sure thing." Hazel approached them with the scissors, her eyes betraying her curiosity. "What's up? You going to give the hero of the hour here a haircut?"

"Nope. I like his hair long." Becca smiled up at him a little too grimly. "Hold still please, Mish."

She reached out and as she pulled the bottom edge of his T-shirt from his jeans, her cool fingers brushed his stomach. Mish nearly went through the roof. What the...?

"Hold still, dammit," she said again, making it an order as she brandished the scissors.

"What—" he started.

"I'm cutting this off of you." She grabbed hold of his T-shirt again and started to do just that. She had to saw at the bottom hem, the scissors were so ridiculously dull.

Hazel laughed aloud. "Rebecca, honey, there's a time and place for everything, but—"

"He was hurt last night," Becca told her assistant flatly. "He was hit by a big chunk of wood running down the river when he jumped in after Chip."

"It wasn't a *big* chunk—"

"And now he's having some *discomfort,*" she glowered up at him. "He thinks he cracked a rib, and he just told me about it now. *Now.* Hours and hours and *hours* later. He can't get out of his shirt without it giving him more *discomfort,* so I'm cutting it off so I can see how bad it really is, okay?"

"I guess that makes sense, but if someone walks in here—"

"Do me a favor, Hazel," Becca said, "and run to my cabin. There're a couple of large, button-down shirts hanging in my closet, toward the back. One of 'em's red. Go and get it for me, please."

"Are you kidding? And miss *this?*"

"Go. Please?" Becca finally managed to cut through the hem, and she put the scissors down on the counter. She took the package Mish was still holding and set it down as well.

"You want me to lock the door behind me?" Hazel was having way too much fun. She winked at Mish. "You know, it's been a *real* long time since Becca's cut off a cowboy's T-shirt. You should be honored. She doesn't do this to just anyone."

"Hazel." Becca closed her eyes. *"Go."* She shook her head as the door closed behind Hazel, purposely not meeting his gaze. "I'm sorry—I didn't mean to embarrass you. Which side is it on?"

Which side...?

"I'm afraid of nicking you with the scissors, so I'm going to tear your shirt—at least up to the collar. But I don't want to bump your broken rib."

"Cracked," Mish corrected her. "Left side." He reached for the cut in the T-shirt. "I can do this."

But her hands were already there. And she tore the cotton upwards, swiftly but carefully.

The sound of the fabric tearing seemed impossibly loud in the stillness of the room. It was a dangerously erotic sound, one that implied impatience and hinted at an intense passion.

They were alone, and this woman he wanted so badly was literally tearing off his clothes. Heat coursed through him, flames licking the desire he'd so carefully concealed, and bringing it to life. Amusement followed instantly, but it wasn't enough to extinguish the heat.

It was hard to swallow, hard to breathe. Her fingers brushed his bare chest as she gave another pull and tore his shirt all the way to his collar. It was that second time that completely finished him off. He desperately tried to fight his growing arousal even as he laughed softly at the absurdity of it all, but it was a losing battle.

Becca was standing close enough to kiss, and Lord, he wanted to kiss her. He wanted to pull her tightly against him, so she could feel just what she did to him. He wanted to wrap her legs around him, cracked rib be damned.

But he didn't. He stood perfectly still, his hands down at his sides, all amusement completely gone as he forced himself not to reach for her. The effort of doing so, however, made him start to sweat.

She made a soft sound of dismay when she saw the colors of his bruise spreading beyond his Ace bandage. Reaching again for the scissors, she began to saw through the heavier cotton of his crew-neck collar.

She had to move even closer to do it, her thigh pressed against his, her breasts brushing his chest. Mish closed his eyes, feeling a bead of perspiration trickle down the side of his face, praying she'd be done soon. He was trying to be good, but he wasn't a saint.

Finally, she cut through. He opened his eyes only when she stepped back, when he heard the clatter of the scissors on the counter. But he was premature—the torture wasn't over yet. Becca moved closer again, and began to peel his shirt off his shoulders.

"Don't lift your arms or try to help," she instructed him softly, her hands cool against the heat of his skin. She worked his sleeve down his right arm, touching him every inch of the way, and then gently pulled the rest of the shirt from his left.

Mish unfastened the bandage himself, stepping slightly back from her, bracing himself for the words he knew were coming.

"God, you call that a *little* bruise...?" Her words were laced with a tough disbelief, but she actually had tears in her eyes.

"I told you, it looks worse than it is." Please God, don't let her start to cry. If she did, he'd never be able to keep from reaching for her.

She blinked them back forcefully, grimly. "That must've hurt like hell. It hurts you right now—even just to stand there, doesn't it?"

She was angry at him, and while anger was better than empathic tears, it could get him taken to the hospital if he wasn't careful.

"Becca, I swear," he said calmly, as matter-of-factly as he could manage, considering the way his heart was still pounding from her touch. "It's really not that bad."

"Bad enough for you to break out in a cold sweat." With one finger, she caught a bead of perspiration that was dripping down his face, holding it out somewhat triumphantly to show him.

That wasn't cold sweat. It was very, very hot, very steamy sweat. But it was probably better that she didn't know that.

"I can't believe you put in a full day of work," she continued, refusing to be calm or matter-of-fact in response. "I can't believe I stood there and watched you mucking out the stalls, and I didn't have a clue you were hurt!" She was so angry her voice was shaking. She crossed to the back of the office, her movements jerky as she opened one of the drawers and took out a key. "As of right now, you're out of the bunkhouse and staying in cabin 12. I'm marking it unavailable on the books—it's all yours until the end of next week. After that, be ready to clear out if we get any walk-ins, but I doubt we will. We're not full up with guest reservations for another month and a half." She slapped the key onto the counter in front of him. "I'm also giving you a week off."

He opened his mouth, and she held up her hand. "At full pay," she added as ferociously as if she'd just informed him he was getting twenty lashes. "And if it doesn't heal enough for you to move without pain by then, I'll give you another week, but you'll have to let the doctor in town check you out first. Does that sound fair?"

"I appreciate your generosity," Mish told her. "But it's *not* fair. Not for you. You're already short-staffed."

She looked startled, as if she'd never expected him to consider that. "I'll take care of your chores."

"Along with your regular job?"

It was insane, and she knew it. "I'll...call Rafe McKinnon. He told me he was going to his brothers' for a few days before he started looking for work up north. I'll give him that raise he wanted. He'll come back in a flash. He had a major thing for Belinda."

"I thought you said the owner didn't want to—"

"To hell with what Justin Whitlow wants," she said fiercely, coming back out from behind the counter. "If he doesn't like the way I manage his ranch, he can just fire me."

With her eyes sparking and her chin held high, she looked unstoppable. If he weren't careful, she would bulldoze straight over him. "You say that as if it would be a good thing." He tried to smile, keep things a little more light.

She glared back at him. "Maybe it would be. If I'm too damned chicken to quit, then I have to make him fire me, don't I?"

"There's a difference between being chicken and being cautious."

Mish didn't know what was happening. Becca was standing still, but she just kept getting closer and closer to him. And then he realized that he was the one who was moving toward her, pinning her back against the counter. He was drawn toward her as absolutely as if he were a magnet and she were true north. He could smell her hair, see every individual freckle on her nose, watch the irises of her beautiful, warm eyes widen as he leaned closer and closer.

He forced himself to stop, just a whisper away from the softness of her lips, and he felt a rush of relief. Another second, and he would have kissed her. Another fraction of an inch and...

She still didn't move, yet her lips brushed against his. He heard her sigh, saw her eyelids flutter closed as he kissed her again.

As *he* kissed *her*. What was he doing? Was he completely insane?

This was wrong. This was crazy. This was...

Incredible.

She tasted as sweet as he'd imagined, her lips introducing him to a whole new definition for the word *soft*.

Three kisses was enough. Lord, it had to be, it was three kisses too many. And he surely—well, *probably*—would've pulled away from her after three, if only she hadn't touched him.

But the sensation of her hands on the bare skin of his arms was one he couldn't deny himself the pleasure of knowing. And when she slid her hands up to his shoulders, and then to the hair at the nape of his neck...

Three kisses became four and five and more and he lost count, lost all sense of up and down, lost himself in the dizzying sweetness of her mouth.

He pulled her close, dying to cup the softness of her breasts in his hands, but settling for the feel of her against his chest. He kissed her longer, deeper, but still slowly, claiming complete ownership of her mouth.

She'd worked his hair free from the rubber band he'd used to hold it back, and as she ran her fingers through it, he knew the truth.

Three *hundred* wouldn't be enough.

He had to stop kissing her. This could have been the rightest wrong he'd ever done, but it *was* wrong.

Her hands trailed down his back, cool against the heat of his skin, and he groaned.

And Becca nearly jumped back, away from him. "Oh, God." She brought her hand up to her mouth, her eyes enormous. "I'm so sorry—did I hurt you?"

He stared back at her. *Hurt* him...? And he realised she wouldn't have pulled away if she hadn't thought she'd somehow hurt his bruised side. If he hadn't made that strangled sound, she'd be kissing him still. He didn't know whether to laugh or cry.

"There's a Jacuzzi up by the swimming pool," she told

him. "Just inside the main cabana. It might help if you spent some time soaking."

"I'm okay." Mish had to clear his throat. "It's not that bad, really."

How was it possible that mere moments ago his tongue had been inside of her mouth, yet now they were talking to each other as if they were strangers?

They *were* strangers.

And he shouldn't have kissed her. "Becca, I really have to—"

The office door opened with a squeak. And Mish quickly turned toward the counter, suddenly extremely aware that he was standing there not only without a shirt, but still nearly fully aroused as well.

"Oh, yikes," Hazel said. "That must really hurt."

He could only hope she was referring to the bruise on his side.

She turned to Becca. "Sorry that took so long. Going into your closet should merit hazardous-duty pay."

"Ha, ha." Becca took the shirt from her assistant. "I've assigned cabin 12 to Mish, at least until the end of the week. He's got some sick days coming to him, as well."

She moved behind Mish, holding the shirt open, so that he could slip his arms into it with relative ease. The soft cotton smelled like Becca. It was like being enveloped by her hair.

As if she'd been touching him forever, she gently turned him to face her. "Need help with the Ace bandage, too?"

Mish glanced at Hazel, who was back at her computer, across the room.

"I need..." What? To take off Becca's clothes? Undeniably. He lowered his voice, leaned closer to her. "To talk to you. Come outside with me for a sec."

It would be private, but not as private as pulling her with him into the back room where he could shut the door and...

Becca glanced at Hazel, too. And she scooped the key to his cabin, his package and his bandage off the counter. "I'll walk you over to number twelve."

"Thanks, Hazel," Mish called, letting Becca open the door for him. Without the bandage, every step he took seemed to jar his side. Of course, it jarred with the bandage on, too.

"Feel better, sweetie. And don't keep Becca out too late tonight."

"Ignore her," Becca said. "You have permission to keep me out as late as you want."

Oh, Lord. Mish waited until they were both several yards away from the office. "Becca, look, I let myself get carried away back there, and I want to apologize."

She stopped short, right there in the driveway. "Are you apologizing for...kissing me?"

"No, I'm..." He briefly closed his eyes. "Yes. Yeah, I am."

Becca started walking again, quickly enough so that he had to work to keep up with her. "That's funny. I didn't seem to think any of those kisses warranted an apology. I mean, jeez. If you're sorry about *those,* well, the ones you *aren't* sorry about must be out of this world."

"Becca, I—"

"That was a joke, Parker. You're supposed to laugh." She turned, slowing her pace as she walked backwards. "I don't suppose you'd want to discuss this over dinner." One look at his face and she turned around again. "Yeah, I didn't think so."

"I meant what I said about the timing being bad for

me,'' he told her quietly. ''I'm sorry if I confused things back there by finding you completely irresistible.''

Becca laughed as she glanced at him, shaking her head. ''Well, there's the prettiest rejection I've ever heard.''

''I *am* sorry,'' he said again. ''I don't know what happened.''

She handed him the key, the package and the Ace bandage. ''The cabin's down to the left,'' she told him. ''I'll have dinner brought to you on a tray tonight.''

''That's not—''

''Don't worry,'' she said. ''It won't be me carrying the tray. I can take a hint—particularly after it's hammered home.''

Mish watched her walk away. ''Becca.''

She turned back, her eyes subdued.

''If it were purely a matter of what I wanted... If there was nothing else to consider...''

She smiled crookedly. ''Get some rest,'' she said. ''It's got to be tiring being so damn nice.''

''It's definitely Mitch's case,'' Lucky said to Wes over the phone. ''Remember that old leather thing he always carried? Called it his bag of tricks? Well, it's here. In bus locker number 101.''

Lucky had lucked out and found Mitch's bag on his fifth try. The locks had been ridiculously easy to pop open—the luck had come from the lack of bus station security guards to question why he was opening locker after locked locker.

''We're going to set up twenty-four-hour surveillance,'' Lucky decided. ''If he's anywhere in this part of the state, sooner or later he's going to come back for his bag. And when he does, we're going to be watching.''

''Sitting in a bus station for hours on end,'' Wes contemplated. "Bob's gonna hate that almost as much as I do."

"You don't have to like it, you just have to—"

"Do it. I know, I know," Wes interrupted. "You've gotta stop reading those Rogue Warrior books."

"Look, since I'm already here," Lucky said, "I'll take the shift till 0100 hours. I'd offer to stay later but—"

"You've only slept an hour in the past forty-eight. Don't be a hero, Lieutenant. I'll be there at 2000."

"Make it midnight, Cinderella, and I'll take you up on that offer," Lucky countered, looking out the grimy windows at the street. "But first trade in the Batmobile for something with tinted windows. This place is a ghost town. We're going to get looked at if we're sitting in here, watching the lockers. We'll need to sit out on the street." They'd have a clear shot of almost the entire bus station if they parked a vehicle in the right place. "You and Stimpy can duke it out over who plays watchdog for the rest of the night. Any word from our beamish, church-going boy, by the way?"

Wes laughed. "Believe it or not, he's taking one of the church ladies to dinner. He left a message saying that we need to talk to a guy named Jarell Haymore. He was on duty the night we think Mitch might've been at the shelter."

"So if Bob's already found that out, what's he doing taking this lady to dinner?"

"Beats me. He gets weird sometimes."

"What'd *you* find?" Lucky asked, his gaze sweeping the bus station. Even when he wasn't looking directly at it, he kept the row of battered lockers in his peripheral vision. Nothing moved. Anywhere. The bus station was as empty now as it had been an hour ago.

"Well," Wes said, "let's see. Mitch Shaw's nickname during BUD/S training? The Priest."

Lucky laughed. "You're kidding."

"Yeah, and you're going to love this. There are still rumors floating around that Shaw either was or *is* some kind of, ahem, shall we say…man of God?"

"A SEAL who's really a priest?" Lucky shook his head in disbelief. "No way, Skelly. That reeks of BUD/S legend. Kind of like the story about the boat team that got so hungry they barbecued the instructor—and were secured two days early, and given shore leave in Hawaii for their ingenuity. I just don't buy it."

"*I've* never seen him with a woman," Wes said. "Have you ever seen him with a woman?"

"Yeah," Lucky said. God, he was tired. "I saw him with his tongue dragging in the dust as he followed Zoe around out in Montana. And you did, too."

"Yeah, yeah," Wes said impatiently. "Zoe Robinson could make a dead man stand up and dance. But Bob and I went drinking with Shaw a few times after we got back to Coronado. He never went home with anyone—not that I ever knew about. And it wasn't a case of no opportunity, if you know what I mean."

"He *is* a covert operative," Lucky pointed out. "He probably knows a thing or two about how to be discreet. Let's keep this conversation moving forward, Skelly. What else did you find out about him?"

"Medal, medal, medal. Every time the guy turned around, he was being awarded another damn medal," Wes said. "Eighteen, to date."

Eighteen. Lucky swore in admiration.

"Yeah. Won his first medal when he was—get this—fifteen years old."

What? "Are you serious?"

"Why would I make this up?"

"Maybe it was a typo, or—"

"It's too unreal, Luke. It's got to be true. Combine that with Shaw having gone into the SEAL program his first year in the navy. In fact, I think he went from the recruiter's office to BUD/S training. How often does that happen?"

"Never?"

"No, it happened at least once. With Mitch Shaw. The man won two more medals straight out of BUD/S. Since then, it's been kind of a yearly thing for him. 'Oh, it's April. Time for another trip to the White House to add to this collection on my chest.'"

Lucky exhaled a burst of air. "Well, if that's the case, I think we can pretty much assume he hasn't sold the plutonium to the first third-world country ready to hand him a suitcase filled with a million dollars in small bills."

"I don't know about that, Luck-meister. It's these superheroes you've really got to watch out for. When they turn, they turn *bad*. Guys like Shaw are lugging around a ton of resentment. You know, 'The United States made fifteen billion dollars because I saved the world, and all I got were these eighteen lousy medals...'"

Lucky laughed. "Yeah, Skelly, right. You keep on thinking that way. This is a man Admiral Robinson trusted with his life."

"That's true," Wes admitted. "Apparently Robinson tapped Mitch Shaw to join his Gray Group at its inception. In other words, Shaw was Gray Group's agent double-oh-*one*. You know, I'm glad I didn't know all this last year. This guy scares me."

"Anything else?" Lucky asked, rolling his eyes. *Wes* was the scary one.

"I've got some feelers out," Wes said. "You know,

asking around, looking for anyone who might've gone through BUD/S with him. But apparently not too many people survived and... Oh, my *God!*''

Lucky nearly dropped the phone. ''What? Skelly—sit-rep! What's happening?''

''Bobby just walked by with...''

''What?! Who?''

''Oh, baby! Bobby's church lady looks like a super-model! She's got long hair and a miniskirt and lo-o-ong legs and...'' Wes started to laugh hysterically. ''I gotta go—maybe she has a sister.''

Wes hung up, and the silence in the bus station was even more complete than it had been before.

Bobby just walked by with a church lady who looked like a supermodel. Go figure.

Lucky and Wes had both made the mistake of making an assumption, while the truth was, there were no real givens in this world.

Bobby had ended up lucky, in the company of a beautiful woman for dinner, while Lucky had wound up alone in a urine-scented bus station.

Lucky would have assumed the odds of that ever happening were impossibly low.

Kind of like the odds of Admiral Robinson's top covert operative selling out his country by selling stolen plutonium to the highest bidder.

God, what if it was true? What if Mitch Shaw *had* turned?

Chapter 6

Mish sat on the porch of his cabin, waiting for the sun to set.

He'd slept fitfully all day, his dreams haunted by violence. He'd awakened countless times, his heart pounding and his side throbbing. He sat quietly now and tried to pull apart the visions into his past that his subconscious had belched up, like malodorous bubbles from a tar pit. Because dreams, although sometimes imagined events, were often based on things the dreamer had seen or done, weren't they?

There had been a man in religious robes, standing bravely in front of a group of men with assault weapons. Terrorists. It had happened in a heartbeat. One of them had raised his side arm and fired a double burst into the man's head. And as Mish had watched, helpless as a child, so filled with fear and horror that he didn't even dare to cry out, the man had slumped, a lifeless rag, to the floor.

The image still made him feel sick.

He'd dreamed of gazing through a sniper scope, dreamed of sighting a target and squeezing the trigger. He'd dreamed of more personal violence as well. Hand-to-hand combat, a martial-arts free-for-all with the only rule being survival.

And he'd dreamed of a woman—his mother? It was hard to say; her face was turned away, and it kept changing. She sat, her head bowed in grief, weeping. When she *did* look up at him, her tear-bruised eyes silently accusing, he realized she was Becca, and he sat up, instantly awake.

It didn't take much to figure *that* dream out. He was trouble. He'd always been trouble, and the only thing he could bring Becca was pain.

A party of riders approached, heading out for a late-afternoon trail ride. Becca led the way, giving him no more than a brief glance, lifting a hand in a vague greeting as she passed.

True to her word, she'd kept her distance all day—except for that one brief appearance in his dreams.

Hazel had brought him both breakfast and lunch on a tray.

Dinner was going to be served in just an hour, but Becca would be out on the ride for most of that time. Mish could go sit with the guests and…

He didn't want to sit with anyone. He didn't want to do anything except get into the ranch office and look at that personnel file. He needed to find out his former address, and then he had to go there—wherever "there" was—to see if anything was familiar to him.

Frustratingly, the package that had come in the mail yesterday had held no answers—only more questions. It had contained only a key.

It was a bank key—the kind that unlocked a safe-deposit box. But there were no markings on it, no note stuck in with it, nothing. It could have belonged to any of hundreds of safe-deposit boxes in any thousands of banks in New Mexico. Or the world. Why keep it only to New Mexico? This key could well have come from anywhere.

It was driving him mad, his complete lack of a past.

Mish had spent some time today gritting his teeth and trying to force himself to remember. Who was he? *What* was he? But the answers continued to elude him.

All he knew for absolute certain was this relentless sense of unease. Don't tell anyone. Don't talk about why he was here. Don't reveal his weaknesses...

The sound of Becca's laughter drifted back to him through the lengthening shadows, and he had to wonder—not for the first time—if maybe, just maybe he'd be better off not knowing.

"Oh, my God, what are you doing in here?" Becca jumped back from the office screen door when she realized someone—Mish—was inside. She grabbed hold of the porch railing to keep herself from falling backwards down the stairs.

"I'm sorry, I didn't mean to scare you." Mish stepped outside. "I was..." He cleared his throat. "I was actually looking for you."

She stared at him. "In the *dark?*"

"Well, no," he said mildly. "Of course not. There was a light on in the back. I knocked, but no one answered, so I went in."

Becca moved past him, trying not to notice how good he looked standing there in the soft moonlight, wearing the red shirt, sleeves rolled up to his elbows. Her heart was pounding, but only because he'd startled her. She refused to let it be for any other reason.

"The door was unlocked?" she asked. Inside, she turned on the lights. *All* of the overhead lights, not just the pleasantly dim one on her desk.

Mish squinted slightly in the glare as he followed her. "I had no problem getting in."

"I'll have to talk to Hazel. This door needs to be locked at night." She shuffled through the papers on her desk, aware that he was standing there watching her, aware that she was wearing her bathing suit under a very short pair of cutoffs, aware that she had virtually thrown herself at him and he had pushed her away.

But he'd just said that he'd come there looking for her. She glanced over at him. "So what's up?"

He had the kind of dark hair and complexion that had helped coin the phrase "five o'clock shadow." It was now after eight, and he had stubble worthy of the cover of *GQ* magazine. He rubbed his chin in a spot where he had a small white scar as he shrugged. "I just, um... I don't know, really. I was feeling a little better, and I wanted to..." He shrugged again.

"I'm glad you're feeling better. You look..." Delicious. "As if you're...feeling better." Oh, God, why didn't she just go over and drool on his boots?

"I'll definitely be back before the week's out," he told her. "Helping in the barn, I mean."

"What are you, nuts?"

He smiled. It was ludicrous. When he smiled he was even more good-looking. "No, just...bored."

"Ah," she said. "Bored." Becca found what she was looking for—tomorrow's sign-up sheet for the tennis court—and she breezed past him toward the door. She held it open and gazed at him pointedly. He got the message and went out. She flicked off the lights, and shut the door behind her, making sure it was securely locked. "Is that why you came looking for me? Because you were bored?''

"Oh, Lord,'' he said. "*No*. Absolutely not. I just… I…''

"Forget it.'' Becca was embarrassed for herself all over again. And angry at herself, as well. She'd practically invited him to kiss her yesterday, and then when he had, she'd stupidly assumed that he'd been as affected by those kisses as she was. They had been nuclear-powered kisses, kisses that completely bulldozed over any of *her* doubts about bad timing. Hey, for the promise of more kisses like that, she would have invented a whole new calendar. It had been well over twenty-four hours since his lips had last touched hers, and her knees were *still* weak.

Yet Mish had said *no thanks* and walked away. It was a new twist on an old story—a man who was in such a hurry to leave he didn't even bother to start the love affair first.

But right now he was blocking her path. "I was just thinking that even though the timing's bad…'' He couldn't quite hold her gaze. "I don't know,'' he admitted. "It feels kind of like playing with C-4…'' He broke off, shaking his head slightly. "I mean, like playing with explosives,'' he continued. "But…''

"You want to go get a drink?'' she asked him. "Or are you thinking we should skip the formalities and just go straight to bed?''

Oops, her anger was showing. But at least she'd managed to get him to meet her eyes. "I'm sorry,'' she said. "That was rude of me, and uncalled-for, and—''

"This was a really bad idea,'' he said quietly. "You're still upset with me, and you have every right to be. I'm really sorry.'' He turned to leave, and this time she blocked *his* path.

She knew he would eventually leave. Call it whatever you like, self-sabotage, a built-in defense mechanism, lowered expectations, whatever, but she simply didn't hook up with guys who were viable candidates for anything long-term. She knew that about herself. She was okay with Mish leaving. In fact, she was practically planning for it to happen.

That was because she was a realist. That was because she faced the truth and was honest with herself.

But there was a very, very small fragment of time in every relationship, right at the very start, where magic *could* conceivably happen. There was a small moment, maybe an hour or a day or maybe even as long as a week, where hope reigned, and possibilities seemed as limitless and wide as the vast New Mexico sky.

And during that moment, happily-ever-after didn't seem as much like a myth. And true love didn't sound quite so much like some con artist's clever lie.

Becca knew, she *knew,* that Casey "Mission Man" Parker's vocabulary didn't contain the word *forever.* But when she'd looked into his eyes as he'd slowly lowered his mouth to hers, something had shifted, and in that instant she'd been filled with enough hope to cloud her 20/20 vision.

She could have squeezed an entire month of hope out of just one kiss.

"How can you just ignore this?" she asked, gesturing between them. Once again she was throwing herself in front of the rejection train, heaven help her. But she *had* to know. "How can you walk away from something that has such incredible promise?"

He smiled, a beautiful, regretful, slightly crooked smile. "Well, that's just it. For someone who's walking away, I seem to be back where I started, don't I?"

* * *

"So where on earth did you learn to swim like that?"

Mish looked down into his glass of beer. He drank imported Canadian beer, he'd somehow known that without really having to think about it. The light from the pool area lit the amber liquid in a way that was completely familiar. Yes, he'd sat in the shadows and stared into many a glass of imported beer and—he tried to make it completely effortless—he'd learned to swim back when he'd...

Nothing. Nothing came.

"I don't know," he told her. "I've been able to swim since before I can remember."

He had to toss the focus back to Becca, but gently. He was treading a conversational tightrope here. If he asked her the obvious questions about herself—where are you from, how long have you worked here—she'd take that as an invitation to simply turn around and throw similar questions back at him.

He didn't want to lie to her, didn't want to make up a fictional past. Yet at the same time, he knew he couldn't tell *anyone* about his amnesia. Not even Becca with her beautiful eyes.

"I bet you can't remember the first time you rode a horse," he said.

She smiled, and he was glad she'd caught him breaking in to the ranch office. If she'd come along two minutes later, he'd have slipped out undetected, and he'd be sitting alone in his cabin, frustrated by the lack of information in his personnel file.

That file had contained a previous address and a phone number in Albuquerque. There was a fax number jotted on the margin that had a Wyatt City exchange. Other than that, his so-called file was absurdly thin. Still, an address and phone number was more than he'd had to go on an hour ago.

And, unlike an hour ago, he was no longer sitting in his cabin, alone.

"Actually," Becca said, "I can remember in complete detail the first time I rode a horse. I was ten, and it was May. It was warm for New York—I can still feel the sun on my face."

She closed her eyes, lifting her face slightly, as if toward the sun, and just like that, everything Mish was feeling flip-flopped. This was a mistake. Yes, he enjoyed Becca's company. He enjoyed it too much.

He knew he should stand up, plead sudden intense fatigue—which would go over better than insanity—and walk, very, very quickly, back to cabin 12.

Alone.

What was he doing, sitting here this way? Letting himself dream about kissing the graceful length of her neck? Letting himself imagine burying his face in the soft, sweet-smelling cloud of her hair? Letting himself remember how it had felt to kiss her, the giddy, breathless sensation of her mouth and body pressed against him? Letting himself fantasize about waking up early, in bed next to her, and watching her sleep?

He was a killer.

Okay, maybe he didn't know that with absolute certainty, but he was pretty close to positive. He'd certainly spent some time in jail—and if he had to guess what for, the carnage that splattered his dreams provided a heavy-duty hint.

"I sat there in a saddle for the first time," Becca continued, opening her eyes and giving him a smile that would have melted a glacier, "with all this power and grace beneath me. I was so awed, so completely overwhelmed, I nearly cried. The horse was a mare named Teacup, and she must've encountered a dozen little girls just like me every day. She was patient and dignified, and whenever she looked back at me, she seemed to smile. And I fell completely in love. From that moment on, my goal in life was to spend as much time riding as I possibly could. Which wasn't easy, considering I lived in New York."

He couldn't keep himself from asking. "In the city itself?"

"No, about forty-five minutes north of Manhattan. Mount Kisco." She paused, and he braced himself. Here it came. "How about you? Where are you from?"

He'd actually prepared for this one. "I never know what to say when people ask me that," he told her. "I've lived in a lot of different places. I'm not really sure which one I'd call home."

Thankfully, she didn't seem to think his evasive answer was odd, and he turned the focus back on her. "But I don't think I've ever been to Mount Kisco, New York. It's hard to imagine a town with riding stables and horses only a few minutes north of New York City."

"The really good stables were in Bedford," she told him. "I used to ride my bike ten miles…" She laughed. "So I could work in the stables for free. In exchange for riding time, you know? Funny, I still work for close to nothing, only these days I don't have a lot of extra time to ride." She rolled her eyes. "Of course, when Whitlow gets back and fires me, I'll have a *lot* of free time, but nowhere to stable Silver."

"Silver's your horse?"

Becca nodded. "Yeah. This summer we're celebrating our seventh anniversary."

"Silver," he said. "Named after…?"

"Yes, the Lone Ranger's horse. Hi, ho Silver, away. Yeah, I know what you're thinking—not very original. But I didn't name him. And I didn't geld him, either. He was already cut when I bought him."

She laughed then. "That's one way to identify a man who's a greenhorn," she continued. "Talk about geldings. He'll wince every time."

Mish laughed self-consciously. "Did I?"

Her smile was so sincere and contagious. "Oh, yeah."

"It seems...so barbaric."

"Stallions can be pretty wild," she told him. "And too much testosterone in one stable can create chaos. They fight, sometimes pretty viciously. And they get...shall we say *amorous* at the most inopportune moments. Like the time that the Mortensons—four kids under age eight— were staying here at the ranch. I swear, every time we turned around, Valiant had broken through his fence again and was mounting one of the mares."

How had this happened? They were sitting here talking about sex. True, it was only about horses having sex, but still...

Mish cleared his throat and grabbed hold of the conversation with both hands. "You know, I just can't believe Justin Whitlow would fire you." He took another sip of cold beer. "This place can't run itself. And from what Hazel's told me, she's not interested in your job."

Becca drew lines of moisture on the plastic table with the bottom of her glass. "I don't blame her—the way things've been going, *I'm* not interested in my job." She looked up at him. "I don't suppose any of the places you've worked recently were looking for a manager?"

Mish forced himself not to shift in his seat. "Not that I know of, no." He finished his beer, knowing that it was time for him to stand up and say good-night. He had to get out of here before her questions got more personal. Or before he did something completely idiotic, like hold her hand. If he held her hand, he would kiss her again. And if he kissed her again…

"Yeah, I didn't think so." She sighed, her chin resting dejectedly in her palm. "God, I despise the whole job-hunting, résumé thing. And the thought of going into a new position, in a new place, expending all that energy, hoping that this time it'll be better or at least *different,* and then…" She sighed again. "It's depressing. Finding out it's all exactly the same. Same struggles, same old boss-induced problems."

"You need to work for yourself," Mish told her. "Buy your own spread."

Becca laughed. "Yes, thank you very much, I should, but last time I looked, the millionaires weren't exactly lining up with marriage proposals. And the bank's not likely to give me a three-million-dollar mortgage with only a beat-up pickup truck as collateral."

He couldn't seem to force himself to stand up. "Is that really what it would cost?"

"I don't know," she admitted. "It's so outside of the realm of possibility, I haven't even checked to see if any local properties are for sale."

"Maybe you should."

"Why torture myself?" she challenged.

"It's only torture if you think in terms of what you don't have. If you look at it as something to strive for, it's a dream. And it's amazing what people can achieve with just a little bit of hope and a dream."

She was looking at him the same way she had back in the barn, the same way she'd looked at him right before he'd kissed her in the office. Her eyes were soft and so impossibly warm.

"What's your dream, Mish?" she whispered.

"Peace," he said. He didn't have to hesitate. "My dream is to find some peace."

Oh, Lord, he was doing it again. He was leaning toward her, closer and closer and... He pushed himself back in his seat and somehow managed to smile. "Peace, and a ride into Santa Fe tomorrow morning."

"Santa Fe?" She shifted slightly back in her own chair. "Are you leaving already?"

She'd moved just slightly, barely noticeably. That and the shade of disappointment in her eyes were almost imperceptible. Yet there was something about her words, something about her resignation that sucker punched him with a double dose of emotion. Frustration. And anger. Anger at himself. Anger at her for guilting him out every time he...

Every time he...

Left...?

What the *hell...?*

"Mish, are you all right?" Across the table, Becca's eyes were wide as she gazed at him.

He took a deep breath, blowing it out hard. "Sorry," he said. "I was... That was...déjà vu or something, I don't know. Weird." He ran his hand down his face. "I'm just...I'm going to Santa Fe—Albuquerque, actually—for a few days. I have something that needs to be taken care of. I figured as long as you're giving me this time off, I might as well put it to good use. I'll be back by Monday at the latest."

She was still watching him closely, concern in her eyes. "Anything I can help with?"

Becca wasn't being nosy. She actually meant it. She wanted to help.

But what would she do if he told her, "Yeah. See, I

have complete and total amnesia. I have absolutely no idea who I am—oh, except for the little clues I've picked up here and there, which lead me to believe I'm a hired assassin and an ex-con. While I go visit the previous address that was listed in my personnel file and try to stir up any suppressed memories, why don't you check out the faces on the most-wanted list in the post office, and see if you can find me there?''

Mish cleared his throat. ''No,'' he said instead. ''Thanks, though.''

She poured the rest of her beer into her glass. ''Well,'' she said. ''I'm actually driving into Santa Fe day after tomorrow, if you want to wait until then to go. I've got to put in an appearance for the Whitlows at a fund-raising dinner for the Santa Fe Opera.''

''Thanks,'' Mish said again. ''But the sooner I get there, the better. I really should go tomorrow.''

''Maybe,'' Becca said, then stopped. She laughed. ''God, this is insane, but... I have an extra ticket to the dinner. The food's great...and I'm just *so pathetic*—I can't believe I'm asking you out *again*.'' She laughed again as she slumped over the table, head buried in her arms.

Mish didn't know what to say.

She lifted her head and looked him in the eye. ''I don't do this with everyone. In fact, I've never done this with anyone. I just...really like you.''

Her words warmed him. She *liked* him. ''I don't know why. You don't know me, Bec. I could be someone awful.''

''No, you couldn't. You're too nice. You have this basic goodness at the core of your being—''

He let loose a pungent curse he rarely said aloud. ''You

don't know that. So I pulled a kid out of a river. That doesn't make me a saint.''

''Maybe not, but it makes you someone I want to know better.'' She leaned toward him. ''Come to this dinner with me—as a friend. We can set some boundaries right now, if you want. No sex. Okay? We meet at the dinner, we leave separately. No pressure, no temptation, even.''

Mish had to laugh at that. ''You know, I think this is a first for me. Being enticed to go out to dinner by the promise of *no* sex.''

Her eyes sparked. ''If you want, we can set different boundaries—''

''No,'' he said hastily.

''I'll leave the ticket at the door for you,'' Becca told him. She stood up, and he rose to his feet, too. ''The party's being held at the Sidewinder Café—it's a restaurant near the center of town. Doors open at six. I'll probably arrive at six forty-five.''

He had nothing to wear to a formal party. And even if he did, he had no business deceiving this woman any further. She thought he was *nice*. He knew—for both of their sakes—he should stay far away from her.

But when he opened his mouth, he said, ''All right. I'll see you on Saturday. At six forty-five.''

He was completely insane.

''Well,'' Becca said. ''Good.''

And she smiled. And when she smiled, her entire face lit up, and as Mish watched her walk away, being completely insane suddenly didn't seem so terrible.

Bobby and Wes climbed into the van, carrying two paper bags from which there escaped an incredibly delicious aroma.

''Hey,'' Lucky said, glancing up from the less-than-inspiring view he had of the bus station lockers. From where he was parked, he could see locker number 101 through the tinted van windshield and through the bus station window. It wasn't the most inconspicuous surveillance setup, but it was better than sitting on the grimy plastic bus-station chairs, in full view of anyone driving by. "I didn't expect you guys for another few hours."

"Man cannot live on M&Ms from the candy machine alone," Wes said, digging through the bags. "So we brought you this celebratory meal from Texas Stan's."

With a flourish, Wes handed Lucky a large container of Texas Stan's four-alarm chili and a plastic fork.

"Bless you, Ren. Bless you, Stimpy. What are we celebrating?" Lucky asked, taking the lid off the container. God, it smelled good.

"Joe Cat called," Wes reported, his mouth already filled with one of Texas Stan's spicy beef enchiladas.

Lucky nearly dropped the chili. "Did Shaw turn up?"

"No," Bob said from the back seat. "The news is good, but not *that* good. The captain had a message for you from your sister."

"Ellen?"

"Yeah," Wes grabbed for one of the sodas, using it to hose down the inside of his mouth. Lucky knew from experience that Texas Stan's spicy enchiladas were only slightly less hot than the chili. "She called to tell you she's getting married."

Lucky laughed at that. "Yeah, right, Skelly. Very funny. What did she really want?"

"We're serious," Bobby said. "Ellie's engaged. I called her from the motel. She sounds really happy."

"The guy's some college geek," Wes reported.

They weren't kidding. Lucky carefully put down his container of food. "Ellen's not old enough to get married.

She's only…what?'' He had to do the math. "Hell, she's barely twenty-two.''

"My little sister, Colleen, is twenty-two.'' Wes took another bite of his enchilada. "Ann frr's hrr errrurr mmrrr.''

"Colleen *is* old enough to get married,'' Bobby countered, completely able to understand him even with his mouth full. "You guys look at your little sisters and see ten-year-olds. It's like you're stuck in a time warp. Other guys look and see two very hot, very full-grown women.''

Wes swallowed and turned to face the back seat. "Colleen? *Hot?* No way. Last time I was home, she skinned her knee skateboarding. She's the world's oldest living tomboy—she doesn't even know she's a girl. Thank God.''

"Oh, come on, Skelly.'' Bobby shifted so that he was sitting forward and the entire van shook. "Remember when we visited her at college? Guys like her. A *lot*. They were always dropping in to her dorm room, remember?''

"Yeah, she's a great mechanic and they came asking her to fix their cars,'' Wes countered. "That's not the same thing.''

"There's no way I'm letting Ellen get married,'' Lucky said grimly.

"Maybe she's pregnant,'' Wes said helpfully. "Maybe the geek knocked her up.''

Lucky glared at him. "You should consider a new career writing greeting cards, Skelly. You always know *exactly* the right thing to say.'' He glowered at Bobby in the rear view mirror. "Why aren't *you* eating?''

"He's having dinner again with the supermodel.''

Bobby smiled serenely. "Her name is Kyra.''

"I hate you,'' Wes said. "First you make me stop smoking, now this.''

"Trade you Kyra for Colleen."

Wes snorted. "Yeah, sure you would." He turned to Lucky. "I got E-mail today from a SEAL went through BUD/S training with the Priest."

Ellen was getting married. Lucky shook his head in disbelief.

"Actually," Wes expounded, "this guy—Ruben is his name—he went through BUD/S, but the Priest—Mitch—didn't."

That caught Lucky's attention. "Come again?"

"Apparently, Mitch didn't make it through BUD/S his first time around. It took him two tries." Wes paused and noisily sucked down half of a milk shake. "It's a great story, Lieutenant. You're going to love this."

Lucky just looked at him. Waiting.

Wes was unperturbed as he searched for a napkin and delicately wiped his mouth. "Ruben told me in this E-mail that the Priest made it nearly all the way through BUD/S—no complaints, not a lot of talking at all. Just silently getting the job done."

"Unlike those of us sitting here who talked nonstop through basic training," Bobby interjected.

"I'm not talking to you anymore," Wes said. "I hate you, remember? You've let a supermodel come between us."

Lucky closed his eyes. "Skelly."

"Yeah. So it's the morning before Hell Week starts, right? And the Priest wakes up, and he's got the flu. Raging fever, intense intestinal distress. I mean, he's sick as a dog. Sicker. He knows if any of the instructors find out, he'll get pulled and stuck in the hospital."

Wes finished the rest of his milk shake. "So," he continued. "He keeps his mouth shut. At least he tries to. But he gets pulled when he starts vomiting blood. Dead giveaway he's got some medical problem. They try to talk him into ringing out, but he refuses. They drag him to the hospital, but as soon as they leave him alone, he breaks out of his room. He goes out the window—and this is with a hundred-and-four-degree fever—and rappels to the ground from the fifteenth floor.

"Ruben told me the Priest just showed up back in Coronado. Middle of the night. He just rejoins his boat team as if he's never been gone. He can barely stand, but there he is. 'Ready for duty, sir!' This time, the instructors figure they'll just wait for him to keel over, but when he falls, he crawls. The tough little sonuvabitch doesn't stay down. So they promise him he can start over again with the candidates from the next cycle, but that's not good enough for the Priest. He won't quit. They end up having to knock him out with a shot of Valium. And when he wakes up, Hell Week's over."

"Oh, man." Lucky couldn't imagine going through Hell Week, that awful endurance test while stricken with the flu.

"He came through the next cycle," Wes said, "head of the class."

For several long moments, they sat quietly.

"Wherever he is," Bobby said, breaking the silence, "I hope he's okay."

Then Wes spoke, voicing aloud the question running through Lucky's mind. "Is it possible for a guy like that to sell out?"

"No way," Bobby said.

Lucky wasn't so sure.

Chapter 7

Becca took a glass of champagne from the waiter's tray, smiling her thanks, trying her hardest to pay attention to Harry Cook as he talked about his granddaughter's first ballet recital.

Harry was a sweet man—generous with his millions, too—and Becca had met four-year-old Lila during last year's Children's Hospital fund-raising picnic. The story Harry was telling was amusing, but Becca was finding it hard to focus.

She turned her back on the arched entrance that led into the restaurant from the lobby, determined not to spend the evening waiting for Mish to show.

Or not to show.

That was tonight's question.

She took a sip of champagne, forcing herself to slow down, to breathe. She usually didn't drink during these parties. After all, she was being paid to attend, to schmooze, to reinforce Justin Whitlow's contacts with the well-to-do population of northern New Mexico.

But tonight, she needed the champagne.

She laughed with everyone else as Harry finished his story, as he did what had to be a rather accurate imitation of Lila's final bow, but then she broke away from the group, heading toward the door to the Sidewinder's central outdoor plaza.

The night air was much warmer than the relentless chill of the restaurant's air-conditioning. And since the long dress she was wearing exposed all of her arms and most of her back, she welcomed the heat.

There were only a few people outside, and Becca was glad to take a breather from the crowd. She sipped her champagne, gazing up at the strings of festive lights that decorated the plaza, dancing in the gentle breeze.

Mish wasn't going to come.

Even if he *did,* he would probably be too embarrassed to enter the high-class restaurant in his jeans and T-shirt.

The moon was a sliver in the sky—far more beautiful than the strings of lights. And the breeze carried the scent of flowers—proof that nature could provide far more enticing decorations for a party than even the chic Sidewinder.

Becca looked up at the moon, refusing to wonder if she would ever see Mish again.

If she didn't, so be it. He'd been around when it had been most important—to save Chip's life. If she had to choose between that and his appearance tonight at this party, well, that was a no-brainer. As much as she liked Mish, she'd take Chip, alive and well, any day. And even though Mish wasn't going to show, well, at least the possibility of his appearance had inspired her to wear this dress.

It had been hanging in the back of her closet for years, hanging in the back of her *mother's* closet since before Becca had been born. Her great-grandmother had made it during the 1930s. It was elegant and graceful and undeniably sexy. Blatantly sexy.

Definitely not something she wore every day.

She heard the door to the restaurant open, like a portal to a different world. The music and laughter was momentarily louder before it closed again, shutting out all but the heartiest laughter and the faint kitchen sounds of dishes clinking together.

Becca glanced up to see a man in a dark suit stop to get his bearings, still standing by the door. He wasn't Mish—his hair was too short, and besides, the suit looked expensive. She looked away. But she could see him from the corner of her eye as he took in the bar on the far side of the plaza, the couples talking quietly in the shadows, the strings of lights, the flowers, the trees, the moon.

He looked at the moon for a long time.

She turned her back to him before he could glance at her a second time.

One thing about this dress, it made men take long second glances. And some men even were bold enough to approach her.

Sure enough, she could hear his footsteps on the bricks, coming closer. He'd started walking toward her.

Becca turned toward the door, ready to nod politely on her way back into the restaurant and…

"Sorry I'm a little late. The bus from Albuquerque had a flat."

Mish?

It was. He'd gotten a haircut. And a new suit. And he was so clean-shaven, he must've stopped for a touch-up in the men's room before coming outside.

"You look incredible," he told her, his voice nearly as velvety-soft as the night.

"You do, too." Her own voice was husky as well.

He smiled crookedly, his eyes crinkling slightly at the edges. "Yeah, I cleaned up pretty well, huh?"

She touched the lightweight wool of his jacket sleeve. "Where on earth did you get the money for this?"

He stepped back slightly, pulling free from her grasp, putting both of his hands into his pockets. A gentle reminder. No sex. No touching. "I called my man Jeeves, had him wire me some funds from my Swiss account."

Becca laughed. "I'm sorry, I shouldn't have asked. It's none of my business."

"Truth is, I had some cash," Mish told her. He'd been hoping he'd find the rest of his clothes and his other belongings—books, at least, because *surely* he had books— at the address listed in his personnel file. But he'd gone all the way to Albuquerque only to find that the address had been a fake. The street existed, but not the number. It had been a business district, filled with rundown pawnshops and seedy topless bars. Everything about it was completely unfamiliar.

The phone number Mish had found in the file had been disconnected, as well.

He'd spent nearly two days wandering around Albuquerque, looking for something, *anything* that triggered any kind of recognition.

The closest he'd come to a flicker of memory had been when he'd gone to the mall and tried on this suit. As he slipped on the jacket and looked at himself in the mirror, he'd gotten the sense that something was wrong. He'd worn suits before, but the jacket had been different. There was something about the neckline or the collar or... He'd stared at himself in the three-way mirror until the fitting-room clerk had gotten nervous, but the answer hadn't come to him. How could a suit jacket be different? Men's jackets had been virtually the same for nearly a hundred years. It didn't make any sense at all.

"How are you feeling?" Becca asked.

"Much better," he told her. "Although I'd appreciate it if you could refrain from elbowing me in the side for another day or two."

She laughed. "I'll try."

She really did look amazingly beautiful. Her dress was a killer, with narrow straps that were barely there, but necessary to hold up the front, like some kind of feat of engineering. The fabric was shimmery—not quite white, not quite gold, but a color somewhere in between that set off her golden-brown curls almost perfectly. She'd actually tried to comb her hair into some semblance of a style, using clips to hold it in place, but it was rebelling. He had to smile.

"You decided to leave your cowboy hat home, huh?"

"No, just out in the truck," she countered.

Mish kept his eyes on her face, away from all that smooth skin, away from the golden-white material that clung enticingly to her breasts and stomach and fell in a smooth sheet all the way to the floor. But he couldn't resist taking a peek at her feet.

"No," she said, "I'm not wearing boots." She lifted her skirt slightly to show him.

Her shoes looked like something Cinderella might wear. Delicate and barely there. As sexy as the dress.

She was smiling at him, and despite the fact that he was playing with fire here tonight, he felt himself start to relax. Albuquerque had held no answers. Maybe he'd never find out where he'd come from, what he'd done. And maybe that was okay.

"Are we allowed to dance?" he asked her.

She knew he was referring to the no-sex rule, and she thought about it. "I think it's probably okay. I mean, as long as we're in public, sure. We can dance. But only after dinner."

Mish had to laugh, and he couldn't begin to guess. "Why only after dinner?"

She finished her glass of champagne and set it down on a nearby table, giving him a smile that warmed him to his very soul. "Because I'm starving."

She headed for the door, and Mish followed her inside. He probably would have followed her anywhere.

"She moved next door when I was in second grade," Becca told Mish.

They'd found a table in a quiet corner of the restaurant, and had talked about books and movies while they'd had dinner. Or rather, she'd talked. Mish had listened.

He was listening still, watching her across the small table, giving her every ounce of his attention. He listened with his eyes as well as his ears, his face lit by the flickering light from a single candle. It was a little disconcerting to be the focus of all that intensity. But it was extremely nice, too—as if everything she had to say mattered. As if he didn't want to miss a single word.

"We were inseparable right through high school," she continued. "And when we went to college, we stayed tight. Peg was going to be a kindergarten teacher, and I was going to be a veterinarian." She had to smile. "Only I hated it. I don't know what I expected—probably a few years of classes and then an internship spent cavorting across the countryside with the doctor from *All Things Bright and Beautiful,* helping birth lambs and foals and bunnies. Instead, I was stuck in a city animal hospital, tending to dogs that had been hit by cars. House pets that had been abused. We had one woman bring in her cat— someone had sprayed him with lighter fluid and set him on fire. It was…'' She shook her head. ''It was really awful. But I was determined not to quit. Being a vet had been my dream for so long. I couldn't just abandon it.''

Mish had been watching her, his eyes the most perfect blend of green and blue and brown, but now he looked down, into his coffee cup. ''It's hard to admit you've made a mistake, particularly on that scale.''

''I think I was afraid of my parents' disapproval,'' she admitted.

He looked up again, into her eyes, and Becca felt the room tilt. ''So what happened?''

''Peg was diagnosed with cancer.''

Mish nodded, as if he'd been expecting her to tell him that awful news about her lifelong best friend. ''I'm sorry.''

''It was Hodgkin's disease. In an advanced stage. She did chemo and radiation, and…'' God, it had been ten years, and Becca *still* had to blink back tears. Of course, she never talked about it, never talked about Peg. She couldn't remember the last time she'd given so much of her soul away for free. But she truly wanted Mish to understand. Because maybe then he'd know why she'd been pursuing him so relentlessly.

''She died eight months later,'' Becca told him.

Silently, Mish reached across the table and took her hand.

Becca felt fresh tears well as she gazed down at their intertwined fingers. His hands were warm, his fingers broad and work roughened. She wanted him to hold her hand, but she didn't want him to do it out of pity.

Gently, she pulled her hand free. ''She knew she was

dying,'' Becca said. ''And even though I'd stopped com-
plaining about school—how could I bitch about something as trivial as boring classes and dull teachers when
she was going through this real life hell?—she knew I
was unhappy. And she made me talk about it. Yes, I hated
school, but I wouldn't quit. I felt trapped by my expectations and my sense of responsibility. And she asked me
what I loved doing best, more than anything else in the
world. Of course, she knew—I loved riding. I told her,
great, who was going to pay me money to ride all day?
And she told me to go be a cowboy, work on a ranch, to
do whatever I had to do—just make damn sure that I was
happy. Life was too short to waste.''

Mish's eyes were beautiful but inscrutable. He surely
understood what she was telling him, but he didn't ac-
knowledge that her words applied to him—to the two of
them and the attraction that simmered between them. And
when he spoke, he surprised her. ''So why are you still
working at the Lazy Eight?''

She didn't answer right away. ''I love New Mexico.''
It sounded exactly like what it was—an excuse for wimp-
ing out.

Mish nodded.

Becca briefly closed her eyes. ''Yes, okay, so I'd be
much happier working for myself. I bought a lottery ticket
tonight. Maybe I'll get lucky and win enough money to
buy my own ranch.'' And maybe Silver would grow
wings and fly. Or—even more unlikely—maybe she'd
wake up tomorrow morning with Mish in her bed.

She looked away, suddenly aware she'd been eyeing
him as if he were the dessert cart. ''I should really go
schmooze.''

''You know, sometimes it works better if you make
your own luck,'' he told her as she pushed her chair back

from the table. "If you seek it out rather than waiting for it to come to you."

Becca touched him then, just lightly, the tips of her fingers sliding down his cheek in the softest caress. "Haven't you noticed me trying?"

She walked away, her heart pounding, before she could see his reaction.

She'd taken the first step across those boundaries they'd set between them and the next move was Mish's. Would he stay or would he run?

Becca knew everyone who was anyone in Santa Fe.

She worked the room like a pro, shaking hands, remembering names, introducing Mish with a brief anecdote about the people he was meeting. "This is James Sims. Don't ever put money on the game if you golf with him. He's good enough to go pro," and "Mish Parker, Frank and Althea Winters. Their granddaughter was just accepted at Yale University. Biochemistry major."

It wasn't an act. She was really good with people. And they all liked her, too. Who wouldn't, with her warm, inclusive smile?

She hadn't expected him to stick around after dinner. Mish had seen the surprise in her eyes as he'd approached her by the bar after he'd had a second cup of coffee— and let his pulse return to normal.

He wasn't sure himself why he hadn't left. Her message had been all too clear as she'd told him the story of her friend's death. Life was too short. Cut to the chase. Take the plunge. Just do it.

And, in case he'd been completely dense, she'd driven the message home by touching him lightly, provocatively. *Come home with me tonight.*

Mish wanted to. He wanted to give in. The temptation

was so strong, it seemed to buzz and crackle around him. He knew he *should* run for the door.

As he watched, Becca let herself be waltzed out onto the dance floor with a man in his eighties.

She sparkled as she laughed with him, and since she was at a safe distance, Mish allowed himself the luxury of aching for her. He longed to lose himself in the sweetness of her body, the warmth of her mouth. It was more than sex, although it was certainly about sex, too—he couldn't pretend otherwise. He burned for her, but he also wanted to lie down with her in his arms, to fall asleep and dream not about the past, but of the future.

A clear, bright future, unshadowed by mistakes and regrets and hidden doubts.

Mish stood there watching Becca, not running anywhere. He couldn't run. He was completely glued in place.

The song ended, and the old man led her back to him.

And then, for the first time in what had seemed like hours, they were alone. The room was clearing out, the party almost over.

"The band's getting ready to pack up," she said, attempting to refasten one of the clips in her hair.

They still hadn't shared a dance. It was probably just as well.

"Where are you staying?" he asked, not touching her for the nine-thousandth time that night. He had to find the strength to stay away from her. She deserved someone better than him.

"I'm down the street at the old Santa Fe Inn. They've just restored it—it's beautiful." She smiled. "Don't worry, I won't ask if you want to come see it." She held out her hand for him to shake. "Thank you for a lovely evening."

Mish gazed at her hand in disbelief. Did she honestly think he would briskly shake her hand and let her walk out into the night, wearing a dress that would draw the attention of every human male within a ten mile radius?

"I'll walk you to your car," he told her.

"I'm parked over at the inn."

Damn. "Then I'll walk you to the inn." Walking her to her hotel would be a mistake. He knew that for a fact before the words even left his mouth.

"You really don't have to," she said as if she could read his mind.

"I won't come inside," he told her. Told himself.

"Well," Becca said as she headed toward the door, "I won't force you to, so you don't have to look so tense."

Mish rolled his head slightly. "I'm not tense."

Becca just smiled at him.

The night air was cooler now, and she took a deep breath as they stepped out onto the street.

A group of men had just come out of a bar named Ricky's across the street, and were heading back toward the center of town. There were four of them, and as Mish watched, they noticed Becca. First two, then three and four. Heads turned, body language changed. Their stares weren't disrespectful, just very, very interested.

And he resisted the urge to put his arm—or at least his jacket—around her shoulders.

She took another deep breath, and her dress clung to her in a way that was hard to ignore. And now he was staring, too.

"It's a beautiful night." She hugged herself, rubbing her upper arms. "I love it when it cools off like this."

"Are you warm enough? I can give you my jacket..."

Becca smiled at him. "Considering we're about twelve more steps from the inn, and considering it's probably all of seventy degrees, I think I'll survive without danger of frostbite, thanks."

Mish could see the sign out in front of the inn. The place was, literally, just a few dozen yards away. In just a few moments, Becca would go inside and he'd be alone.

"Why did Justin Whitlow want you to come to this party tonight?" he asked, hoping maybe she'd linger, praying that she wouldn't. "I mean, was the point just to keep his name on the tip of everyone's tongue, or was there something else you were trying to do?"

She gazed up toward the moon. "Whitlow's actually trying to arrange a fund-raising event for the opera at the Lazy Eight. He gets to be the big generous benefactor that way, because he'd donate the facility. Except, of course, people would have to stay over. And then there would be the publicity he'd get for hosting the event. Not to mention the bonus of showing off the ranch to all those Santa Fe Opera supporters who have money to burn."

"Money to burn."

She turned to glance at him, amusement in her eyes, a small smile playing about the corners of her lips. "Yeah. Amazing concept, isn't it? But nearly everyone I introduced you to tonight has more money than they know what to do with."

Mish touched her. For the second time that evening, he couldn't help himself. He just stopped short and took her arm. "There's your answer, Becca."

She didn't know what on earth he was talking about. But she didn't pull away. Her skin was so soft beneath his fingers, he was momentarily distracted, temporarily thrown.

She was standing close enough to kiss, and the way she was looking up at him—eyes wide, lips slightly parted—

he nearly gave in to the temptation to cover her mouth with his own.

But he didn't kiss her, though he didn't release her, either. "You just spent four hours tightening your relationship with dozens of men and women who have—in your words—'money to burn.' Come on, Bec, don't you get it? These people *like* you. If you went to them with a plan to buy a spread and turn it into a vacation ranch, you could very well find yourself all the financial backing you'd need right here in Santa Fe."

She was wary, keeping her natural enthusiasm buried, at least for the moment. "I'd need to work it all out— down to the last detail—before I started asking anyone for money. I'd have to find a piece of property..." She shook her head. "God, I don't have time to go driving halfway across the state to—"

"Use the Internet," Mish interrupted. "The computer back at the Lazy Eight office has Internet access, doesn't it?"

"Actually, it doesn't," Becca told him. "But I just got access on my laptop. I'm trying to create a website for the Lazy Eight. In my spare time." She laughed. "I hear myself say that, and I sound completely insane. *What* spare time?"

He finally let go of her, and took a step back. When she laughed, he found her irresistible, but kissing her now would only complicate things beyond belief. "When we get back to the ranch tomorrow, we can use your laptop to search for properties listed for sale."

"My laptop's upstairs in my hotel room," Becca told him.

Upstairs. In her room. Mish didn't say anything, didn't move. He just looked at her, imagining the hushed quiet of this four-star hotel's rooms, imagining one that smelled faintly of her unique brand of shampoo, imagining dim lights, a king-size bed, Becca turning her back to him, his fingers finding the tiny zipper pull at the back of her dress and...

"I've only been on-line a few times," she continued. "Is it really possible to do that kind of a property search?"

Mish nodded. "Yeah, I think so. We'd just need to use a search engine. Plug in the information we're looking for and..."

She was looking at him curiously. "Where did you learn about the Internet?"

Um. Good question. It was just one of those things he knew, like the waist size of his jeans. He shrugged. "I don't know. I just...picked it up here and there, I guess."

"Would you mind coming up and..." She broke off. "I'm sorry. This can wait for tomorrow." She looked chagrined. "I didn't mean to make you uncomfortable."

"If you like," Mish said, "I can come up for a few minutes—help you get signed on and started." But then he would leave.

"This isn't just a ploy to get you up to my room," she told him earnestly.

Mish laughed. "I know." He—and she—would be safe as long as he didn't kiss her. And he *wasn't* going to kiss her. "I won't stay long."

Chapter 8

"Okay," Mish said, "here we go. This looks more like the kind of place you're looking for."

Becca inched her chair even closer to the computer screen. She'd long since kicked off her shoes, and she curled her feet and legs underneath her long skirt.

Mish had thrown his jacket onto the bed at least forty-five minutes ago, and had loosened his tie and rolled up his sleeves to his elbows.

It was amazing. He worked the keyboard and mouse of her computer the way Becca handled horses. It was as if the computer were a part of him, a permanent attachment.

She had to laugh. Her new ranch hand was a secret computer nerd.

"Look," he said, doing something with the mouse and making new pictures flash on the screen. "This one looks really great. The price seems right. It doesn't have a *whole* lot of acreage, but it borders a state park, so—"

"It's in California," Becca realized as she leaned even closer. "Down near San Diego."

"It's beautiful down there," Mish told her, doing something with the mouse and the computer to mark the site so that she could find it again.

"God, but California...?" Becca shook her head. "Everyone I know is here in New Mexico. I don't know anyone who lives in California."

"I live in California," he said. His hands suddenly stilled on the keyboard and he looked up at her. "I'm from California." He laughed.

What was he telling her? That he wanted her to move to California to be near him? It didn't make sense. He didn't even want to kiss her. Why would he want her to live near him?

"San Diego," he told her. "I lived there when I was a kid. We had a beach house. It was..." He laughed again. "I actually remember this. The ocean's so beautiful and..."

He was gazing at her, but he quickly looked away, returning his attention to the computer screen as if he'd just realized how close together they were sitting.

"I should go," he said quietly. "I've already stayed too long."

"You know, I think that was the first time I've ever heard you volunteer information about yourself," Becca mused.

He shrugged, forced a smile. "I don't have a whole lot to tell." He rubbed his forehead as if he suddenly had a headache.

"I've been trying to guess," she said, resting her chin in her hand. "What exactly did you do, Mish? Something you're still paying penance for? Is that why you turned down Ted Alden's check? You don't drink—at least not heavily. I've never seen you drink more than a single beer. Tonight you only had soda even though there was an open bar. And you've made no attempt at all to replace your stolen driver's license. I don't know a single man who wouldn't have put a priority on getting his license back. Unless he didn't have one. Unless it had been revoked. Maybe for D.U.I. Am I getting warm?''

Mish sighed. ''Becca—''

She touched him. She put her hand on the taut muscle of his suntanned forearm, wanting to touch him despite the fact that he'd pushed her away every other time she'd reached out for him.

''It doesn't matter to me,'' she told him quietly. ''Wherever you've been, whatever you've done, it's irrelevant. Whatever mistakes you've made, they're in the past. I like who you are right now, Mish. I don't care where you went to college, or if you dropped out of high school, or got left back in second grade. I'd love to know those things about you, sure, but only if you want to share them with me. If not, that's okay, too.''

She slid her hand down to his, and Mish turned his arm over so that their fingers could interlock. He stared down at their two hands, knowing the inevitable. He and Becca had been barreling toward this moment from the instant he'd agreed to attend the fund-raising dinner with her. Despite everything he'd told himself, he'd known it from the start. He was here, in Becca's room, because he couldn't stay away.

''I don't know many men—or women—who would've jumped into that river after that boy. It was dangerous as hell, and you didn't even hesitate.''

''I'm a strong swimmer.''

''You're a good man.''

He levelly met her gaze. "If I were a good man, I'd say good-night right now and leave."

"I said you were good. I didn't say you were a saint."

She was close enough to kiss, and he knew, unless he did or said something soon, that she was going to kiss him.

"I can't give you what you deserve," he whispered. And then he kissed her, because he couldn't wait for her to kiss him, not one second longer.

Her lips were as sweet as he remembered, her mouth eager, hungry. She melted against him, her arms slipping up around his neck, pulling him closer.

He'd meant to kiss her softly, sweetly. Instead he almost inhaled her, his hands sliding against the smooth fabric of her dress, against the soft warmth of her body beneath.

Her bed was three steps away. All he had to do was lift her up and...

He pulled free, breathing hard. "Becca..."

Her brown eyes held a clear echo of that powerful kiss's molten heat. "Stay with me tonight."

"Just tonight?" His voice sounded husky to his own ears. "Is that really what you want—a one-night stand?"

"I'm looking for a lover—and a friend—who'll stick around only until it's time to leave," she admitted. "But it's impossible to know when that time will be, especially when a relationship is just starting. Still, I would hope it wouldn't be after only one night."

"So you want a...relationship."

Becca laughed at that. "You say it as if it has a capital *R*. As if it's something enormous and terrifying."

He couldn't joke about it. "Isn't it?"

"No! I hate to break it to you," she said, "but we've already *got* a relationship. We've had one from the moment you walked onto the Lazy Eight and asked for Becca Keyes.'' She shifted impatiently in his arms, tightening her grip on him, moving closer when he would have set her aside. ''All I want is to change the parameters of that relationship to include long stretches of time that we can spend naked together. But that time's not infinite. Frankly, I don't believe in forever.''

She held his gaze as if she were trying to convince him of the truth she spoke by letting him see into her soul. ''Honest, I'm not looking for true love, Mish. I promise you, when the time comes, I'll let you walk away.'' Her eyes were gentle then as she pushed his hair back from his face. ''You don't have to worry about hurting me.''

She kissed him. Softly, then harder and deeper, and he kissed her back until the room spun, until he couldn't breathe, until he thought his heart might explode in his chest. He should make a break for the door and not stop running until he hit the other side of town. Because he could taste forever in her kiss. Despite everything she'd said, it was back there. A hint of promise that made him want... Made him want...

It couldn't be... Was the bittersweet longing that he could practically taste his *own?* He nearly laughed aloud.

Wouldn't *that* be the ultimate in irony? Here was this fabulous woman giving him everything he could possibly want from a lover—including the serenity of knowing she had no expectations—and *he* was the fool who was falling hard.

Becca broke their kiss and pulled back to gaze searchingly into his eyes. She shook her head at all the doubt and confusion he knew was swimming there.

''How can you possibly kiss me that way and still resist this?'' she asked. She laughed in disbelief. ''Maybe you *are* a saint.''

He *wasn't* in love with her. He was infatuated, sure. He was wildly attracted, without a doubt. But *love...?* He barely knew her. No, this was about sex, about chemistry, about attraction. It had to be.

So why *was* he resisting?

"There's a lot I can't tell you, Bec," Mish confessed, torn between wanting to open up about his inability to remember his past, and that intense conviction deep in his gut that he shouldn't breathe a word about it to anyone. "About myself, I mean, but...I do know I'm no saint."

"Then stay," she whispered. "Please." Her gaze dropped to his lips, and for a fraction of a second, time hung.

Anticipation surrounded Mish breathlessly, heart-poundingly. She'd told him she didn't need to know more about him than she already knew. She'd told him she wasn't looking for more than a short-term lover. She'd given him permission to keep his secrets to himself, guilt-free.

And then she leaned forward and kissed him again.

And it was all over.

Even back when he'd first walked into the inn, there had probably only been a six-percent chance that he would walk back out of this hotel before dawn. But that chance just dropped to zero.

His willpower had been completely shattered.

He wasn't going anywhere.

Except maybe to heaven.

He pulled her hard against him, filling his hands with her softness, sliding his palms along the bare skin of her arms and back, breathing in the familiar, sweet scent of her hair as he kissed her again and again and again—deep, ravenous, soul-reaching kisses that shook him to his very core. He felt her hands at his throat, unfastening his tie, pulling it free, then worrying the buttons of his shirt.

She seemed determined to get his clothes off him, and as far as brilliant ideas went, he was right there with her, one-hundred-percent. He found the zipper at the back of her dress and unfastened it, then pulled back to yank his unbuttoned shirt free from his arms.

She gasped as her hands touched his Ace bandage. "Oh, no, I forgot all about... I didn't hurt you, did I?"

He had to laugh. "You're killing me," he told her, "but not the way you mean. I'm fine."

"Honest?"

This was one thing he *could* be honest about. "Yes."

"And you'll tell me if it hurts?"

He laughed again. "It hurts, but—"

"Not the way you mean," she finished with him, laughing, too.

Her smile grew slightly wicked, and he watched, spellbound, as she rose to her feet and pushed the thin straps from her shoulders. Her dress fell off her in a sheet, pooling at her feet, leaving her naked save for a pair of shimmering silk panties.

She was beyond beautiful, and he reached for her, needing to touch the smoothness of her skin, the soft fullness of her perfect breasts, needing to hold her close, to feel her naked against him.

She touched him, too, with her hands, with her mouth, slowly running her fingers up his arms, across his shoulders, down the muscles of his bare chest, gently across his bruised side, driving him half-mad from the sensation.

How could something that felt so right be so wrong?

And it *was* wrong. Despite all that she'd told him, he knew it was wrong to make love to her without telling her the truth, without admitting that he didn't know what that truth was. Who was he? He honestly didn't know. Becca thought he was a good man. He strongly suspected otherwise.

Mish had reason to believe he'd done terrible things in his past, and here he was, right on schedule—giving in to temptation again.

Except when Becca kissed him, it didn't feel wrong. When Becca kissed him, when she touched him, it felt right in a way he'd never experienced *right* before.

And dammit, he wanted more.

He pulled her down with him onto the bed, kissing her, touching her as she cradled him between her legs. He could feel her heat as she pressed herself up against his arousal, and the sensation was dizzying and so perfect, he wanted to weep.

He felt her reach between them, felt her unfasten his belt, his pants, and then she was touching him, her fingers against his skin. It felt impossibly, paralyzingly, mind-blowingly good.

This woman wasn't looking for forever. She expected this fire they were fanning to life between them to burn hot and white, and then burn out. She had no misconceptions where this love affair was concerned, and she wouldn't be hurt when he left. She wasn't in love with him—at least not really. She didn't believe in true love.

Becca tugged at his pants, and he rolled off her to help her push them down his legs. Together they pulled off his boots, took off her panties. And then, finally, they were both naked. Mish pulled her on top of him, kissing her, desperate to be inside her, surrounded by her slick heat. He could feel her against him. All he had to do was shift his hips and...

But she moved when he moved, lifting herself away from him. "Whoa," she said, laughing. "Wait a sec—

safe sex, birth control! I've got condoms in my bag. Don't move, okay?''

Mish was staggered. He couldn't have moved if he'd wanted to. A condom—he'd completely forgotten about using one. He'd been more than ready to make love to Becca, despite being totally without protection. If she hadn't stopped him...

She pulled a foil-wrapped package from her purse, and came back to the bed, tearing it open.

"I'm sorry," he said, his voice hoarse as he pushed himself up on his elbows. "It's been a while for me, and I wasn't thinking."

"I hope you don't mind wearing this," she told him, kneeling beside him. "Because I'm afraid it's non-negotiable."

"No." He pulled her toward him, unable to keep from touching all that smooth, soft skin. "I never mind being forced to do something intelligent. I seriously don't know how I could have—"

She smiled at him, amusement dancing in her eyes—she was so beautiful. "Considering I was trying to drive you to distraction, I can't really complain when it worked."

"Distraction, huh?" Her thighs were smooth against him, her breasts so soft in his hands. He bent to kiss her, to draw her into his mouth. She moaned, and just like that the pulsating fire was back, heat flickering white-hot through his veins. "I'm just glad you had a condom," he murmured.

She handed it to him. "I always keep them on hand," she breathed, "in case Brad Pitt comes to town."

Mish lifted his head, and Becca laughed. "Just checking to see if you were still paying attention," she told him. "If you want to know the truth, I bought a box because despite all my promises to be good, despite all the times you told me *no,* I still had designs on you.''

She'd spoken the words lightly, but he touched her face gently, his eyes almost soft beneath the heat of his desire. ''I didn't tell you no because I didn't want you. You *do* know that, Becca, don't you?''

She knew it now and she was glad—so glad—that she hadn't given up.

She kissed him, tasting his hunger for her, feeling his need in the way that he held her, the weight of his desire.

Becca reached between them—he was taking too long—and helped him cover himself. She straddled him then, rolling him over onto his back as she kissed him, his arousal sinfully hard against her stomach.

He explored her body with his hands and mouth as if he were a starving man at a banquet, as if he would never be able to get enough of her.

It was an incredible turn-on—the way he looked at her as if she were the sexiest woman he'd ever seen, the way he touched her as if she were some kind of goddess or angel or...

''Becca,'' he breathed, and she loved the way her name sounded in the midnight velvet of his voice. He reached between them to touch her intimately, lightly first, then harder. ''Please, may I—''

She would have agreed to anything, promised him everything else. *''Yes.''*

He lifted her up then, turning them both over so that he was on top of her, his weight between her legs. She raised her hips to meet him and, oh, the look in his eyes was nearly as incredible as the sensation of him, thrust hard and deep, inside of her.

He held her gaze as he began to move, and the connection between them was so profound, her heart was completely in her throat. How could this be? This was supposed to be...well, if not casual, then at least *ordinary*. She hadn't anticipated feeling as if her entire soul were exposed to the elements. She hadn't dreamt that this man's kisses might resurrect all of her long-buried hopes of happily-ever-after.

That was crazy. This was sex. It was *great* sex, but it *was* only sex.

But as Becca looked into the eyes of this man who was making such wonderful, exquisite love to her, she saw possibilities that made her breath catch in her throat. She saw her future stretching out before her, and for the first time since forever, her journey was not a solitary one.

She laughed aloud. They *were* crazy, these thoughts that were invading her.

But when Mish smiled, too—his eyes crinkling at the edges with his pleasure and joy—she knew she was in trouble.

Big trouble.

He somehow knew just how to move to please her most—long, slow strokes that stole the air from her lungs, that left her dying for more.

And when her release ripped through her, it tore her open, scorching her very soul. She closed her eyes and clung to him, feeling him explode as well.

And when he lowered his head and kissed her, she closed her eyes and let him claim her mouth as thoroughly as he'd just claimed her heart.

Chapter 9

Mish could smell the fear.

It hung, sharp and unmistakable, in the small room. He'd been trapped there for hours with the others. There were twenty-four of them—mostly women and young girls. Some had been weeping continuously. When one of them left off, another started in.

He was numb.

The man in the religious robes lay on the floor where he'd fallen, half of his head blown away, his hands outstretched, wide and reaching, surprised by his own death.

He'd died trying to negotiate the release of the women and children. But the terrorists would not negotiate. They all knew that now.

And so Mish waited. He sat with his back against the far wall, and he waited, trying not to shake. He looked at the walls, at the ceiling—anywhere but at that pool of darkening blood on the floor.

But then the door opened, and everything moved too

fast. A black man, an American, scrambled up from the hostages—launching himself at the men with guns. Shots were fired as Mish lunged to his feet. The American staggered back, but not before wrenching an assault weapon from one of the terrorist's arms.

More gunshots. The American went down hard, the weapon skittering across the floor.

Toward Mish.

He didn't think. He reacted, picking it up, his finger squeezing the trigger before he'd even got it aimed. The force pushed the barrel up as he fired, and he fought to push it down, sweeping the entrance to the room, spraying the terrorists with bullets, splattering the back wall and doorway with their blood and brains.

Someone was screaming, the voice raw and guttural with rage, but barely loud enough to be heard over the deafening machine-gun fire.

But then it was over. The men on the floor before him were undeniably dead. He'd killed them. He stopped shooting and realized that the voice—and the rage—were his own.

The American was bleeding badly, but he grabbed another assault weapon and kicked the door shut.

"Good job," he told Mish through the blood that bubbled on his lips. "Way to send them straight to hell, Mish."

Mish stared at the bodies, stared at what he'd done.

He'd killed them. God help him, he'd pointed the weapon, and taken the lives of three human beings. He may have sent them straight to hell, but what had he done to his own soul?

And he turned, because over on the other side of the room, the dead man in the robe was pushing himself up and off of the floor. The half of his face that was left was frowning, and he raised his hand, pointing accusingly at Mish. "Thou shalt not kill," he intoned. "Thou shalt not kill."

He took a step toward Mish, and then another step. And Mish realized with a jolt of shock that the man wore a liturgical collar, streaked bright red with blood.

And what was left of the dead man's face might as well have been his own.

Mish sat up in bed, his heart pounding, gasping for air.

Someone stirred in the bed beside him. Becca. It was Becca. She sat up, too, hesitantly touching his back. "Mish, are you all right?"

The hotel room came into focus, dimly lit by the first light of dawn that streaked in through the tops of the heavy window curtains.

Mish fought to control his ragged breathing, fought to bring his pulse back down to normal. "Nightmare," he managed to say.

"A bad one, huh? Want to talk about it?"

He pushed his sweat-soaked hair back from his face with hands that were still shaking. "No," he said. "Thanks."

She put her arms around him and lightly kissed his shoulder, and he turned toward her, grabbing her and holding her far more tightly than he had a right to, kissing her far more proprietarily than he should have. But he desperately needed grounding, desperately needed her.

"Mmm." She smiled up at him in the slowly growing light as she ran her fingers through his hair. She didn't seem to mind the dampness. "I'm sorry you had a nightmare, but I'm not sorry you woke me up, especially when you kiss me like that."

She was naked. They both were. And as Mish gazed

into her eyes, detailed memories of the power and passion
of last night came crashing back, full force.

He had made love to this woman, and she to him, in a
way that had been beyond description, beyond compari-
son.

And she deserved to know the truth about who he
was—or who he wasn't.

He'd stared at the ceiling for a good portion of the
night, struggling with wanting to tell her of his missing
past, and this overpowering sense of knowing—this absolute *conviction*—that he would not be allowed to tell
her anything about himself, even if he knew.

She kissed him, pulling him back with her against the
pillows, intertwining their legs. "I've got a few days off
coming to me," she murmured. "What do you say we
order a steady supply of room service, tell them to hold
all my calls, and just stay here until Tuesday morning?"

Mish wanted to do it. He wanted to hold the world at
bay for two days straight. And why couldn't he? As far
as he was aware, he was the only one searching for himself.

And who could know? Maybe he'd find himself here
in the safety and warmth of Becca's eyes.

And if not, maybe he'd have figured out a way by then
to tell her who he feared he was.

"'Til Tuesday sounds great," he whispered between
kisses. In truth, it sounded about a lifetime too short, but
that wasn't something he'd ever dare admit, either to her
or to himself.

He kissed her longer, deeper, willing himself to stop
thinking, to just *be*.

With Becca's eager help, that wasn't hard to do.

The call from Joe Cat came in just after dawn.

Lucky had only been asleep for about twenty minutes,

but he snapped instantly awake—especially after he heard the Captain's familiar New Yawk accent.

"More of Shaw's funny money turned up," Joe Cat said without ceremony. "This time in a men's clothing store in Albuquerque. Two bills."

Lucky turned on the light next to the motel-room bed. "We'll go check it out, but I'm not going to leave that bag in the bus station locker without a baby-sitter. I got a gut about this one, Cat. Mitch Shaw has had that bag for a long time. If he's alive, he's coming back for it. I've buddied up the surveillance—Bobby and Wes are watching the station right now." He started pulling on his pants. "But I could head north in about five minutes."

"No, stay in Wyatt City," the captain commanded. "Crash and Blue are already on their way to Albuquerque." He gave a disparaging laugh. "I'd be with 'em, but the admiral's allegedly flying in today. I need to be on hand to give him a sit-rep. I just thought it'd be smart for you to know Shaw's still fairly local. In state, at least."

Lucky kicked his pants back off and settled back on the bed, phone tucked under his chin. "Unless he's dead and someone else is spending his money."

"Yeah, I think we've got to consider that possibility," the captain said seriously.

"But what if he's not dead?" Lucky asked. "Is there a chance he's trying to send some kind of message to us by circulating those bills?" Surely Mitch knew which of the bills he carried were fake and which weren't.

"That's what I keep coming back to," Joe Cat said. "What if Mitch Shaw located the...missing material?" Even though it was a secured line, he was careful not to use the word *plutonium*. "What if he's in deep with the people who have control over that material, and can't check in? Using the money might be his way of flagging us down, getting backup into the area.''

"Except we spoke to a guy named Jarell at the homeless shelter," Lucky reported. "He remembers seeing Mitch. He was brought in late at night, barely conscious, apparently falling-down drunk, with the fight kicked out of him. Jarell only saw him that one night, said he left before breakfast, said as far as he could tell, Mitch was alone. He also said Mitch left a jacket behind, but Jarell wouldn't give it to us—he wouldn't even let us look at it.''

"Get it," the captain said.

"Yeah," Lucky told him. "I'm working on that. But that church has something going on 24/7. There's always someone there, so we're going to have to get creative. But don't get your hopes up, Skipper. Even after we *do* get it, chances are that jacket's not going to tell us jack.''

Joe Cat sighed. "I don't know this guy Shaw at all. Is he a heavy drinker? Is he into drugs at all? Is it possible he's gone on some kind of binge?''

"I've never seen him have more than a single beer," Lucky said.

"Which could fit into the pattern of a problem drinker," the captain pointed out. "He keeps it under control, until suddenly he can't anymore. And then it's not one beer, it's a dozen, and he's off and running.''

"Jarell said he was so skunked, he couldn't even remember his own name." Lucky shook his head. That was hard to imagine. Quiet Mitchell Shaw completely out of control.

"There's a question I haven't been able to stop thinking, Luke. Do you think he might've turned—you know, embraced the dark side of the force?''

Lucky closed his eyes. "I don't know, Obi-Wan," he

said. "The admiral's not going to like this, but I don't think we can rule out that possibility at this point."

The phone rang.

Becca opened her eyes and found that she'd fallen asleep draped half on top of Mish. It should have been uncomfortable to sleep like that, her leg thrown across his thighs, her head resting on his shoulder, but it wasn't. She fit against him perfectly.

His eyes were open, and he gave her the sexiest, sleepiest good-morning smile as she reached across him for the telephone.

She couldn't resist and she stopped to kiss him, hoping that whoever was calling would just give up and go away. But they were persistent and the phone kept ringing.

"I knew I should have told the desk to hold my calls," she complained with an exaggerated sigh as she picked up the phone. "'Lo?" she said into the receiver, pulling the cord back with her, settling into the warmth of Mish's arms.

She could feel his arousal, heavy against her thigh, feel his fingers trailing lightly, deliciously down her back from her shoulder to her rear end and back again.

"Becca? This is Hazel. I'm sorry, did I wake you?"

Becca sighed, but even the thought that her assistant wouldn't have called unless there was a real problem at the Lazy Eight wasn't enough to detract from the pleasure of Mish's touch.

"It's nearly eight, and I thought you'd be up," Hazel continued apologetically. "I'd offer to call back later, but this really can't wait."

"What's the problem?" Becca had to work to keep her voice even and controlled as Mish lowered his head to her breast. He kissed her lightly at first, then slowly drew her nipple into his mouth. She bit back an exclamation, and he lifted his head, smiling at her like the devil incarnate.

Like an outrageously handsome devil incarnate.

"We seem to have something of a mystery on our hands," Hazel told her.

Mish lowered his head and kissed his way down her stomach, stopping to explore her belly button with his tongue.

"Oh, God," Becca said. "Hazel, are you sure I can't call you back in just a few minutes—an hour tops—I promise?" Mish kissed the inside of her thigh, and she closed her eyes. "Please?"

"Becca, it's about that Casey Parker. That Mish character. Did you know that he's gone? He cleared out of cabin 12 the day before yesterday, and I've seen neither hide nor hair of him since."

Becca laughed. Hazel's big mystery was no mystery. Becca knew exactly where Casey Parker was—*and* exactly what he was doing.

And, oh, she liked what he was doing, but she pulled back from him, shaking her head, widening her eyes. No way could she talk on the phone while he did that.

He grinned at her and her laughter bubbled over again. "Hazel, I'm sorry. I thought I mentioned it to you. Mish had some business to take care of in Albuquerque. He should be back at the ranch on Tuesday."

"Well, it's going to be interesting when he returns," Hazel said, "especially if the man who was just here at the office decides to come back, too. Because then we'll have *two* Casey Parkers on our hands."

Becca could see the promise of paradise in Mish's eyes. He was behaving himself, lying down at the end of the bed, lightly stroking her foot. But despite his distance, he was obviously distracting her, because Hazel's words just didn't make any damn sense. "I'm sorry. *What* did you say?"

"Two," Hazel repeated. "Casey Parkers. Pretty bizarre mystery, huh? A second Casey Parker just showed up at the Lazy Eight, claiming you'd hired him on as a ranch hand. He was looking for a package that was supposedly waiting for him here at the office. He was pretty bent out of shape when I told him we'd filled our quota of Casey Parkers for the month and I'd given that package to the first one. I even had to call Rafe McKinnon down to the office to flex his muscles."

Becca sat up, her full attention on Hazel's words. "Is he still there?" she asked. "Call the sheriff and—"

"He's gone. He drove off in a wild hurry after he found out there'd been a Casey Parker here before him. I don't know *what's* going on."

"He's an imposter." Even as she said the words, Becca knew they made no sense. Why would someone show up at the ranch pretending to be Casey Parker?

"*Some*one's an imposter," Hazel said. "And that's why this phone call couldn't wait. Becca, I know there was something brewing between you and this Mish. Promise me you'll be careful if you see him again today?"

"Hazel—"

"Because Casey Parker Number Two had picture ID. He had a driver's license," Hazel told her. "He was a big guy with a gray beard and a beer belly, and it was *definitely* his picture on that license."

And Mish had had no ID at all.

He was sitting on the end of the bed, watching her.

He'd been listening to her end of the conversation. He

knew she'd been talking about him and all sense of wicked play had disappeared.

"Are you sure?" Becca whispered. She pulled the sheet up so that it covered her, and Mish looked away tiredly, almost guiltily—as if he somehow knew exactly what Hazel was telling her.

"Honey, I used to work in the sheriff's office over in Chimayo. This license looked legit. It wasn't tampered with in any way that I could see. They have those fancy hologram thingies on 'em, you know, to keep people from messing with 'em." Hazel sighed. "You *were* planning to see him again, weren't you? That Mish? I *am* sorry about this."

"Thanks for calling," Becca managed to choke out before she hung up the phone.

Mish didn't look at her. He just sat on the bed, staring down at their clothes, still strewn on the floor where they'd left them last night.

"So. You want to tell me who you really are?" She'd meant to sound tough, but her voice shook slightly and ruined her delivery. "Seeing as how you're *not* Casey Parker?"

He looked up at her then, his eyes filled with regret and...shame?

Becca let herself get good and mad, fighting the tears that were on the verge of exploding from her eyes. Damn right he should feel shame!

"Maybe I should get dressed," he said, reaching for his clothes.

Becca scrambled out of the bed, pulling the sheet with her, and grabbed his pants away from him. "Oh, no, you don't. You're not going to leave before you at least give me *some* kind of explanation."

With shaking hands, Mish pulled on his shorts. Had he

really thought he could have this woman without giving her anything of himself in return? Had he really thought he could hide here with her, safely cocooned from the real world, from the truth?

But the real world had reached out and somehow she now knew more about him than he did. How and what didn't matter. He should have known it would happen. He should have protected her from this.

And he would have, if only he'd stayed away from her. He should have been strong enough to resist the magnetic attraction he felt for her, that dizzying pull of longing. Instead, he'd given in to what *he* wanted, what *he* needed. And he'd hurt her. Badly.

Selfish. He was a selfish son of a bitch.

And in one brief moment, all of the magic of the night was gone, as if it had never existed, never been real. They'd shared something wonderful, something he'd longed to hold on to, something fragile and perfect that now lay crushed and broken at his feet. And he'd done that as surely as if he'd stomped on it with both heels of his boots.

"The real Casey Parker showed up at the ranch," Becca said, her voice thick with betrayal. "You had to have known that was bound to happen."

"I didn't," he said loudly, more forcefully than he'd intended. He stood up, pushing his hair back from his face, feeling as if he might be terribly, violently sick. Lord God, he'd been so selfish.

"You didn't?" Her voice rose, too. "Dammit, I *know* you're smarter than that. You *had* to know Casey would show up sooner or later."

He wasn't Casey Parker. He'd suspected that for a while. The name had seemed so unfamiliar. But still, he'd hoped.

God, he'd hoped. But hope wasn't enough. Not anymore.

So now what?

Although his back was to her, he could see her reflection in the big mirror that hung above the dresser. She was gazing at him with such hurt, such accusation in her eyes.

He still couldn't tell her the truth. He wasn't supposed to tell anyone why he was in New Mexico—he couldn't remember why, but he knew that he wasn't supposed to talk about it with a strength that was overpowering. Still, to walk away, leaving her to think that he'd purposely deceived her... He couldn't do that, either. How could he?

He stood there, stomach churning, sick to his soul, head bowed and shaking, unable to stay, unable to leave.

"You know," she said, her voice shaking, too, "if you'd come to the ranch and introduced yourself to me, if you'd been honest about who you were, I would have hired you. I don't understand why you had to lie."

What could he tell her? "Maybe I should just go. I can't tell you what you want to know."

Disbelief colored her voice. "You can't tell me your *name?*"

He glanced up and saw that she was crying. She tried to hide it by brusquely, almost savagely, wiping her tears away as she still clutched the sheet around her.

"Call me old-fashioned," Becca said sharply, "but I at least like to know the *name* of the men I've had sex with."

His name. Mish looked up, and came face-to-face with himself in that mirror.

He was still a stranger to his own eyes. Hard and lean and dangerous, with his morning stubble thick and dark

on his angular face, his hair wild, messed from sleep, his
eyes bitter, soulless, he looked to be the kind of man who
would lie his way into a woman's bed and leave her with
little regard for her feelings in the morning.

He stared into those eyes, praying for a glimmer of
memory, a whisper of a name. Some small fragment of
truth that he could give her...

Mish.

Mission Man.

"Just tell me your name," Becca whispered.

He stared harder, fists tight, teeth clenched, hating himself, hating the stranger staring tauntingly back at him, no
longer praying to God but *demanding* the answers he
sought. Who the hell was he?

Mission Man.

An echo of Jarell's voice whispered the nickname, and
his anger and frustration erupted.

"I don't know my damn name!" He exploded, spinning and hitting his reflection with his fist.

The mirror cracked, cutting his image in two. He hit it
again, harder, and it shattered, the glass slicing his hand.

Becca backed away, shocked by his outburst, staring at
this suddenly wild-eyed stranger whose blood dripped
from his fingertips onto the carpeting.

"I don't know who the hell I am!" he shouted hoarsely.
"I woke up nearly two weeks ago in a homeless shelter
with five thousand dollars, a handgun in my boot, directions to the Lazy Eight with your name on it, and no
memory of anything important—including my own name!
You say I'm not Casey Parker? Well, guess what? This
is news to me, too!"

Becca clutched her sheet around her, watching him,
ready to run if he suddenly came toward her. Could what

he'd just said possibly be true? Did he have some kind of amnesia? It sounded so amazing. And yet...

He was standing there, shaking like a wounded animal, his eyes filled with tears, unable to meet her gaze. "Just give me my pants, and I'll go."

"Where?" she asked quietly, her heart in her throat. She had been furiously angry with him, but if what he was saying was even remotely true...

He looked up at her. He didn't understand.

"Where will you go?"

He shook his head. He was so upset he couldn't even answer her. One of his tears escaped, and he wiped it away with a shaking hand. This couldn't be an act, it couldn't be. He was as upset by this as she was. More.

She didn't know much about mental illnesses, but it was possible this man she'd given a piece of her heart to last night was sick in ways she couldn't even imagine. If so, then he needed help.

And if not... He'd had a gash on his head when he'd first arrived at the ranch. It was mostly healed now, but what if the blow he'd received *had* taken away his memory?

She tried to imagine what that might be like, how terrifying and awful and strange. How completely alone he must feel....

Either way, she had to get him to a doctor. She had to convince him to go with her to the hospital.

"If you don't have anywhere to go, then it doesn't make sense for you to leave," she told him, keeping her voice low, as if she were gentling a frightened horse. The first thing she had to do was calm him down. Then she had to find out if he still had that gun he'd mentioned. Guns and high emotions never mixed well.

She stepped closer, holding out her own hand to him.

"Come into the bathroom. Let me look at your hand. It's bleeding."

Mish looked down, as if noticing his injured hand for the first time. He looked at the mirror, looked at her. "I'm so sorry, Becca."

"Come on," she said. "Let's make sure you don't need stitches. And then we can talk and try to figure this out."

"I should just go. I'll leave money to pay for the mirror—"

"No," Becca said. "I want you to stay."

He started to argue, but she interrupted. "Stay," she said again. "I think you owe me at least that much."

Mish nodded. For a potentially crazy person, his gaze was remarkably steady now. "Becca, do you believe me?"

Becca turned away as she led him into the bathroom. "I'm still working on that."

Chapter 10

Becca had put clothes on. Jeans and a T-shirt. She sat across from Mish, her legs curled underneath her as she gazed at him.

Mish, too, had pulled on his pants. Like her, his feet were bare. The shirt he'd worn last night, the one she'd helped peel off of him, hung open as he gazed down at his bandaged hand and tried his best to answer her questions.

He'd told her about waking up at the homeless shelter, of the old man who'd named him Mission Man, of the way "Mish" had somehow seemed both wrong and right. He'd told her of his confusion and shock at seeing his unfamiliar face in the mirror. He'd tried to put into words what it felt like to remember nothing but trivial details of his past. And he'd apologized again for deceiving her.

She cleared her throat. "Before—you said you had a gun."

He glanced up at her and tried not to think about the

way she'd looked, lying back, naked, on her bed. It was crazy. They'd made love twice, last night and early this morning, and he was still dying for her touch. He still wanted more.

Like *that* was ever going to happen again.

He cleared *his* throat. "Yeah. A small handgun. Twenty-two caliber. It was in my boot with the cash and that fax that had the directions to the ranch."

"Where's the gun now?"

"Back at the Lazy Eight. In my private lockup in the bunkhouse. I wasn't comfortable... I didn't think it was appropriate—or even legal—to carry it around."

Becca nodded, trying very hard not to look relieved.

Mish couldn't keep from smiling crookedly. "Makes you nervous, huh?" he asked. "The thought of me walking around with a weapon?"

She answered honestly, glancing involuntarily at the shards of broken mirror that still littered the dresser. "I'm sorry, but, yeah."

"You don't have to apologize. If our roles were reversed—"

"If our roles were reversed, *I* would have already checked myself into a hospital."

Mish shifted back in his chair. "I can't do that."

"Of course you can." She leaned forward. "Mish, I'll go with you. I'll *stay* with you. The doctors will—"

"Call the police," he finished for her. "They'll have to. Bec, I was shot. They'd need to report it." He hesitated. Lord, why not just tell her? He'd already revealed too much. "The truth is, I'm probably someone you wouldn't want to know. I've had these dreams..." Telling her about them in detail would be too much. The awful images already haunted the hell out of him—no need to haunt her as well. "They're...violent. *Really* violent."

"That doesn't mean anything. I've had violent dreams and—"

"No, this is stuff—at least some of it—I know I've seen. I've also dreamed of…" He couldn't look at her. "Prison. I've done hard time, Bec. I can't believe I would dream about it in that kind of detail if I hadn't."

She was silent.

"I think if I dig back and uncover my past, I'm going to find out that I'm not a very good person," he told her quietly. "So let's go back to the ranch. Maybe if I'm lucky Casey Parker'll be there. I can give him that package that came for him, and ask him what his fax was doing in my boot—maybe find some answers. Then I'll take my things and clear out. And you'll be done with me for good."

Becca pulled her knees in close to her chest, encircling them with her arms.

"Or," he said, "if you'd rather, I'll leave now, find another ride back. I can arrange to be gone before you return on Tuesday."

He could walk out that door in a matter of minutes, and Becca would never see him again. And this was supposed to be something she'd *want?*

She felt her eyes fill with tears, and she blinked them furiously back. She stood up, unable to sit still another moment longer, wishing this room were bigger, knowing that even if it were the size of a stadium, she would be drawn toward him.

"Why didn't you tell me any of this last night?" she asked, forcing herself away from him, moving over toward the window. "We talked for *hours* at that party. I can think of ten different times that you would've had a perfect segue to this subject." She turned to face him. "'Funny you should mention your childhood in New

York, Becca, because you know, since a week ago Monday, I can't remember anything about mine. In fact, I couldn't even remember my name until I came to the ranch and you called me Casey Parker...'''

His eyes looked suspiciously red, too. ''Would you have believed me?''

''I don't know. I might've, yeah. I believe you now, don't I?''

''I don't know. Do you?''

She let out a burst of air that was nearly a laugh. ''No. Yes. I don't know. I think, amnesia? But then I think, it sounds so crazy, it's *got* to be true.'' She couldn't figure out *why* he would make up this outlandish story. It wasn't to gain sympathy points to get into her bed. He'd already been there.

The truth was, she *did* believe him. She trusted him on a level that went beyond logic. Despite his conviction that he'd been to prison, despite his belief that he was some kind of criminal, Becca trusted him with every fiber of her being. And maybe that was just because of sex. Maybe it was just her hormones blocking all common sense. If love was blind, then lust surely was like being in a sensory deprivation tank.

But when she looked into Mish's eyes, she believed him, whether she wanted to or not.

Maybe he was a con man, maybe he was seriously mentally ill, maybe she was going to get badly burned. But she was damned if she wasn't going to see this through to the end, find the facts that would either prove her wrong and label her a fool, or provide the missing pieces in Mish's past. Either way, she'd come out further ahead than she would by walking away right now.

Or letting him walk away.

Becca turned back to the window, feeling a sense of

calm at her decision, feeling the pressure of her impending tears lessen. "I'll call Hazel, tell her to page me if Casey Parker shows up at the ranch again. I'll have her offer him some kind of financial bonus if he'll stick around until we show up."

"He left the ranch?"

She looked up at the perfect blue sky, wondering at the sudden note of interest that rang in his voice. "Hazel said he got out of there pronto. Apparently he was ticked off by the fact that another Casey Parker had been there first." She turned to face him, certain she looked like hell, but grateful that at least she wasn't crying. "I think we should take a drive down to Wyatt City. Check out this shelter, try to talk to the men who brought you in."

Mish looked as emotionally exhausted as she felt. "We?"

"Yeah," Becca said. She crossed her arms so he knew she meant business. "Unless you lied and last night really *was* just a one-night stand."

He shook his head in disbelief. "Becca, didn't you hear anything I said? I'm probably one of the bad guys. I need you to stay away from me."

"Maybe," she said. "But what about what *I* need?"

Wyatt City was as dusty and run-down as Mish remembered it.

Except he only remembered it from the time he walked out of the First Church Shelter to the time he left on the Greyhound to Santa Fe.

It was one of those towns with a Main Street that hadn't had a face-lift since most of the buildings went up back in the late fifties, early sixties. It was crumbling. A true work in progress, as far as ghost towns went.

The old movie theater was boarded up, as was the

Woolworth's. Both looked as if they'd gone out of business a decade or two ago, and the space hadn't been rented out since then. A liquor store was doing a thriving business, as was an adult-video rental place, and a bar.

"Have you considered the possibility that you lived here?" Becca spoke for the first time in what seemed like hours. She took a right turn on Chiselm Street, where a row of post World War II adobe-style houses had been turned into offices. A palm reader. A chiropractor/masseuse. A tax attorney. A tattoo parlor. "You might have an apartment somewhere in town. Or a room. Or..."

"Yeah," he said. "I guess it *is* a possibility." He didn't want to tell her about his hunch, his sense that he'd come to Wyatt City for a reason. A reason that he didn't know, but couldn't talk about just the same.

"Oh, no!" She pulled to the side of the road and hit the brakes a little too hard. She looked at him, her eyes wide. "You could have a *wife*. You could be *married*."

"I'm not," he told her. "I don't know how I know that, but—"

"You *can't* know it," she told him. "Mish, the only things we absolutely know about you are that you've never learned to ride a horse, you were here in Wyatt City for some reason two weeks ago, and that you aren't Casey Parker."

"If I *am* married..." He shook his head. "No, I know I'm not. I'm always alone. I live alone. And lately I work alone. I don't know how I know that, because I don't even know what it is I do." But he could guess. The list of possibilities was nice and short. Burglar. Thief. Con artist. Assassin.

"But if that's not enough for you," he continued, "then last night..." He squinted as he looked out of the truck's windshield at the setting sun glinting off the still hot

street. "I don't know, I guess you probably could tell—
it's been a long time for me. Since I was with a woman."
He glanced at her, embarrassed to admit it. "Since I even
wanted to be with a woman."

She laughed, a giddy burst as she tipped her head forward to rest on her folded arms on the steering wheel.
"That's very flattering, Mr. I-know-damn-well-I'm-a-sex-
god-but-I'll-pretend-to-be-humble, but the fact is, you
can't *know* you're not married if you've got amnesia."

"No, there are some things I *do* just know. I know it
sounds unbelievable, that I could know what size jeans I
wear, but not even recognize my own face in a mirror. It
doesn't make any sense, but Becca, I'm telling you, I
know."

She was peeking out from beneath her arm, and he held
her gaze. "And I'm not pretending anything," he added
softly. "It *had* been a while for me. I wanted to make
love to you all night long, but somehow the night got
away from me."

Lord, what was he doing? She was wary of him, wanting to keep her distance. So why was he saying things
like that, things that would draw her back into his arms?

Because he wanted her in his arms. And he had absolutely no willpower where this woman was concerned. He
knew the best place for Becca to be was dozens—hundreds—of miles away from him, yet he couldn't stop himself from wanting to hold her.

She lifted her head, still watching him. He could see
the heat of her attraction for him in her eyes, doing battle
with her wariness.

He could see paradise lingering there as well, just a
kiss and a heartbeat away.

He turned away. "The church is in this neighborhood,
not too far from the bus station."

Becca hesitated, but he didn't look over at her again, and finally she put her truck in gear.

"Jarell? He's a popular man these days," the woman who worked in the church office said with a chuckle. She pulled a file folder from a rickety old cabinet, and flipped through the pages. "He's a volunteer, so I can't guarantee his hours won't change, but let's see..." She frowned. "No, he's not working at the shelter this evening—actually, not until Wednesday night."

"Isn't there any way we could get in touch with him tonight?" Mish asked.

The woman shook her head, smiling apologetically at both Mish and Becca. "I'm sorry, we can't give out personal information about our volunteers. But there's a good chance he'll be in the kitchen tomorrow afternoon. There's a church dinner tomorrow night, and no one can make meat loaf like Jarell. At least not meat loaf for two hundred."

Tomorrow afternoon. Becca looked everywhere but at Mish. If they had to wait until tomorrow afternoon to talk to Jarell, that meant they'd have to spend the night here in Wyatt City.

She stood quietly aside as he thanked the woman, then followed him out of the church and into the hot evening air. They walked in silence until they got to Becca's truck, parked just down the street from the bus station.

Mish turned to face her. "When we left Santa Fe this morning, I didn't think quite as far as tonight. I'm...sorry. I'll pay for the motel rooms."

Rooms. Plural. Did he really want to stay in separate rooms tonight? Was it possible that, unlike her, he hadn't spent the entire day bombarded by vivid memories of sensations from the night before? Could it be that, unlike her, he wasn't dying for the chance for them to kiss again?

All day long, all she wanted was to take him in her arms and kiss him.

Becca closed her eyes. Please, God, let him be right. Have him not be married...

"We should go have dinner and—"

"Does it make sense," Becca interrupted him, trying to sound matter-of-fact, when in truth her heart was pounding, "to pay for two when we're probably going to end up in one? Rooms," she added, probably unnecessarily.

His eyes looked luminous in the early evening light. "Do you really want that? Even knowing...who I am?"

She reached for his hand. "You say that as if you're convinced you're some kind of monster. Why? Because you were carrying a gun and you don't believe in banks? For all we know, your license to carry that gun was in your wallet, which was stolen. Yeah, the bullet wound on your head is a little harder to explain away, but it *is* possible that you were simply in the wrong place at the wrong time, isn't it?"

"Becca—"

"So, okay, you dreamed of prison. I've rented movies enough times to be able to have pretty vivid dreams of prison, too. Dreams are *dreams,* Mish. They're not the same thing as memories. I sometimes dream that my teeth are falling out. It happens to be a common stress dream, with no basis in reality, fortunately." She took a deep breath. "So, yes, I really want us to get a room. *A* room. A room with a shower, a pizza and a cold six-pack of beer. Let's lock ourselves in and forget about all this for a few hours. You know, for someone with amnesia, you're not very good at forgetting things."

Mish smiled, and her heart leapt. But then his smile faded. "What if it turns out that I'm someone terrible? What if I'm an assassin? A hit man?"

Becca had to laugh. "Only a man would what-if himself into the middle of a Clint Eastwood film. And that guy over there? See him? The one climbing into that van with the tinted windows?" She pointed down the street.

As they watched, a man with short brown hair and a barbed-wire tattoo encircling his upper arm, carrying a cardboard tray with three large coffees, climbed into the back of the van. Another man, this one a movie-star-handsome blond, climbed out.

The blond looked as if he could make a fortune on the rodeo circuit from just his smile, but he wore sneakers on his feet instead of cowboy boots, and a baggy pair of cargo shorts instead of jeans. His shirt hung open, revealing a chest of *Baywatch* quality. He made half circles with his head, as if relieving the kinks in his neck as he made his way across the street to the Terminal Bar. It was named after its proximity to the bus station, no doubt, rather than its dire medical condition.

"They're not just waiting for the bus from Las Vegas, for the shorter guy's wife Ernestina to return from a visit to her sister, Inez, who's a dancer at Caesar's. No, they're probably sitting there, staking out the bus station on the off chance *you'll* show up. Right?"

Mish looked at the man heading into the bar. His eyes narrowed, and he looked closer.

"Mish." Becca pulled his chin so that he faced her. She kissed him lightly on the mouth to get his attention completely. "What if you're *not* a hit man? What if you're the UPS man? Or what if you sell washers and dryers at Sears? Or maybe you're extra-adventurous and you specialize in overnight fresh fish deliveries to towns like Las Cruces and Santa Fe?''

He smiled at that, and she unlocked the door to her truck. ''If you want, we can drive around for a little while. See if anything sparks a memory.''

Mish nodded, glancing at the van sitting in front of the bus station. ''Yeah,'' he said. ''I'd like to do that.''

Becca climbed into the truck and started the engine, switching on the air-conditioning right away. God, it was hot.

Mish swung himself in the passenger's side, picked her beatup cowboy hat up off the seat between them, and put it on his head, tugging the brim low over his eyes.

And as they drove past the van, he slouched way down in his seat.

''Today I am a very fountain of information,'' Wes said as Lucky swung himself back into the van after making a quick pit stop at the Terminal Bar. ''The captain called when I was taking a nap. I don't know how he does it, but somehow he always knows when I'm sleeping.''

''That's why he's the captain and you're not,'' Bobby pointed out. ''He knows when you are sleeping. He knows when you're awake...''

''What did he say?'' Lucky asked. ''Did he talk to Admiral Robinson?''

''He knows if you've been bad or good—no, wait,'' Bobby said. ''That's Santa Claus, not Joe Cat.'' He smiled. ''I always get them confused.''

''Yeah,'' Wes said, ''they're both so jolly. Well, Santa's jolly. Joe's not. In fact, he's getting pretty fed up and put out by the way the top brass are jerking him around. I don't know how many days running this is that first they tell him, yes, Robinson's on his way, only to call him later and say, no, he's been detained again.''

"Any word from Albuquerque?" Lucky asked.

"Crash and Blue reported in. No sign of Mitch," Wes told him. "But he *was* there. At least the shop owner described someone who looks just like him, down to his pretty green eyes.''

"That's good," Bobby said. "That's great. He's alive.''

"Yeah, but the mystery thickens," Wes reported. "He spent nearly four hundred dollars. Bought himself a nice suit, a coupla shirts, some underwear. Total came to three and change, yet our boy used two of the counterfeit bills with two that were unmarked. What's up with *that?* And why's he buying a suit?''

"A few days ago, I wished I'd brought a suit with us from California," Bobby said. "Because I—"

"Had a date with the supermodel," Wes finished for him. "Yeah, rub it in."

"Okay, so maybe there's a woman involved," Lucky said. "We need to make sure we look at everyone passing by. Mitch could be with a woman."

"Or maybe he was just getting himself a disguise. If *I* wanted to disguise myself," Wes pointed out, "first thing I'd do is buy myself a suit. Make myself look like a business geek. No one would ever recognize me."

Lucky stared out the tinted window at the bus station. Mitchell Shaw was out there. Somewhere. Lucky had had a gut feeling that he'd come back for his "bag of tricks." But maybe he wouldn't. Maybe he and his new suit were long gone, the missing plutonium with him. Maybe the somewhere that Mitch was, was on the other side of the world.

"Did the captain give us any orders?" Lucky asked.

"Sit tight," Wes said. "Just sit tight."

"Stop," Mish said. "Bec, stop here!"

Becca slammed on the brakes.

The lengthening twilight was casting odd shadows in an alleyway that was probably poorly lit at best, even at high noon.

Mish climbed down out of the truck and went between two buildings, one brick, one wood. The pavement—what little was left—was pitted and cracked. The scent of rotting garbage filled the air. It was familiar, as was the latticework of the fire escapes that decorated the outside of the brick building.

Mish closed his eyes to see the image of those iron stairs and landings lit by a stormy night sky that flashed with lightning and...

Yes, he had been here before.

He knew without looking that a few steps farther in, behind the dumpster, was a basement door—once painted a bright red, long since faded by the heat—that stood ajar.

"Mish?" Becca had parked the truck and now followed him.

It was getting darker by the minute, and he moved cautiously past the Dumpster, with its sound of rats scurrying away. He moved closer and...

A basement door.

Ajar.

Faded red.

"I've been here." He was certain now. He turned to Becca. "I remember..."

What? What did he remember?

He closed his eyes. Thunder and lightning. His clothes soaked almost instantly after the downpour started. He'd been following...

Following… Lord, he couldn't remember who he'd been following or why he'd been here.

"I had my weapon drawn." Somehow he knew that. He'd gone down the steps to the basement door, and he'd hidden deep in the shadows, his handgun held ready.

Nothing had moved. Nothing. The storm raged for many long minutes, and still he stood frozen, waiting, watching.

But the man he had followed and was waiting for to return—and it *was* a man—had vanished.

Finally, Mish had crept out. Up those concrete stairs and into the puddles of the alleyway.

Something had made him turn. Some instinct, or perhaps a sound he'd managed to hear beneath the pounding of the rain.

But he'd turned, and lightning flashed, and he saw the face of the man he was after for the briefest split second— before the muzzle flash from the man's handgun exploded his night vision, before the bullet from that weapon knocked him over and out.

He focused everything he had in him on that scrap of memory, on that split-second exposure of a face.

Forty-five to fifty years old, heavy set, graying beard, thinning hair. Small nose in an otherwise puffy face. He'd been up above Mish, on the roof.

Mish scanned the roof, scanned the windows of the brick building. He longed for the feel of a weapon in his hands—not that wimpy little .22 he'd found in his boot and left back at the ranch, but a *real* weapon. A Heckler & Koch MP-5 room broom. Or even an MP-4. Something with a real bite, something that would fit comfortably in his arms.

Then it hit him—he was actually standing here, wishing he had an assault weapon.

An *assault* weapon.

Who the hell was he?

"Mish, are you okay?"

Nothing moved along the roof-line now, and Mish could see, even with the rapidly falling shadows, that it had been sheer luck that had enabled the bearded man to get the jump on him. It was also equally sheer luck he hadn't killed Mish.

Or maybe it wasn't luck. Maybe it was just ineptitude. Or amateurishness.

But if the bearded man had been a real shooter, he would've made damn sure he'd finished Mish off before he'd left the scene.

The scuff of a boot against the pavement made him spin around in a defensive crouch and...

Becca.

Her eyes were wide as she gazed at him, as he quickly straightened up.

"What do you remember?" she asked quietly.

"I wasn't here making a delivery for UPS, that's for damn sure."

Chapter 11

"Please," Mish said.

His steak was as untouched as her grilled-chicken Caesar salad. Why had they bothered to come to this restaurant anyway, if neither of them intended to eat?

Becca thought wistfully of that pizza and beer she'd hoped to share with him, preferably while naked on a motel-room bed.

"You want me just to leave you here," she repeated. "To go back to the Lazy Eight tonight. Just...that's it? Good luck? So long? You're on your own? Thanks, but I'm no longer needed?"

It had been too many hours since Mish had gotten close to a razor, and with all that stubble on his face, he looked positively dangerous.

Except for his eyes.

Mish's eyes gave him away.

And his eyes told her he wanted her to stay.

But he leaned forward now, to convince her otherwise.

"It's not as simple as what I do and don't need, Bec. For all I know, this guy—the man with the beard—is still somewhere around here. In town. Nearby. I don't know. But I *do* know that if I'm his target, I don't want you anywhere near me."

Becca sighed and gave up even toying with her salad. "So we're back in that Clint Eastwood movie, huh?"

"He shot me," Mish said flatly. "He looked at me, he aimed, and he discharged his weapon. And…"

It was her turn to lean across the table. "And *what?*"

He lowered his voice, looking away from her, the muscles in his jaw clenching. When he looked at her again, his eyes were bleak. "And if I had had the chance, I would've aimed and fired my weapon at him."

"Now, is this an actual memory we're talking about, or is this another of those things you just somehow *know?*"

"I'm sure you're very funny, but I don't happen to find any of this humorous," he said tightly.

She reached for his hand. "I don't mean to be such a smartass, I just…" She exhaled noisily. "Mish, I don't want to get in my truck and just leave you here. *I* still haven't given up on the UPS-man scenario."

He squeezed her hand slightly before he let her go, his eyes dark with regret. "I would have shot him, Bec," he said quietly. "And yes, that's a solid memory."

Odd, that part seemed to have been edited out of the version he'd first told her, after they'd left the alley and gotten back in her truck. Becca tapped her fingers on the table. "What else do you remember from that night?"

"I was carrying my .45—I don't know what happened to it. It must've been stolen with my wallet. The .22 in my boot was just a backup, but…I remember wishing I had an MP-5."

"MP-5?"

"Heckler & Koch MP-5," he told her grimly. "It's a German-made assault weapon. A machine gun. It's called a room broom, because you use it at a relatively short range to clear a room."

"Clear a room?" She was starting to sound like a parrot.

Mish nodded. "Yeah, it means just what it sounds like." He gripped his water glass tightly as he brought it to his mouth and took a sip.

"I have this recurring dream where I'm in a room," he told her. "Locked in with these other people. The door bursts open, and these men come in carrying assault weapons. There's a struggle, and one of the weapons—it's an Uzi. God, how do I know the names of these things?" He took a deep breath and when he spoke again, his voice was matter-of-fact. "In the struggle, an Uzi is kicked toward me, and I pick it up, and I use it to clear the room of the men with the weapons. One sweep with my finger on the trigger, and I kill them all. That's what it means to clear a room."

Becca shook her head, refusing to believe that could have happened—at least not as emotionlessly as he made it sound. "Mish, I know you're trying to prove that you're a terrible person, but you should hear some of *my* dreams. There's this one where I'm in a furniture store and—"

"I recognized the men in that van today," Mish told her.

That...van? She didn't say the words aloud, but she was certain they echoed on her face.

"The one with the tinted windows. Parked by the bus station?" he clarified. "I don't know where I know them from—both the shorter man with the tattoo and the man with the light-colored hair—but I definitely know them from somewhere.''

Becca didn't understand. ''Why didn't you say something to them? Approach them, find out who they are? Maybe find out who *you* are?''

''They were definitely running some kind of surveillance,'' Mish told her. ''And I know you were joking this afternoon, but it's possible they are looking for me.''

''Surveillance?'' Becca was incredulous. ''How could you know *what* they were doing in that van? You couldn't see inside. I'm sorry, Mish, but—''

''I didn't have to see inside. I knew there were three men, even though I didn't see more than two—because Tattoo brought three cups of coffee with him. Three *large* cups, which I took to mean they were planning to stay awhile. Blondie shook his muscles out when he got out of the van—they'd obviously already been there for some time. So long, in fact, he was in a rush to get into the bar and use the head.''

''Use the…? What's a *head?*''

''Men's room,'' he said. ''Lav. It's called a head on a ship.'' He rolled his eyes. ''Great. Now I'm a sailor.''

Becca laughed. She couldn't help herself.

Mish smiled, too, but it faded far too quickly. ''Becca, go home.''

She rested her chin in the palm of her hand, clearly going nowhere. ''What if you don't remember anything else?'' she asked. ''What if the rest of the details of who you were don't ever come back to you?''

Mish shook his head. ''I haven't really thought in terms of a worst-case scenario.''

''Maybe,'' she said softly, ''not remembering wouldn't necessarily be the worst-case scenario.''

He gazed at her for a moment, clearly understanding

what she was getting at. He'd thought it himself, many times. If he never pushed to find out the truth, if he just let go of whatever he'd done or been in the past, if he started over, from scratch...

"It would be kind of like being born all over again," Becca continued. "It could be a blessing. If you honestly think you did such terrible things..."

"You make it sound so tempting," he whispered. "But I'm here. I can't leave Wyatt City without at least talking to Jarell."

"Ah," she said. "There you go. Now you know exactly how *I* feel."

She met his gaze staunchly as he searched her eyes.

After several long moments, he nodded. "All right. I'll get us two rooms for tonight."

He was determined to keep his distance. Becca nodded, too. She'd let him win that battle.

For now.

Mish flipped through the TV channels twice more, but it was just like playing a game of solitaire that had run its course. Nothing new or interesting had magically appeared.

An infomercial on selling real estate. A late-night talk show with some actress who had a body like a POW-camp survivor—emaciated and bony and completely unappealing, compared to Becca's soft curves.

Compared to Becca's lush breasts and soft thighs and...

Mish changed the channel, shifting uncomfortably on the bed, refusing to think about Becca, naked in his arms.

The movie channel was showing a romantic comedy about a man who, after only one glimpse of a beautiful young woman, knew that she was his destiny. From what Mish could tell from the few minutes he'd watched earlier, the hero was determined to win the girl's heart by any means, including outright deceit. He lied about his name, his identity, his profession, his past.

Mish watched for a few more minutes before turning off the set in utter disgust. He knew how the movie would end. True love would triumph and the girl would forgive the hero.

But real life didn't work that way. Real life was filled with unmendable hurt, with unforgivable wrongs, with irreparable damage.

And most people didn't get a second chance at *anything*.

He lay back on the bed, aching with an awful emptiness, staring up at the plastered ceiling, knowing full well that he was one of the lucky ones. He'd been given a second chance—a chance to detach himself from all of the wrongs he'd ever done. A chance to start fresh, to live clean, to do right.

So what was he doing? He was lying here, nearly jumping out of his skin, desperate to cross the motel courtyard and knock on the door to room 214.

Becca's room.

She'd wanted to spend the night with him again. She'd told him so. But he'd turned her down, obsessed with the idea of protecting her from himself.

He'd checked them into their rooms, said good-night, and then he'd taken a long, cold shower. He'd shaved, too, although for what reason, he had no clue. He was here for the night. Alone.

And Becca was in her room. Alone. Way on the other side of the motel complex.

But now he lay here—alone—unable to think about anything but the softness of Becca's lips, the perfect fit of his body to hers, the sparkle of her eyes, the satisfied smile that curled her lips after he…after they…

Oh, Lord. He had to stay away from her. He *had* to.

Mish stood up, unable to keep from pacing. He was unable to stop himself from pacing right over to the TV where his room key sat, pocketing the key and pacing right out the door.

Room 214 was on the other side of the swimming pool, up on the second floor. He found the room without even counting windows—he already knew where it was. Behind the heavy draperies, he could see the glow of her light still on. She was awake.

Okay, he'd go over and knock on the door, ask her if she wanted to meet at the Waffle House for breakfast in the morning.

Mish crossed the courtyard, went up the stairs. He could hear the sound of a radio playing from inside room 214, heard Becca singing along. She had a sweet voice, low and musical.

He stood, leaning his head against her door, listening to her sing, and he knew without a doubt that he hadn't come here to talk about breakfast.

He'd come to stay until breakfast.

He couldn't do it. Try as he might, he couldn't stay away from her. Try as he might, he wasn't worthy of this second chance he'd miraculously been given.

Because here he was, yet again, right on schedule, giving in to temptation, choosing to do wrong instead of right.

He didn't know his name, but he knew with a gut-clenching certainty that before this was through, he was going to hurt this woman.

How hard could it be *not* to knock on her door? All he had to do was put his hands in his pockets or behind his back. And then he had to turn away, not think about the fact that she would probably greet him with a kiss, pull him into her room, surround him with the sweet scent of her freshly washed hair, the paralyzing softness of her smooth, clean skin. She would fall back on her bed with him, wrap herself around him and…

Mish couldn't turn away. And he couldn't keep his hands behind his back. He lifted one, about to rap loudly right next to the sign that said 214, but he never got the chance.

The door opened.

And Becca stood there, wearing cutoff jeans and a halter top that showed off a pair of smooth, bare shoulders that looked too damned good even when covered by a perspiration-stained T-shirt. She was carrying an open pint of ice cream, a plastic spoon stuck in the top.

"Mish! You startled me!" She was surprised to see him. And pleased. *Very* pleased.

"Yeah," he said, jamming his hands into his pockets and taking a step back from the door far too late. "Hi. Sorry. I realized we never talked about the morning. I didn't want to wake you up too early if you wanted to sleep in and…"

And she knew exactly why he was standing there, knew it had nothing to do with making plans for the morning. Mish could see her awareness in her smile, in the warmth of her eyes.

"I was just coming down to your room," she told him. She held out the ice cream. "I thought maybe you might want to share this with me. It's so hot tonight, and…"

And she'd intended to come to his room and share more than ice cream. He knew that, too. And she knew he knew…

"They were all out of cones," she said, "but I figured

we could just spread it on ourselves. Take turns licking each other clean...?''

Mish laughed. He couldn't help himself.

"So," Becca said, her lower lip caught between her teeth as she tried not to smile. "Are you coming in, or what?"

He was coming in. She knew it and he knew it. Mish lost himself in her eyes. "Why can't I stay away from you?" he whispered.

"Why would you want to?" she countered just as softly.

And as she reached for his hand and tugged him gently into her room, closing and locking the door behind them, Mish couldn't remember why he'd even considered staying away. She set the ice cream down on top of the motel television and he drew her into his arms. As she melted against him, he slowly lowered his mouth to hers and then, if he hadn't had amnesia already, he would have contracted a full-blown case of it right then as he lost himself completely in the sheer sweetness of her kiss.

As Mish kissed her, Becca tugged him toward the bed, afraid that he might come to his senses and walk out the door. She knew he was afraid of hurting her. She knew he wouldn't quite believe her even if she told him again that she wasn't looking for more than a low-maintenance, high-passion, short-term love affair. At this point, she wouldn't quite believe herself.

Last night had been incredible, even with the secrets that had hung between them. Tonight promised to be even more amazing.

Except tonight, she was the one with the secrets.

Mish's fingers were gentle as he worked to loosen the knots in her halter. His eyes were as warm as his hands as he pulled her top free. And as he drew in a sharp breath at the sight of her bare breasts, he made her feel like the most beautiful, most sexy woman in the world.

He touched her gently with his mouth and his hands, taking his time to look at her, to really take her in.

Becca tugged at the hem of his T-shirt, trying to pull it up, and he yanked it over his head. And then she was touching him, too, sliding her palms across his gorgeous tanned muscles, kissing him just as lightly, taking her time to look at him as well.

The bruise on his side was starting to fade. His muscles were amazingly well-defined, as if he had stepped out of an anatomy textbook. Or a J. Crew catalog. Arms, shoulders, pecs, he was sheer perfection right down to the six-pack of muscles that made up his abdomen.

But his eyes were as soft as his body was hard. And it was his eyes that held her captive.

All night long, he'd told her this afternoon. He'd wanted to make love to her all night long.

He lowered his head and lightly touched the tip of her breast with his tongue as he found and slowly unfastened the top button of her shorts.

All night long…

Becca pulled his mouth to hers and kissed him just as slowly, languidly, leisurely drinking him in.

It was as if the entire world had gone into slow motion, and with that, all of her senses had heightened.

She could hear the sound of their quiet breathing, the sound of her zipper being pulled down, tantalizingly slowly. She could feel the slightly callused roughness of his fingers against her skin. The delicious chill of the conditioned air against the tongue-wetted tips of her breasts. The satin-over-steel silkiness of his back beneath her hands. The baby-smoothness of his cheeks against her face…

He'd shaved for her. He'd come to her reluctantly after trying for hours to keep his distance. And yet, he'd recognized the futility of his resistance enough to shave before coming to her room.

It was silly, really. That he'd shaved was no big deal. It was simple consideration. A small sign of kindness, of *caring,* yet it brought all of her emotions bubbling to the surface.

He *cared.* She knew without a doubt that he desired her, but to know that he *cared*...

Becca was in too deep. She was in serious trouble, if the fact that this man had shaved for her was enough to bring tears of joy to her eyes. But she couldn't stop what she was feeling. It was far too late.

She was falling in love with this man without a name. She was completely enthralled with the gentle warmth of his eyes, with the way he truly listened whenever she spoke, with the fact that despite the absolute goodness that seemed to shine from within him, he was *not* an angel. Despite his good intentions, he was drawn to her as completely and powerfully as she was drawn to him. And try as he might, as much as he wanted otherwise, he hadn't been able to stay away.

He drew her shorts and her panties slowly down her legs, and she took close to forever to help him rid himself of his jeans. Then, skin against skin, she touched him, breathed him, kissed him, completely on fire, yet preferring this slow, intense burn to a white-hot flash of flame that would end far too soon.

No, she didn't want this to end.

She had no idea what tomorrow would bring, and more than half hoped this Jarell from the homeless shelter would provide no answers to Mish's many questions. His talk of machine guns had made her uneasy. Those were the weapons used by the survivalists who lived in military-style compounds in the mountains. They were all-or-nothing organizations and Becca had no desire to join one—no matter how desperately she loved this man.

Oh, yes, she loved him desperately. How could she have let that happen?

When she first asked him to have dinner, she'd imagined she'd love him just a little. A safe amount. Enough to justify giving in to this intense physical attraction, but not so much that she would feel this shortness of breath, this lack of control.

She'd wanted a brief entanglement with a handsome stranger. True, she'd wanted more than shallow sex, but she'd wanted nowhere near this Grand Canyon of emotional attachment.

But it was okay. It was going to be okay, because there was no way in hell Mish was going to fall in love with her. Becca could deal with a one-sided love affair. What she *couldn't* handle was hoping against hope that she had, in fact, at long last, found true love.

Because despite how much she hoped, true love didn't exist. And she and Mish would part, just later rather than sooner. And crushed hope was far worse than no hope at all.

Mish pulled back from their endless kiss, their languorous embrace, and as she gazed into his eyes, her heart twisted in her chest.

"I want you," she whispered, knowing he would misunderstand, but needing to say it, say *something,* all the same.

He kissed her again, then reached across her for the condoms she'd left on the nightstand. She closed her eyes, pressing herself against him, feeling the hard length of his heat parting her, dangerously close to penetration. She was more than ready for him, in every possible way.

It had to be biological—some kind of nesting instinct that was kicking in as her thirtieth birthday approached.

He pulled away from her to cover himself, and she resisted the urge to cling to him. She knew he would be back in a matter of moments. Still, she would use this as practice for the real thing, for when they would part for good.

He held her gaze as he came back to her, as he joined her in one slow, perfect thrust.

It was too good, too perfect, and Becca pulled him to her and kissed him, afraid of what he might see if he looked too close.

She shut her eyes and loved him.

All night long.

Chapter 12

"**M**r. Haymore?"

"Only folks call me Mr. Haymore be bill collectors and magazine salesmen." The tall African-American man stood at one of the sinks in the church kitchen. His back was to Mish and Becca, but he didn't turn around. He kept right on washing stalks of celery as he spoke. "If you're here on that sort of business, you might as well just walk right back out the door. You'll have to catch me some other time. But if you're here for something friendlier, call me Jarell, wash your hands and roll up your sleeves. I could use some help chopping this celery. Got two hundred forty people to feed tonight, and time's wasting."

Mish moved to the next sink over and started washing his hands. "Jarell. I spent the night at the shelter here two weeks ago. Do you remember me by any chance?"

Jarell's face broke into an enormous smile. "Well, I'll be! If it isn't Mission Man! Mish! You are looking *good,* my man! Out of uniform, but still doggone *good!* Staying clean, I'll wager.'' He held out a big wet hand for Mish to shake, then pulled him in for an embrace. ''Glory be, it *is* a good day!''

''Out of uniform…?'' The words had a strangely familiar ring to them.

''Yeah, you're here for your jacket, aren't you? I'm afraid it's pretty badly stained, though, and…'' Jarell caught sight of Becca as he released Mish. ''Hey, who's this?''

''Becca Keyes,'' Mish told him. ''A…friend of mine.''

She met his eyes briefly in acknowledgement of his hesitation, and he felt a wave of heat as a vivid memory of the night before flashed through him as clear as day. He could see Becca shattering as she sat astride him, head thrown back, breasts taut with desire as he, too, exploded in perfect slow motion. Friend, yes, but friend wasn't a big enough word for what she was to him. Except *lover* didn't quite cover the intensity of their relationship, either.

Jarell wiped his hands on a towel before enveloping Becca in a welcoming hug.

''Did I leave…a jacket here?'' Mish asked.

''I knew you'd be back for it.'' Jarell picked up a knife and set to work chopping celery. ''You were pretty out of it the morning you left. You were wearing it when you came in, along with a shirt, but they were both soaking wet so Max and I took 'em off you so as you wouldn't catch a chill. I apologize for not reminding you of that in the morning, although, like I said, I'm pretty sure the jacket's ruined.'' He set down the knife and wiped his hands again as he headed toward the office door. ''I'll get that for you.''

''Thank you,'' Mish said. His jacket. And a shirt. He

had no idea what they would look like, but maybe—just maybe—they would trigger more memories.

Becca touched his hand. ''Don't expect too much,'' she said softly.

He forced a smile. ''I never do.''

''Here you go,'' Jarell said, coming back into the room, carrying a plastic grocery bag. ''If you get it cleaned, it'll keep you warm at least. Not that you're needing to stay warm with this heat wave we've been having.''

Mish took the bag from Jarell, glancing inside. The jacket was black. From what he could tell, a plain suit jacket. Nothing special, nothing strange. He felt a rush of disappointment. Still, maybe Jarell could provide some other information.

Becca had picked up a knife and started chopping celery, earning one of Jarell's million-dollar smiles. Mish was afraid he'd cut off a finger if he tried to help, afraid his hands were actually shaking. Please, Lord, let him either find some answers or the peace to live with never knowing the truth....

''I was wondering,'' Mish said, ''if that one night was the only time I stayed at the shelter, or...'' He cleared his throat, ''I know this sounds awful, but I was wondering if I spent the night here any time before that.''

Jarell blew out a stream of air as he began cutting celery again. ''Whew, it was a bad one, huh? Mish, I can't tell you how often I've seen it happen. A good man gives in to the temptation, takes a drink and ends up on a binge, God knows where.'' He laughed ruefully. ''Then he spends the rest of his life unable to reclaim those days of blackout, always wondering just where he was and what kind of trouble he got into while he was gone.'' He sighed again. ''As far as I was aware, the first time you used a bed at the First Church shelter was the only time. The

night you were brought in was my fifth night on in a row.
Rico's brother got arrested down in Natchez, and I was
covering for him, working more nights than usual. So unless you were drinking hard for more than a week, and
sleeping somewhere else, which of course is entirely possible…'' His eyes were dark with sympathy. "How many
days of blackout you trying to recall?"

Becca was watching him, and Mish glanced at her only
briefly. He liked Jarell, but the truth made him uncomfortably vulnerable. He didn't want to tell anyone about
his amnesia. "Too many," he answered vaguely.

"Hmm." Jarell frowned down at his celery. "Is it good
news or bad news if I tell you a couple of men were in
here a few days ago, flashing your picture around, looking
for you?"

Damn. "One of them have barbed wire tattooed around
his biceps?" Mish asked, managing to sound matter-of-
fact. "Other one blond, dresses like he comes from California?"

"Barbed-wire tattoo, yes," Jarell said.

Becca exclaimed softly, and Mish looked up to see her
nursing her finger where she'd nicked it with the knife.

"But his friend was Native American. Big man. Dark
hair. Quiet. Reminded me of Chief from *Cuckoo's Nest.*"
Jarell gestured with his head toward the sink. "Run it
under cold water," he advised Becca. He glanced back
at Mish. "They also wanted to know if you'd been
here more than just one night. They seemed friendly
enough…"

"But…?"

"But dangerous," Jarell admitted. "It was just a hunch,
a gut feeling, but they were the kind of guys you'd want
to make sure were playing on your team. Whether the
game's softball or something else, you wouldn't want 'em

to be part of the opposition." He paused. "You want to leave a message in case they come back?"

"No," Mish said. "Thanks, but I know where to find them."

"You want me to tell 'em you've been here if they come back, asking, or…?" The old man's eyes were knowing. He'd done his share of hard, harsh living.

Mish shook his head. "I'd appreciate if it you could forget to mention we were here, but I wouldn't want to ask you to lie."

Jarell smiled. "Wouldn't have to lie. I'd just have to start spouting scripture. I'm sure you know what would happen then. They'd be done with their questions soon enough."

Mish laughed. "I'd appreciate it."

"No problem, my man."

Mish glanced inside the bag again. He wanted to examine the jacket and shirt more closely, but not here. Somewhere more private. Like maybe back in Becca's motel room. Maybe after they'd pulled the curtains and spent an hour or two naked….

He was staring at her. And she was gazing back at him, trepidation in her eyes.

She hadn't truly believed him when he'd told her about recognizing the men in the van. But she did now. And now she was realizing that—what had she called it?—this Clint Eastwood thing wasn't a movie, but was, in fact, Mish's real life.

Mish pulled his gaze away from her, and forced a smile in Jarell's direction, holding out his hand again. "Thank you so much. For everything."

Jarell slapped him five. "You're welcome so much. I'm glad I could be of help."

Mish opened the door to the parking lot and stepped back, waiting for Becca to go first.

"Just remember," Jarell called after them. "One day at a time, Father. Just one day at a time."

"Father?" Becca said. Had Jarell just called Mish *Father?*

Outside the church kitchen, the early-afternoon sun seemed brain-searingly bright. Mish was scanning the surrounding neighborhood, as if searching for any sign of the tattooed man or his friends from the surveillance van. God, could those men really be looking for Mish?

Mish shook his head, obviously distracted. "He's full of weird nicknames."

She unlocked the passenger side door to her truck, then crossed around the front. "Why did he call you Mission Man?"

Mish reached across the cab to unlock her door. "I don't know." He glanced down at the bag he was holding before he went back to scanning the world outside the truck's windshield. "Do you mind if we go back to the room?"

"So we can pull the curtains and hide?" she wondered aloud as she started the truck and pulled out of the parking lot. "Mish, maybe you should just walk up to these guys, find out who they are and why they're looking for you."

He was silent, unwilling to give her a long list of reasons why approaching these men could be a terrible mistake. It was possible they had been sent to fix the bearded man's botched job. Maybe they would grab him, pull him into the van, drive him someplace isolated and pop him— plug two bullets into the back of his head. It was also possible that before they did that, they'd take him somewhere isolated and ask him questions he couldn't possibly answer, no matter the pain they inflicted upon him. And wouldn't *that* be fun?

But the thought that they might get their hands on Becca and threaten her safety to get him to talk made his blood run cold.

"Or maybe," Becca said, "we should just get our things, check out of the motel, and go back to the Lazy Eight. You can work for me as long as you want to—as long as you need to. If you want, I could teach you how to care for the horses. I could teach you to ride. I could—" She broke off, as if suddenly aware of how desperate she sounded. "I like you, and care about you," she tried to explain. "You know that. I haven't exactly tried to hide that from you. All I'm saying is that if you *do* want to put whatever this is behind you, I'm here to do whatever I can to help."

Mish felt a rush of emotion that pressed behind his eyes and made his chest feel constricted. *I'm here...* He didn't have to be alone in this—he *wasn't* alone. Yet at the same time, he felt this odd mixture of disappointment and relief because she hadn't told him that she loved him. The disappointment didn't make sense—he was already terrified of hurting her, terrified of getting her inextricably involved in any of this, of putting her into physical danger.

And heaven help them both if she decided that she loved him....

"Thanks," he told her. "I just...I want to look at this jacket and shirt before I decide what my next move is going to be."

"I don't suppose there's a name tag sewn inside the jacket?" Becca laughed. "Probably not. It's probably been a few years since your mother sent you to summer camp."

Mish couldn't manage more than a wan smile. "Look, Bec, I know you need to get back to the ranch—"

"I can call Hazel, find out what the guest load is like, find out if I can take a few more days. Last I knew, the week was only lightly booked, so unless we've had a party check in at short notice, I won't need to get back right away."

She pulled into the motel lot and parked near her room, turning to look at him almost challengingly. "Unless you still want me to leave."

Mish got out of the truck, unwilling to sit there on display, where anyone could see them. "I don't want you caught in the crossfire. If someone's gunning for me—"

"Then let's both leave Wyatt City." Becca had to run to catch up with him. "Right now."

He unlocked the door, and they stepped into the room.

It was welcomingly cool and soothingly dark after the harsh brightness of the afternoon heat. They'd left a Do-Not-Disturb sign on the door, and the bedcovers were still rumpled from the night before, the colorful wrappers from the condoms they'd used still scattered on the floor.

Mish locked the door behind them, aware that they'd also locked the door the night before, aware that he wanted her again, just as badly as he'd wanted her last night.

More so.

And she knew it, too. She kissed him lightly, brushing both her lips and body against him in a message that was impossible to miss. And in case he *did* miss it, she said, "Why don't we wait to leave until tonight? We can take our time, take a nap—maybe catch a few hours of sleep."

Mish caught her, pulling her tightly against him, kissing her hard, letting her feel what she did to him. "Sleep?"

Becca smiled, glad he was no longer trying to ignore

the attraction that sparked and ignited between them with little more than eye contact. "I did say *maybe*. But…first things first."

She pulled away from him, picking up the plastic grocery bag from where it had slipped out of his hands and taking it to the little table by the window. "Oh, *this* is what I smell." She pulled the jacket out, held it up. It was stiff, encrusted with mud, stained and spotted. And it smelled *bad*. "Wow, if you smelled even slightly like this when you woke up in the shelter, I've got your nickname figured out. Jarell wasn't calling you Mission Man, he was calling you *E*mission Man."

She handed the jacket to Mish, who winced. "Whoa, man! I'm sorry—I can take this outside if you want."

"I can handle it. I work with horses," she reminded him as she pulled the shirt out of the bag. "You know, I was kidding about the name tags sewn in, but sometimes cleaners stencil part or even all of a customer's name onto the tail of a shirt."

Yet there was nothing there. The white shirt itself was unsalvageable, permanently stained dark brown in places from blood. Mish's blood.

He'd been shot and left for dead, bleeding in an alley. The thought made her a little light-headed.

"Check the pockets of the jacket," she told him, trying to sound as if searching articles of clothing for any identifying marks was something she did every day. "I didn't check the pockets."

"Empty," he reported. "But…"

Something in his voice made her turn toward him.

"I think there's something sewn into the lining. Here at the hem."

He held it out to her, and sure enough, there *was* something hard in there. Something small, but something that didn't bend.

"I have a Swiss army knife in my bag," she told him, but he'd already torn the lining open.

It was a key. An oversized key that might unlock a hotel room or a locker, with the number imprinted right on it: 101.

Mish tore the lining completely out of the jacket, but there was nothing else hidden there. No notes, no messages, no nothing.

As Becca watched, Mish hefted the key in his hand. "How much do you want to bet this key fits one of the lockers at the bus station?" He sounded so grim, considering they'd just found a major clue.

"But that's great," Becca said. "Isn't it?"

He didn't say anything, and she realized, *bus station.* The men in the van had been parked outside of the bus station. Was it possible they knew Mish had something— a suitcase, a duffel bag—stashed in one of the lockers? Obviously, from the look on his face, Mish thought it was.

He picked up the plastic bag, ready to stuff the ripped jacket and shirt back in, but Becca could tell from the way he was holding the bag that there was something else still inside. He pulled it out. Like the shirt, at one time it had been white and…

Mish stared at it.

Becca stared at it, too, reaching behind her for the bed. She had to sit down. "Is that…yours?" she asked inanely. Of course it was his. He'd been wearing it. It was stained with his blood.

She'd never seen one up close before, but there was no doubt in her mind as to what it was. A liturgical collar. Some kind of clip-on version. The kind that a priest would wear.

A *priest*.

With any other man, Becca might have laughed at the absurdity of the joke, but with Mish, it just was possible.

And it all suddenly made sense. His quiet watchfulness. His compassion, his gentleness. His ability to listen.

Jarell had known, and had called him *Father*.

Mish looked stunned. "No," he said with conviction. But then he added a whole lot less certainly, "I don't think…"

He sat down next to her.

On the bed.

On the bed where they'd made love last night and again this morning and—oh, God, what had they done?

"Well," Becca said shakily, "I guess you were right about not having a wife." She laughed, but it was borderline hysterical and tears filled her eyes. She closed them tightly, forcing herself not to lose it. However upsetting this was for her, it had to be ten times worse for Mish. "Let's go to the bus station, find out if this key does fit one of the lockers. Okay? Let's go right now, see what's in there."

She didn't know what else they would find. God, what had she done?

"It doesn't make sense," Mish said, as if he hadn't even heard her. "If I'm a…" He took a deep breath. "I'm not. I *know* I'm not. Because why would I have a gun in my boot? How could I know so much about weapons and ordnance and… What about all this money I'm carrying? No. I'm not. I'm—"

"If you are a…priest…" She had trouble saying it, too. "*I'm* the one responsible for making you break your vows. I seduced you. This isn't your fault, it's *mine*." Try as she might to be tough, she couldn't fight her tears. They escaped and she dissolved. "Oh, Mish, I'm so sorry."

"Hey." Mish put his arms around her, pulling her close as she cried. "Shhh. Bec. This is going to be okay. I promise. Even if I *am* a..." He took a deep breath and let it out in a burst. "Look, what we've shared was amazing. It wasn't wrong. It was special and perfect and... It was a gift, Becca—something most people don't ever get to experience. And no matter what I find out about myself, I'm not going to regret it. I refuse to regret it. Not ever."

She lifted her head and gazed up at him, her face wet. And Mish's stomach twisted. Lord help him, he hated that he'd made her cry. "Do you remember *anything* about—"

He cut her off. "Bec, it's blank. I swear. If I remembered anything at all about *any* of this, about *anything*, I would've told you by now." He laughed ruefully. "I can't even remember the last time I went to church."

"You tried to stay away from me. On some level you must've known." Fresh tears flooded her eyes. "And I just wouldn't let up. I wouldn't take no for an answer."

"It's okay," he said desperately. "Please, don't cry. This *is* going to be okay."

"How can it be okay?" she asked quietly, "when I'm still dying to kiss you?"

Mish couldn't answer. All words deserted him. But he *knew* that—as much as he wanted to—covering her trembling mouth with his would not be an appropriate response in this situation.

But for several long seconds, as he gazed down into her eyes, he teetered on the edge.

Becca yanked herself away from him, out of his arms and halfway across the room.

"I'm in love with you, dammit," she told him fiercely, turning to face him, to glare at him. "How is *that* going to be okay?"

* * *

Mish watched the van from the roof of Jerry's Tire Center through a pair of binoculars he'd picked up at Target, the last remaining department store in the dying town.

The van was still parked near the bus station.

And inside the bus station, through the window, Mish could see a row of beat-up lockers. Locker number 101 was down near the floor, four from the right end, about two and a half feet high and a foot and a half wide. The men in the van—Tattoo, California and the Native American man—had an unobstructed view of it.

Coincidence? Maybe. But Mish wasn't going to take that chance.

He had to get what was inside of that locker without getting caught. But how?

Create a diversion simply by walking by and letting the surveillance team get a clear view of his face? Lead them on a chase while Becca went into the bus station with the key and...

No. What if there were more of 'em? What if someone else was watching locker 101, too? Mish wouldn't risk putting Becca into that kind of potential danger. No way. Uh-uh. No thanks.

She loved him.

Mish couldn't remember the last time he'd felt both hot and cold simultaneously, the way he'd felt when Becca had let that little bomb drop. He couldn't remember ever both wanting and not wanting something—some*one*— quite so badly.

He had to get whatever was inside that locker. Now, more than ever, he *had* to find out the truth about himself.

He was going to have to evade the surveillance team in the van on his own.

And he knew just how to do it.

Funny, he knew all sorts of breaking-and-entering tricks. He knew how to move silently, knew how to evade capture and escape detection.

But try as he might, he couldn't remember any but the simplest of prayers.

He was no priest.

But he just might be the devil.

Chapter 13

Lucky sat in the van, drinking what seemed like his four-teenth cup of coffee in the past four hours, working hard to stay alert.

That was the hardest part of standing watch or doing surveillance. Staying not only awake but attentive.

He ran disaster scenarios—it was called war-gaming. He planned, down to the exact detail, what he would do should Lt. Mitchell Shaw suddenly appear, walking down the street. He planned what he'd do if Mitch just instantly appeared at locker 101.

He planned for Mitch to come exploding down from the low-hung, sound-deadening ceiling tiles, for him to grab his bag from the locker and be yanked by a rope back up to the bus station roof.

And he planned for his next phone call from Joe Cat.

Lucky had arranged today's schedule so that Bobby would come and relieve him in enough time for him to dash back to the motel and be ready and waiting for the captain's phone call.

With luck, Admiral Robinson would have arrived in California, and this entire mess would be cleared up with some simple explanation. Mitchell Shaw was following Gray Group procedures for going deep undercover—procedures that the admiral had failed to tell the captain about before he left. The possibilities were limitless.

And then he and Bobby and Wes could get the hell out of this dust bowl, and get back to the ocean. After this, they all deserved a silver-bullet assignment. Something that involved a lot of scuba diving in a location that looked a lot like Tahiti with crowds of beautiful women...

"Movement inside," Wes droned. "Heading directly for our locker."

The approaching woman had the shuffling, painfully slow walk of someone who carried seventy-five unnecessary pounds on legs that were getting too old to support that much excess weight. She was wearing a blue dress that hung down almost all the way to the floor from a rear end the size of a VW Bug. She wore ankle socks with a little lace trim and a beat-up pair of running shoes. She had a baseball cap on her head, straggly dark hair coming out the back, and she wore enough makeup to win first-runner-up in the Tammy Faye look-alike contest. She carried a black plastic trash bag—the ultimate in high-fashion luggage.

As Lucky watched, she did a U-turn away from the lockers and he felt himself relax. She went to the Greyhound counter instead and bought a ticket, taking her money from a bejeweled change purse and counting it out painstakingly slowly.

Ticket in hand, she struggled her way to the hard plastic

chairs near the pay phones and wedged her enormous rear end into one of the seats.

There was no one else around. The next bus—the 4:48 daily to Albuquerque—wouldn't be ready to board for another twenty-five minutes.

Lucky swore aloud. "I actually know the daily bus schedule," he said when Wes looked up.

"I do, too." Wes grimaced. "Guess we could always get a job here in the event of more military cutbacks."

"Oh, sure," Lucky said. "I'm already looking forward to coming back to Wyatt City—but only after I'm *dead,* thanks. How can people live without an ocean?"

In the bus station, the woman with the trash bag pushed herself up and out of her seat.

"Got me," Wes said. "Speaking of the ocean, mind if I hop out and take a leak?"

The woman headed toward the lockers, directly toward number 101, and parked herself right in front of them. Her derriere was so incredibly *grande,* Lucky couldn't see what the hell she was doing there.

He swore again. "Wait," he told Wes. "I've got to get a closer look."

"At *her?* I'm sorry, I'm sure she's a very nice lady, but she's not exactly Mitch Shaw's type. I mean, we're supposed to keep our eyes out for someone he'd buy a new suit for. Someone he'd possibly sell out his country for and—"

"Wait here, because she's blocking our view," Lucky ordered, already out of the van. "I'll be right back." He headed toward the doors to the bus station, feeling every muscle in his body screaming from lack of exercise.

He walked past the lockers, past the heavy woman, into the middle of the room, then spun in a full circle, as if he'd come in and was now searching for someone. Of course there was no one around. Even the ticket-counter clerk had disappeared into the back.

Lucky moved toward the woman. "Excuse me, ma'am. Have you seen a woman with a baby?" He gave her his best sheepish grin. "I was supposed to pick 'em up an hour ago, and time just kind of got away from me."

Everything was cool. He could see as he got closer that the old woman was taking what looked like dirty laundry and a collection of old magazines from her Hefty bag and storing it in locker number 99. It was down low, right next to 101—which was still tightly shut and locked.

The woman looked at him and shook her head.

Blue eye shadow. Who the hell had ever invented blue eye shadow? Lucky didn't mind it so much when it was applied sparingly, but this woman's eyelids were nearly neon. And the fact that her face was powdered an almost solid pink sure as hell didn't help.

And hey, she smelled as if she hadn't bathed in about four months. Imagine winning the bad-luck lottery and riding in a bus all the way to Albuquerque next to that magic.

Lucky took a step back.

"No, sorry. Haven't seen anyone." She sounded as if she'd smoked three packs of Marlboros a day for most of her seventy years.

"That's okay," Lucky said, backing away. "That's... fine. Thanks anyway."

He pushed his way out the door, taking a deep lungful of the hot air reflecting off the sidewalk. It didn't smell too fresh either, but it was a definite improvement over what had last invaded his nostrils.

He climbed into the van and turned the air-conditioning up to maximum. "You can go on, hit the head," he told Wes. "She's just a bag lady."

''I coulda told you that.'' Grumbling, Wes left through the back door.

Through the windshield, through the bus station window, Lucky watched the aromatic woman close the locker, carefully pocket the key and shuffle toward the ladies' room.

And once again, nothing in the bus station moved.

Wes came back in one-point-four minutes, carrying several cans of cold soda, bless him.

The stinky bag lady didn't emerge from the ladies' room for another twenty-three minutes.

When she finally did, she was still carrying her plastic trash bag. She worked her way back to the lockers and planted herself in front of locker 99 again. She worked her magic, fussing with the trash bag for many long minutes.

Finally, when the 4:48 was starting to board, she moved away from the lockers, shuffling with her plastic bag toward the bus, leaving locker 99 empty and open behind her.

It could probably use a good airing out.

As Lucky watched, the woman went out the big glass back door and disappeared around the side of the waiting bus. He could see the bus shake slightly, and he could imagine her hauling herself up, one step at a time, trash bag clutched in her hands.

It was still early. There would be about ten or fifteen minutes before two or three people would make the last-minute dash for the bus.

Lucky settled back in his seat.

''So. Figured out what you're getting Ellen for a wedding gift yet?'' Wes asked, clearly bored out of his mind.

''Yeah,'' Lucky said grimly. ''I'm getting her an appointment with a psychologist because anyone who gets married at her age is obviously insane.''

''Ah,'' Wes said. And wisely, he fell into silence.

Twelve minutes passed, each one endlessly long and desperately boring.

Lucky watched the lockers, watched the bus station, forcing himself to stay awake, to stay in battle-ready mode, war-gaming all the scenarios all over again. Of course, if *he* were Mitch, he'd wait until dark to show up. If he were Mitch...

There they came. A station wagon filled with young women. Three were going to Albuquerque, two were staying behind. Lucky watched as they bought tickets in a flurry of movement and chaos and big hair. Hugs. Kisses. Waving, the three travelers disappeared around the side of the bus, climbed on and...

It was only a matter of seconds before they came back into the station.

Lucky was too far away to read their lips, but their expressions and gestures as they spoke to their friends were obvious. They didn't like the way the 4:48 smelled.

Back to the desk, back to the clerk. Pointing toward the bus, talking, talking.

The ticket clerk shook his head, shrugged, pointed to the bus driver, a handsome young Mexican-American man who smiled at the women. And just like that, the mood changed from indignant to a little less uptight. Everyone flirted a little bit. The women explained about the smell— complete with the gestures, but with smiles, too, this time—and the driver nodded, flexed his pecs, straightened his shoulders and disappeared around the side of the bus.

The women hovered, fixing their big hair, adjusting their bras beneath their shirts, moistening their lips, waiting for their hero's return.

One minute turned into two into three...and then he was back, holding what looked to be a torn suit jacket between one thumb and forefinger, and...

A black plastic trash bag...?

"Oh, *damn*," Lucky said, scrambling out of the van. He ran into the bus station, ran past the women and the driver, out the side door and around the waiting bus.

The door was open, and he launched himself up and into it and...

The bus was empty. It was absolutely empty.

He searched it, rushing all the way to the back, but the foul-smelling woman in the big blue dress wasn't on the damn thing.

He swore again, taking the stairs off the bus in a single jump, heading back into the station.

The driver had set the plastic garbage bag next to the overflowing trash can, and Lucky grabbed it, opened it and...

A giant blue dress. Little lacy ankle socks. A baseball cap. Old magazines, and a fine collection of rags.

And—all the way at the bottom—the key to locker number 101.

Wes had come inside, and he watched as Lucky grimly took the key and opened the locker.

Empty.

Mitch's so-called "bag of tricks" was gone.

"Son of a bitch!" Lucky swore. "*Son* of a bitch!"

The foul-smelling woman had been Mitch Shaw.

There was no point looking for him. A man who'd been trained in covert ops like Mitch would be long gone. Or hidden so completely even Lucky and Wes wouldn't find him.

Wes followed Lucky back to the van, climbed in silently.

"He looked right at me," Lucky fumed, as he started the engine. "He *had* to have recognized me. I mean, he *knows* me, we've sat in meetings together. What the hell is going on?"

"We have to call the captain," Wes said quietly. "I don't know, Lieutenant, but maybe we've got to stop thinking about Mitch as one of us, and start thinking of him as the enemy. If he *has* sold out…"

Lucky nodded. This wasn't going to be easy. Damn, telling Joe Cat that he'd let Shaw get past him wasn't going to be easy, either. "I never thought I'd say this, but I'm going to recommend to the captain that it might be time to get FInCOM involved."

Becca drove north along state roads as the sun sat low in the sky.

Mish sat in silence next to her, the leather bag he'd found in the bus station locker at his feet.

He hadn't said more than twenty words to her since she'd dropped her little bomb back in the motel room. And two of those words had been an apology. Becca shook her head. She'd told him that she loved him, and his response had been *I'm sorry*. Still, she supposed that was a good thing. She didn't know what she would have done if he'd told her he loved her, too. It was too terrifying to consider.

The truth was, she didn't *want* him to love her, too. Even if he'd been just a normal ranch hand, just a regular guy, even if he hadn't come to her with amnesia and a bullet wound—yes, even a priest's collar—she wouldn't want him to love her, too.

Love was too risky. It was too uncertain. When she planned for her future, she didn't want to leave that great big unknown black hole of uncertainty gaping out in front of her, the one with the caption under it that read: *What If He Stopped Loving Her?*

Mish was sorry that she loved him, and she was sorry, too. But at least she knew what her future held in store for her. She knew that sooner or later—and probably sooner, from the way things were going—Mish would leave. And she would miss him. She already missed him. From the moment she'd seen that collar, their relationship had changed drastically, and she missed feeling free to touch him, to take his hand, to look into his eyes and dream about the night to come.

But there was no way she would do that now, not without knowing for sure who he was, *what* he was.

Their journey together had come to an end, and soon—possibly in hours—they would part. And she would feel like hell for a few weeks or months, until the day when she woke up and found she could think about him without aching. Then she would find she could wonder fleetingly where he was, and smile at the way he'd briefly touched her heart and her life.

But before that could happen, before she let him walk away, Becca wanted to know the truth. She wanted to know who he really was. She wanted to know what was inside of that bag.

Back in the motel room, Mish had beat a quick retreat after his apology, telling her that he was heading to the bus station. He intended to find out if the key they'd found in his jacket actually opened a locker there. How he was going to do that without the men in the van noticing him, he didn't say. He'd simply told her to meet him in two hours in the parking lot of the closest thing to an upscale bar Wyatt City had, over on the north side of town.

And then he'd left, taking his shirt, his jacket and that unmistakable, unforgettable collar along with him.

Becca glanced at him, glanced down at the bag at his feet. Supple, tanned leather covered a harder surface. It wasn't a gym bag as she'd first thought. It was some kind of hard case. And it looked as if he'd had it and used it for a long time. "Is there a reason you haven't opened that?"

He turned to look at her. "I'm afraid of what I'll find inside," he told her quietly.

Becca nodded, forcing her eyes back onto the road. "I am, too." There was a pull-off up ahead—an old abandoned gas station, the garage boarded up. She slowed and pulled into the dusty, potholed driveway, the truck bouncing until she stopped and put the engine into park.

She didn't turn off the engine. They both needed the air conditioner running.

She took a deep breath. "Mish, what happened between you and me... We're the only ones who know about it. No one else ever has to..."

She could tell from his eyes that Mish knew what she was doing. She was giving him permission to turn his back on her, to deny that their relationship had grown beyond the physical—or at least that it had for her.

"If we both agree it never happened," she continued, "then—"

"But it did happen," he interrupted her. "Bec, I know you think otherwise, but I'm not a priest. The collar was just a disguise. I'm...good at disguises. I know how to change the way I look so completely and...I wish I were a priest. Because then at least I'd have more options right now. I'd have the hope of someday having you in my life. I could make a career change." He tried to smile. "Take you up on your offer to teach me how to care for horses."

Was he saying...? "You'd want that?"

"I want *you*," he said simply.

Becca's heart nearly stopped. She'd said those exact words to him, and she'd meant...

"But it won't be easy to walk away from who and what I think I am," he told her. "It might be flat-out impossible. And I won't put you in danger. I don't really know who the hell I am, but there are people looking for me, Bec. Dangerous people. And I want to be far away from you when they finally catch up with me."

She didn't know what to say, didn't know what to do. He'd spoken of "someday," implied they could have a *future.*

Becca turned away, suddenly wanting that future so desperately, her stomach hurt. Oh, that was bad. That was very bad. She couldn't have this man. And even if she could, she'd never wanted her happiness to depend on any one person. And yet here he was, saying that he would give up everything, if only he could, just to be with her.

"I know what's inside this case," Mish told her quietly. "I haven't opened it, but I still somehow know. I knew when I first saw it. It's got a combination lock, but that's not a problem because I know the combination, too."

He swung it up between them on the bench seat.

"There's a change of clothes inside," he continued. "Jeans and a T-shirt. Two clean pairs of socks. A pair of boots and extra laces." He spun and set the combination, and the lock popped open. "My H&K MP-5 assault weapon."

Mish opened the lid. Sure enough, the leather covered some kind of metal. This was no lightweight suitcase. This was heavy-duty. As Becca watched, he reached inside and took out something that was wrapped in dark fabric.

"And an overcoat so I can carry it concealed."

The dark fabric was, indeed, some kind of lightweight raincoat. And inside it was...

An extremely deadly-looking submachine gun.

"Oh, my God," Becca breathed.

"I'm not a priest," he said. "I wore that collar as part of a disguise. Are we clear about that?"

She nodded.

"Good." He smiled tightly. "No way am I going to have you spend the rest of your life thinking what we shared was any less than perfect."

Mish set the weapon down on the floor at his feet. He pulled a tightly rolled pair of jeans out of the case, along with another, smaller gun in a leather shoulder holster. Clips of ammunition—enough to outfit a small army. Boots, as he'd said. Rolled-up socks. A vest of some sort. A medical kit. A passport.

No, not one passport—seven. Mish had *seven* passports. As Becca silently watched, he flipped through them. His picture was on them all, but each of the seven names was decidedly different.

Becca had to ask. "Do any of those names—"

"No. They don't sound familiar. Not even the one with the Albuquerque address." Mish loaded everything back into the case. "I knew," he said quietly, "but I was hoping I was wrong."

Becca shook her head. "The guns don't prove anything. I mean, maybe you're a...a..."

"A thief instead of a killer?" he suggested.

"A gun collector."

Mish laughed, examining the machine gun before wrapping it in the raincoat again. "This weapon's sanitized— all serial numbers and other identifying marks have been filed clean. Same goes for the handgun. And I bet if we look at the .22 I left back at the ranch, we'll find the same thing.'' He closed the case, spun the combination lock. ''Apparently I collect illegal weapons, which is, of course, illegal in itself.'' He set the case back down on the floor. ''I want you to drop me at the next town and go back to the ranch.''

Woodenly, Becca put the truck into gear. First he was a ranch hand who didn't know a damn thing about horses, then he was a hero who saved a young boy's life. Then he was a man without a past, without the faintest clue who he'd been and where he'd come from. Then he'd been a priest. She'd been so positive he was a priest. But no. He was, in truth, some kind of master of disguises, someone who needed seven passports and seven names and three deadly guns.

And two extra pairs of clean socks.

The socks gave him away.

Mish wanted her to believe he was some kind of a monster, and maybe he had, in fact, done some terrible things in his past, but he was, first and foremost, a man. A man she had only ever seen act gently and kindly.

She held tightly to the steering wheel. ''You're going to Albuquerque to check out the address on that passport.'' She knew him well enough by now to know he couldn't let that go, even though it was probably just another false lead.

''Yeah. And no, I don't want you to drive me there.'' He knew her pretty well by now, too. ''You can drop me at Clines Corners, but that's as far as I'll let you take me.''

Clines Corners was on Route 40, right where 285 cut up toward Santa Fe. He'd be able to get a ride to Albuquerque from there, no problem.

Becca glanced at the clock on the dash. They were at least three hours from Clines Corners. She had a solid three hours to convince herself that the best thing she could do for both of them would be to say goodbye and let him go.

She knew it was the right thing to do.

So why did it feel so wrong?

Chapter 14

The door opened, and the American leapt.

The assault weapon skittered across the floor, and Mish didn't think. He just picked it up and fired.

A spray of bullets, a spray of blood.

So much blood.

"Good job," the American told him through the blood that bubbled on his own lips.

Mish stared at the bodies, stared at what he'd done.

And on the floor, his father's hands started to twitch. Mish backed away, but he couldn't get far enough. He would never get far enough away. *Thou shalt not kill.*

The American's voice was tight with pain. "Way to send them straight to hell, Mitch."

Mitch.

He awoke with a start, drenched with sweat despite the truck's powerful air conditioner.

The sun had set, their headlights the only light for what

had to be miles around. Becca's face looked ghostly in the dim glow from the dash. "You okay?"

He was still breathing hard, his hands shaking as he took his can of soda from the cup holder and took a sip. "Mitch," he managed to get out. "My name. I had a dream…"

"Oh, my God! Mitch," she tried saying it aloud. Laughed. "*Mitch.* Of course. No wonder Mish sounded so familiar to you." She turned toward him eagerly. "What else do you remember?"

Did he remember more than that one awful day? He tried to think back to the alleyway, to the man with the beard. But there was nothing there. No connection. He couldn't even grab hold of his last name. It was out there, but just beyond his grasp.

He shook his head. "I dreamed about… About my…father. He was shot. Killed."

"Oh, God," Becca breathed. "Are you sure it wasn't just a dream? Sometimes—"

"I don't know, Bec, it seems so real. I've dreamed about it a lot, although I didn't realize until now that he was my father. And it always happens the same way, as if it's a memory. I mean, yeah, some of it gets weird, like I know my father's dead, but then he stands up and it's pretty grisly…" He took another sip of his soda, trying to banish that image from his head. "I think it's more than a dream. I think some of it happened."

Becca glanced at him again. "Were you… Did you actually see him—his body—after he died?"

"I think I was there when he was killed."

"God, Mitch."

"I was fifteen." Mitch watched the lines on the road, brightly illuminated by the headlights but quickly fading into nothing as the truck moved forward into the night.

How old was he now? Thirty-five was the number that came to him first. It seemed to fit. Twenty years since he'd first picked up a weapon and pulled the trigger and...

"Can you...tell me about it?" Becca's voice was so soft, so uncertain.

And ended a human life.

Mitch looked at her sitting there behind the steering wheel. She tried so hard to be tough and strong, when in truth the past few weeks had been devastatingly difficult for her. But her resilience shone through. She looked tired, yes, but gloriously undefeated, and Mitch knew without a doubt that she wasn't going to take Route 285 to Santa Fe and to the Lazy Eight when they hit Clines Corners.

No, she was going to stick with him. She was going to take him all the way, wherever he needed to go, and maybe even then some.

But it was only a matter of time before the gang in the surveillance van outside the Wyatt City bus station discovered that locker 101 had been emptied out beneath their noses. And it was only a matter of time before the search for him intensified.

And while Mitch still didn't know what he'd done to spark a manhunt, he did know one thing without a doubt.

He was *not* going to put Becca into any danger.

Even if that meant disappearing into thin air the next time they stopped for gasoline. Even if it meant leaving her without an explanation, without even saying goodbye.

He didn't want to do that. He didn't want to leave her wondering. He'd given her so little as it was.

Can you tell me about it, she'd asked. And he knew that this was really all he had to give her. This small piece of his past that he remembered, this awfulness, this terrible thing that—he suspected—had helped shape him into the person he was today.

"Yeah," he said. "I'd like to tell you. But it's pretty intense, so if you want me to stop…"

"I'll let you know," she told him, and he knew that was the last he'd ever hear of that.

"I was fifteen," he said again. "I don't remember exactly where we were, but we were overseas, I think somewhere in the Middle East. My father was a minister and he'd recently won this position as part of a multidenominational peacekeeping group. It was a really big deal— he was so proud."

It was strange. Telling her about it was helping him to remember. He could recall the open airport where he and his parents had first arrived. He could remember the scent of exotic foods cooking, the swirl of colors and people. He remembered his disappointment when the hotel they were brought to was a tall, modern building rather than something ancient and mysterious.

"We'd been there for about two weeks, when my father took me to lunch at the downtown McDonald's. We were both dying for a Big Mac. I remember we'd ordered burgers from the hotel room service, but they were strange. My dad thought maybe they were cut with horse meat. And I remember my mother rolling her eyes, taking a bite and telling us it was just the local spices. But my father had the afternoon off, so the two of us took a bus from the hotel down to the market. He was…very charismatic. I remember he had everyone on the bus singing the McDonald's theme song. And most of the busload of people followed us into the restaurant, too. Some American businessmen. A group of tourists—mothers and teenaged girls from France, I think."

He could remember the menu hanging above the counter, the words both in English and something undecipherable.

"I didn't see them come in," he continued. "There was this loud noise—that was the first I knew of any trouble. The sound of weapons being fired. My father pulled me down, but it was over before it even began. Terrorists killed the security guards at the doors. They'd taken control of the McDonald's—the symbol for all things American. And we were their hostages."

The truck moved onward through the night. A sign appeared out of the blackness. Clines Corners, twenty miles.

Becca was silent, just letting him tell the story at his own speed.

"They took us into the back, out a doorway into the main part of the building. The guards there were dead, too. It was obvious this had been planned, that this attack hadn't been just a spur-of-the-moment event. They led us into a storage room that had been cleared out. There were no windows and only that one door—like I said, they planned it well. Some of the women and children were crying, and the terrorists seemed on the edge, too, shouting for everyone to be silent, and my father stepped forward.

"He tried to calm everyone down, started talking about the women and kids, trying to convince the terrorists' leader that they should let them go. And I remember..."

Is that your dad, kid?

"There was a man standing behind me. A black man. An American. He must've been in the McDonald's when we arrived—I didn't remember seeing him on the bus."

Tell your dad to back off. The American's eyes and voice had held an urgency.

"He told me to tell my father that these terrorists wouldn't negotiate, that they didn't respect his cross or his collar, that the fact that he was American put him in extra danger."

Tell him. Now.

Dad. ''So I stepped toward my father, tried to take his arm and pull him back into the crowd.''

His father had turned just a little, the sweat glistening on his brow. *Stay back with the others, Mitch.*

''He wouldn't listen to me.'' Mitch could remember his own fear. His sense of panic as he saw the intense concern in the American's face, saw the horror in his dark brown eyes. And he knew even before he turned back that his father was as good as dead.

''It happened so fast. The terrorist lifted his side arm and fired. Two bullets. Right into my father's head. One second he was standing there, and the next...''

He'd crumpled to the ground, lifeless.

''It was so unreal,'' Mitch said, his voice tight with anguish. ''It didn't seem possible that he was really dead. I mean, how could he be dead? He was *so* alive. But there was blood. I didn't know it at the time, but we'd been sprayed with it. All I could see was this pool of red on the floor, beneath him. I wanted to go to him, to help him, to stop the bleeding, but the American pulled me back, into the crowd. He put his hand over my mouth.''

God, kid, I'm sorry. The American's voice had been nearly as rough as his hands.

Let me help him! Mitch had struggled.

''And he told me my father was dead.''

Don't do this, the American had hissed.

''He told me if I made too much noise, they'd kill me, too.''

I don't care! Mitch hadn't gotten the words out from behind the man's huge hand, but he knew the message had been understood.

''He told me to think about my mother, think about

how she was going to feel losing both her husband and her son on the same day.''

Stop being so damned selfish, boy, and you calm yourself down.

''He told me I couldn't help my father now.''

''Oh, Mitch, I can't believe you had to live through that.'' Becca's eyes glimmered with sympathy.

''They locked us into that room,'' he told her, ''and I sat on the floor, trying not to cry, trying not to look at my father. They just left his body there. One of the women had draped her scarf over his head and face, but...''

But that pool of blood had remained.

''The American was making a circuit of the room, trying to convince the others that we had to fight back, and that the moment to strike was as soon as the terrorists returned, as soon as they unlocked the door. He told us he knew about this group of zealots. He knew of their leader, knew that they weren't going to let any of us go free.''

The American told them that when the terrorists returned, the killing would start.

''He said that he was going to fight. But no one else seemed up to it. Everyone was afraid. I was afraid, too.''

But Mitch had looked at his father, at this man who had been so good, so strong, so caring. He'd been killed as if he were little more than a bug to be stepped on. And Mitch had looked up at the American.

I'll fight, he'd said. *I'll help.*

''Thou shalt not kill,'' Mitch told Becca. ''If there was one thing my father believed more than anything, it was in nonviolence. Guns and weapons and war had no place in his world. But I wasn't in his world anymore. And I wanted to kill the men who had taken him from me.''

The American sat down next to him. *Okay. Let's kill*

them, Mitch. You channel that rage, kid. Make it work for you.

"The American man asked me if I'd ever fired an automatic weapon." Mitch laughed. "In my house? I hadn't even seen one up close, let alone held one."

The force of the discharge pulls the muzzle up, the American had told him. *You've got to work to keep it down. And aim for the center of the body. Don't go for the head. It's amazing how often the enemy pops back onto their feet after a shot to the head with something as lightweight as a nine millimeter. And we don't want that, you copy?*

"He gave me a crash course in handling an assault weapon, and I pointed out that a lot of good it was going to do us to talk about firing one, since we didn't have one to fire." Mitch shook his head. "But he told me he had a plan."

"He told me about something called PV—*point of vulnerability.* and AV—*area of vulnerability.* He explained that there was always a point in which an attacking force was temporarily at their weakest. He told me when the terrorists came back, their PV would be when they first came into the room. And that's when we were going to hit them—when they were close together, coming through the door, when it was hardest for them to maneuver."

Mitch had looked at the American through the haze of anger and grief that seemed to rise like a mist from his father's prone body. "It seemed absurd. Out of a roomful of people, virtually sentenced to death, the only ones willing to fight back were this one older man and me. A kid who planned to major in philosophy and religion in college. I didn't know for sure, but up to that point, I had been pretty certain I would follow in my father's footsteps. I had this faith in God, and it seemed it was only a matter of time before I received the call and..."

He laughed again, but there was no humor in it. "I received a call that day, that's for sure. My father and his words and his faith couldn't save us—he couldn't even save himself. But with a weapon like those machine guns... Yeah, I received a completely different kind of call."

Becca reached across the bench seat and found his hand. He held onto her tightly, seeing the lights from the truck stop up ahead, and knowing it was just a matter of minutes now before he had to walk away from her for good.

"The American—I wish I could remember his name!— he was ready for them, and when the terrorists opened the door, he launched himself at them. It was a suicide play. He knew he was going to be shot. But he'd hoped to grab one of their guns and throw it toward me, and somehow he did. And when that weapon came sliding across that tile floor toward me, I didn't hesitate. And I left my father's world for good, Bec. I picked it up, and I fired. I leaned on the trigger, like the American had told me. I pulled the muzzle down, and I swept it across those bastards, all jammed together in that doorway, and I sent 'em straight to hell."

A spray of bullets.

A spray of blood.

So much blood.

Blood...

"I killed all three of them. And with the hostages armed on the inside, we held off the terrorists until the marines stormed the building. The American died on the way to the hospital. He and my father were the only casualties among the hostages."

"I don't know," Becca's voice was quiet in the darkness. "I might be tempted to call you a casualty, too."

"Yeah," Mitch said just as quietly. "In a way, I guess I died that day, too." He pointed to the exit that was approaching. "We could use some gas—and a cup of coffee would be something of a blessing right about now."

He could feel her eyes as she glanced over at him, and he carefully kept his gaze on the road in front of them.

In silence, she took the exit, braking at the Stop sign at the end of the long ramp. The truck stop was brightly lit, and she pulled into the parking lot, into a slot by the restaurant door.

She still had his hand, and when he would have turned away to open the door and climb out, she tugged him toward her. She pulled him into her arms, wrapping him in her sweetness and warmth.

"Thank you so much for telling me," she whispered, and she kissed him.

Mitch lost himself in the softness of her lips. That she would want to kiss him after all he'd just told her was amazing to him. And he knew more than ever that she wouldn't willingly go back to the Lazy Eight without him.

So he held her tightly and, without her knowing it, kissed her goodbye as gently as he could.

"I met Mitch Shaw at his father's funeral." Admiral Jake Robinson sat at the head of the table in the Gray Group's makeshift temporary headquarters at Kirtland Air Force Base in Albuquerque.

After calling Captain Catalanotto, Lucky and his team had been ordered to Holloman AFB, pronto, where a special transport had been waiting to whisk them up to Kirtland. It was the power of the Admiralcy in action. When they landed, they were escorted posthaste from the transport to this office, where they were joined by the captain, and Blue McCoy and Crash Hawken, the two SEALs from Alpha Squad who'd been sent to look for Mitch in Albuquerque.

"The vice president of the United States was at the funeral, too," the admiral told them. "And he shook the kid's hand and told him he was very sorry for his loss, told him there was going to be a ceremony in Washington, and the president of the United States was going to present Mitch with a special version of the Medal of Honor.

"And Mitch looked him right in the eye and told him thanks, but no thanks. He didn't deserve it. His father did, though. His father had died believing in the power of good over evil. The way Mitch saw it, the Reverend Randall Shaw had died sticking to his belief that nonviolence was the only option. Mitch, however, believed that by killing those terrorists, he'd given in and used evil to fight evil. He didn't want a medal for that.

"I introduced myself to him," Jake told them. "I wasn't an admiral at the time, but I'd been heavily decorated from my time in Vietnam. Still it was obvious that he wasn't interested in talking to me—until I told him I was a friend of Senior Chief Fred Baxter, the man who'd died helping Mitch save those hostages' lives. After I told him that, he took a walk with me, and I had the chance to tell him that Freddie was a Navy SEAL, told him a little bit about what that meant. And I told him that Fred was getting a medal, too. Posthumously. And Fred deserved that medal, absolutely, without a doubt. Because Fred Baxter, like me, like most SEALs, believed in something just as absolutely as Mitch's father believed in nonviolence. Fred believed in the power of gray."

Jake looked around his room. "You guys know this. In our world there's no such thing as black and white.

There's no clear line between right and wrong, especially when the outcome affects millions of lives. And so we operate in that narrow band of gray. Mitch was fifteen when he first stepped into that world.

"I don't know what he's doing right now," the admiral continued. "I don't know what the hell he's up to, but I can tell you with complete confidence, gentlemen, that he has *not* sold out, that he remains faithful to both God and country. He's worked closely with me since the conception of the Gray Group—in fact, he gave it its name. I trust him as I trust myself. There *will* be an explanation for his behavior, I guarantee it. I know you're not going to like this, but I suggest we sit tight, give him space to operate, and wait for him to contact us."

Lucky looked at Joe Cat, waiting for the captain to make an alternative suggestion. When he was noticeably silent, Lucky cleared his throat. "Admiral. Sir. Aren't we, um, forgetting about that plutonium floating around out there, about to fall into the wrong hands?"

Jake stood up. "Gray Group operatives have infiltrated an arms dealer's organization—the very one that will be attempting to broker the deal. The client's a political faction in an Eastern European country and we've been keeping tabs on them as well. The exchange was supposed to take place yesterday, but the seller cancelled at the last minute—which leads me to believe that the seller no longer has possession of the plutonium, and that Mitch Shaw does. But a new meeting's been set up for tomorrow. In Santa Fe. Which means that sometime before tonight and tomorrow, Mitch could well be calling in for some help. And gentlemen..." He looked around the table, meeting each of the SEALs' eyes.. "When he needs us, we'll be ready."

* * *

Becca knew what Mitch was doing. She knew, without a doubt, that he was kissing her goodbye. If she let him get out of the truck, he was as good as gone.

She held him tightly, knowing that if she didn't speak now, she'd regret it for the rest of her life.

"Don't go." Her voice shook.

He didn't try to pretend he didn't know what she meant. "I have to, Bec."

She was glad he didn't pull back, glad he couldn't see the tears in her eyes as she did the one thing she swore she'd never do—beg a man to stay. "We can start over. Go away together. We can hide. There's got to be a million places two people can lose themselves in this country. No one will ever find you, we'll be careful and—"

"Spend the rest of our lives looking over our shoulders? That's no way to live."

Becca closed her eyes, feeling her tears escape. "Please…"

"I can't. Not knowing who's after me, or why… It would drive me crazy. Bec, I have to find out who I am." He pulled away from her gently, opening the glove compartment and taking a folded piece of paper out. "I wrote this letter," he told her. "It's to Ted Alden. I've explained the situation as best as I could, and I've asked him to invest the money he wanted to give me in your ranch— the one I know you're going to buy someday. However he wants to set it up is fine. I want you to send this to him along with that check he wrote, okay?"

"No," she said. She wouldn't take it from him, so he put it back in the glove box. "No, it's not okay!"

He opened the door and stepped out into the night. "I love you."

It was what she'd both dreaded and hoped to hear.

Becca squinted at him through both the glare from the overhead light and her tears. "Then how can you *leave?*"

He lifted his case up and out of the truck, his face in the shadows. "How could I stay?"

He closed the door, and Becca scrambled out of the driver's side, wiping furiously at her tears. "Mitch!"

But the parking lot was empty.

He was already gone.

Chapter 15

Mitch couldn't sleep.

He'd toyed with the idea of not getting a motel room because he knew he'd never get his eyes shut tonight.

The Albuquerque address on the passport hadn't been real. Oh, it was a residential neighborhood, but—surprise, surprise—the house number didn't exist. And even though Mitch had walked around in the darkness for close to two hours, he hadn't felt even the faintest flash of familiarity from anything.

He'd walked back to the part of town that was lit by cheap motels, late-night bars and all-night coffee shops. He'd gotten his coffee to go, and paid the extra money for the motel room.

Not because he wanted to sleep.

Because he wanted to look through his suitcase again. See if there was anything he'd missed.

So now he sat on the sagging double bed, surrounded

by the contents of his leather case. His...bag of tricks?
Grab your bag of tricks, Lieutenant...

Lieutenant?

He'd set the weapons aside, but now he picked up the
MP-5. His "room broom." It fit comfortably, easily in his
hands.

His father would have been shocked.

He put it down, and unrolled his jeans. He hadn't had
a chance to go through the pockets and...

He nearly missed it. It was a small photograph in the
back pocket. The torn corner of a picture—just the head
and shoulders of a man.

The face was shockingly familiar.

Shaggy hair, full beard, florid features...

Casey Parker.

The name came to him in a flash of certainty that
chilled him to the bone.

Casey Parker was the man who had shot Mitch in that
Wyatt City alley. He was also the man who had come to
the Lazy Eight ranch, looking for the package that was
supposed to be waiting for him there—the package Mitch
had taken in his stead.

He still had the key that had been in that envelope. He
was carrying it in his pocket.

Mitch took it out and looked at it again. It was, without
a doubt, the kind of key a bank issued with a safe-deposit
box. What was in that box, Mitch could only guess.
Money, maybe. Or the take from some robbery. Jewelry.
Something valuable. Something that had started all this.
Something Parker had already tried to kill Mitch over.

And it was only a matter of time before Parker returned
to the Lazy Eight, looking for this key.

He wouldn't find it, but he would find Becca.

All alone. Unsuspecting. Virtually defenseless.

Mitch threw his things back into his leather case and jammed his feet into his boots. He had to get to the Lazy Eight.

Before it was too late.

Becca opened the ranch office early, just as the sun was coming up.

The sky was heavy with clouds. A storm was brewing. Most likely it would rain hard and heavy starting sometime within the next few minutes and clear up before lunch.

She wished she could say the same about her own dark disposition.

She'd spent a restless night, tossing and turning in her bed, and she'd been exhausted when her alarm had gone off. But it was better to get up and get to work instead of hiding out by sleeping in. Besides, this way she'd be good and tired when tonight rolled around. And maybe she'd fall straight into a dreamless sleep without even thinking once about Mitch.

Hah. Fat chance.

But she had to stop thinking about him. It was entirely likely she would never see him again, so she'd better learn to stop thinking about him. She knew she could do it. And once she learned not to think about Mitch, well, then she'd be on her way to learning to live without him. She could do anything, if she put her mind to it.

And right now she'd stop thinking about Mitch by focusing on all the work she had to do to catch up around here.

The storm clouds were so dark, Becca had to turn on the light over her desk just to see.

She sat down, uncertain of where to start, and knowing

without a doubt that such a dilemma wasn't worth crying over. Yet here she was, on the verge of tears. Again.

Damn Mitch.

And double damn herself for being so stupid as to fall in love with him.

Work had piled up in her in-basket over the days she'd been gone. Her E-mail alone was enough to occupy her for most of the morning. She'd start with that. She scrubbed at her eyes and blew her nose soundly. She was determined to work in the office only until ten. If she could get enough done now, she'd give Belinda the morning off and take the guests on the morning trail ride herself, provided the weather complied. She could use some quality time with Silver and...

The office door squealed as it opened, and she closed her eyes, desperately hoping that whatever problem was walking into the office at 5:06 a.m. could be dealt with quickly and efficiently and...

"Becca, thank God."

Mitch? She turned around so quickly, she nearly fell out of her chair. It *was*. Mitch had come back.

As she stood up, he dropped his case on the floor and moved toward her, coming right up and over the counter that separated them. And then she was in his arms.

"Are you all right?" he asked, pulling slightly back to look down into her eyes. He touched her face, her hair. "Please tell me you're all right."

She nodded. Yes. Now she was very, very all right. "Thank you," she said, kissing his neck, his ear. "Thank you, *thank* you for coming back."

He caught her mouth with his, and the fire that raged to life between them ignited instantly. And as the entire world seemed to swirl and shift around them, as Becca melted against him, she wondered how she could even have *thought* she could learn to live without him.

And in that instant, she knew the awful truth. She'd found her true love. And he loved her, too. Given the opportunity, Mitch would stay forever.

Please, please, give them the opportunity...

He pulled away from her far sooner than she would have liked. "Becca, I remembered something."

She could tell just from looking at him that it wasn't something good.

"It was Casey Parker who shot me. I still don't remember why, but he meant to kill me. And I've got to believe that he'll be coming back here. He's going to want his key."

And Becca knew. Mitch hadn't come back to the Lazy Eight because he wanted to. He'd come because he'd had to. If he'd thought she was safe, she *would* never have seen him again.

But he *had* come back. And she had to make the most of this opportunity to convince him to stay.

Mitch released her, and she let him go, watching as he picked up the phone on Hazel's desk. "What's the sheriff's number?"

"It's right there," she told him. "On that list. Mitch, we've got to talk."

He found it and punched in the buttons.

"What are you doing?" she asked, realizing that he was dialing the sheriff's number.

He was listening to the phone ring, and he met her gaze only briefly. "Calling the sheriff."

"Obviously. Mitch—"

"Yeah, hi," Mitch said into the telephone. "I'm calling from the Lazy Eight Ranch. We've got a major problem here, and I was hoping the sheriff could come out as soon as possible…?''

He wanted the *sheriff* to come out here? If the sheriff got involved, then Mitch would…

''Well, let's start with attempted murder,'' Mitch said to whoever was on the other end of the phone. ''Is that worth waking up the sheriff over?''

Mitch would have to admit to having amnesia. He would be investigated. His fingerprints would probably be run through the computer and…

And then they'd finally know who he was.

But so would the sheriff.

''We'll be waiting for him in the ranch office,'' Mitch said, and hung up the phone. He turned to face Becca, answering her before she even asked. ''I'm turning myself in.''

She shook her head, unable to say anything, unable even to speak.

''I thought hard about it the entire way out here. It's the right thing to do,'' he told her. ''I should've done this weeks ago. I still don't remember much of anything, but that doesn't mean I shouldn't have to take responsibility for the things that I've done.''

''You're jumping to conclusions here.'' She finally found her voice. ''You may not have done anything wrong at all.''

''How about possession of illegal firearms?'' he asked. ''We'll start there. Somehow I doubt we'll end there, though.''

He went out into the main part of the office, walking around the counter this time. Becca followed. ''You don't have to do this.''

''Yes, I do.'' He pulled open the screen door. ''I'm

going to get my .22 from the bunkhouse lockup, so I can turn it in with the weapons in my bag.''

The first crack of thunder rumbled in the distance, ominous and foreboding as Becca followed him outside into the eerie early morning light, and back toward the barn. The wind was starting to kick up, sending clouds of dust scooting across the dry yard.

''This is really the only way I can start over,'' he told her. ''Yes, it feels like I've been given a second chance, because I don't remember my past, but it's not real, Bec. If I really want a second chance, I've got to do it right. And that means facing up to whatever I've done, and paying the price. Lord knows I don't want to go back to prison, but if I have to, so be it. Because when I get out— if I get out—*that's* when I'll be able to make a fresh start.'' He smiled at her, that crooked half smile she'd come to know so well. ''Besides, I'd face more than hard time to be sure that you were safe.''

Becca caught his arm. ''That's why you're doing this, isn't it? Because you don't think I'll be safe from this Casey Parker if you don't.''

He gently pulled free. ''It's also the right thing to do.''

Becca watched as he disappeared into the bunkhouse. ''Dammit, Mitch!'' She ran to catch up with him, following him inside, lowering her voice, aware that the other ranch hands would be rising soon. ''You don't even know that Parker's going to come back here.''

''Becca, go back to the office.''

She rounded the corner that led to the common area and the ranch hands' private lockers, and stopped short.

Mitch was standing absolutely still, staring down the muzzle of a very, very deadly-looking handgun. It was bigger than the one Dirty Harry used in her favorite Clint

Eastwood movies, big enough to blow an extremely fatal hole in Mitch, should the man holding it pull the trigger.

And the man holding it looked as if he'd enjoy doing just that. Big and beefy, he had at least five inches and seventy pounds on Mitch. But he was older, with a beard that was graying, and eyes that seemed almost lost in the fleshy folds of his face. Casey Parker. It had to be.

"She's not part of this," Mitch said to the man.

"She is now," he answered.

Becca saw Mitch's gaze flicker toward the lockup where his handgun was stored, saw him reject the option of going for it, thank God. One gun was bad enough.

"You know why I'm here," Parker said.

"I guess you want the key." Mitch glanced at Becca. His eyes were filled with meaning, filled with a private message. *Be ready to run.*

"Good guess," Parker said.

And she knew exactly what Mitch was planning to do. Point of vulnerability. Just as the man he'd called "the American" had done, he was going to wait for Parker's PV and he was going to attack, giving Becca a chance to run to safety. And, like the American in his dream, it was likely that Mitch would be shot and killed.

Becca shook her head, just a tiny shake, barely discernible. *No.*

"Becca will have to go and get it," Mitch told the man. "I left it in the glove compartment of her truck."

Parker laughed. "Maybe we should try this again." He swung his gun so that it pointed directly at Becca's chest. "Give me the key."

Mitch nearly stopped breathing. He knew it didn't take much, just the gentle pressure from a finger, to end a human life. And as long as Parker had that gun aimed at

Becca, it could happen. In half a heartbeat, she could go from living to dead.

Thunder rolled, closer still.

"My pocket," Mitch said through a throat tight with fear. "It's in my front pocket."

"Get it. Move slowly."

"Point the gun away from her first."

"Give me the key first," Parker countered.

Mitch did, holding it out to Parker on the palm of his hand. If only he could get him to come close enough...

But Parker laughed. "Toss it to me. *Gently.*"

"Point the gun away from her." Mitch knew it was futile. He knew Parker was going to keep that gun aimed at Becca until this was over. And how it was going to end, he didn't want to try to guess. The sheriff was due to arrive any minute, and he didn't even know if *that* would be a help or a hindrance. All he knew was that the next time Parker aimed that gun at him, he was going to rush him, take him down, take him out. Before the bastard had a chance to hurt Becca.

"Toss it," Parker demanded.

Mitch did. He watched the gun while Parker caught and examined the key, but although it swerved, it swerved only slightly.

Becca had been silent all this time, but now she spoke up. "Mitch doesn't remember you. He doesn't remember anything from before he was shot. He doesn't even know his last name. If you just leave, we won't tell anyone or—"

Parker laughed. "Oh, that's good. I suppose you'll give me your promise, too, huh? Well, for someone who doesn't remember, Mitch here has sure managed to screw me up big-time. No, we're going to go for a ride in your truck, Becca dear. Come over here."

Thunder cracked nearly overhead.

"Becca, don't move." Mitch knew that once Parker had Becca close enough to press the gun against her head, the man would never be vulnerable enough for Mitch to attack.

"Becca, come here," Parker said again. "Now."

He swung his gun toward Mitch, who knew this was it. It was now or never.

But before he could launch himself at the gun, Becca dashed forward and got in the way.

And *now* turned bleakly into *never.*

"Out the door," Parker ordered Mitch, Becca tight against him, the gun tucked up under her arm, nearly completely concealed from anyone who might be outside in the yard. "Into the truck."

It was starting to rain. Just a few big drops here and there from a heavy green sky that looked ready to open up. Lightning forked, making the air seem to crackle around them.

Becca's truck was parked near the office. Mitch took his time walking toward it, staring down to the end of the long driveway, praying for a sign of the sheriff's headlights through the unnatural early-morning darkness.

Nothing.

"Get in the truck—you're going to drive," Parker told him. "Keep your hands on the steering wheel where I can see 'em at all times. Take 'em off, and I'll shoot her right here."

Mitch got in and clung to that wheel. *I'll shoot her right here.* Instead of waiting to shoot her out in the middle of nowhere, where no one could see or hear.

Parker pushed Becca into the middle of the bench seat and climbed in behind her, his gun never moving from her. If he squeezed the trigger, a bullet would go straight into her heart.

"Start the truck," he ordered Mitch.

The keys were hanging in the ignition, where Becca had left them. Ranch rules—in case someone needed to move the truck fast. "I'll have to take my hand off the steering wheel," Mitch said. He had to get Parker to point the gun at him instead of Becca.

"Just one hand," Parker warned him. "Do it."

Mitch could feel Becca's shoulder pressed against him, her leg against his thigh. He started the engine, flipped on the windshield wipers and headlights, put the truck into gear.

"Head away from the buildings," Parker ordered.

Mitch pulled off the driveway, pointing the truck toward Finger Rocks, toward the dry riverbed. If it wasn't flooding yet, it would be soon. And maybe...

They drove in silence for quite some distance, the rain starting to fall harder now against the windshield.

Mitch glanced up. He could see Becca's eyes in the rearview mirror. She knew where he was heading, knew how deadly the arroyo could be.

"Don't get out of the truck," he told her.

Parker laughed at that. "You're in no position to be giving orders."

Mitch glanced into the rearview again, and she nodded. Her lips moved. *Love you.*

She thought she was going to die.

But she wasn't. Not if he could help it. Not even if he had to die himself to keep her alive.

"Stop up here," Parker finally said. "This is far enough."

Lightning flashed, and Finger Rocks loomed, still too far away. Mitch hadn't yet reached the edge of the dry riverbed. He could see up ahead that the water wasn't running. Yet. He just had to go a little farther…

The rain was starting to fall even harder on the roof of the truck, tiny bits and pieces of hail bouncing off the hood.

"I said, *stop*."

Mitch took his time hitting the brakes, slowing to a stop. Any second now the sky was going to open up in a deluge so severe, visibility was going to drop to close to zero. In the meantime, he kept his hands on the steering wheel where Parker could see them.

"Get out of the truck," Parker ordered.

Mitch leaned forward to look at him across Becca. "I'm going to have to take my hands off the steering wheel."

"One hand at a time," Parker said. "Move slowly. Open the door. And then step back from the truck—keep your hands where I can see them."

Mitch knew what *he'd* do if he were Parker. He'd make Mitch back far enough away so that when he pulled his gun from Becca's side, Mitch would be too far away to be able to attack. And he'd shoot Mitch from inside the truck, make sure he was dead before pulling Becca out, thus completely eliminating his point of vulnerability.

"I love you," he told Becca, needing her to know.

"Lovely," Parker said. "Move."

Mitch moved *very* slowly as he put the truck into park, still praying that the rain would help him out. *Please God…* If ever he needed a little divine assistance, it was now.

He opened the door and stepped out of the cab and moved back from the truck and…

God was on his side. Lightning cracked, thunder roared,

and the rain came down as if someone had turned on a giant faucet overhead. Mitch was instantly soaked.

And nearly completely hidden by the deluge.

He heard Parker swear as Mitch dropped to the ground, scrambling swiftly and silently beneath the body of the truck. "Where the hell did he go?"

"I'm not getting out," Mitch heard Becca say, bless her. "You're just going to have to shoot me right here— and get the truck all gross and smeared with blood. And that'll go over really well with the state police when you're stopped for that rear taillight that's out."

He heard Parker curse. "You're getting out of this truck if I have to pull you out by the hair!"

Becca screamed as he did just that, but she knew that she was right—he *wasn't* going to shoot her in the truck. He needed it to get wherever he was going. Probably only as far as to his own vehicle, parked somewhere outside of the ranch's fences. Still, the last thing he wanted to do was get her blood on his clothes. And he *was* going to kill her. She had no doubt of that.

The rain drummed on the roof, and the thunder cracking directly overhead was loud enough to wake the dead.

"Where did he go?" Parker demanded. "Where did that son of a bitch disappear to?" He pulled his gun out from her side to get a better grip on her and yanked her out into the rain.

This was it.

It was Parker's point of vulnerability. His gun waved in the air as she fought him, and Becca knew Mitch would be ready and waiting.

And he was.

He appeared with a flash of lightning, pulling Parker away from Becca, leaping on top of the man's gun as he wrestled him down into the arroyo.

The gun went off, and Mitch jerked—oh, God, he was hit. But he'd somehow managed to grab the gun and fling it, hard, into the rocks and rubble that made up the dry riverbed.

But it was dry no longer. The water was rising, and Becca peered through the rain as Mitch, despite being shot, splashed and wrestled with Parker.

"Get away!" he shouted, his voice barely audible over the roar of the rain. "Becca—take the truck and *go!*"

Chapter 16

Up on the riverbank, Becca stood still, frozen in the truck's headlights.

Dammit, why didn't she take the truck and get herself to safety?

Mitch fought Parker with a desperation, aware that his arm was bleeding, aware that the pain and the light-headedness he was already feeling from the shock were putting him at a disadvantage, aware that his opponent was trying to get to the place where they'd both last seen his gun bouncing off the rocks.

Parker was relentless, hitting Mitch hard, again and again, in the spot where the bullet had nicked him.

Nicked was an understatement, but Mitch was well aware it could have been far worse. A weapon like that, fired at close range, could blow a man's arm clear off. He'd been lucky.

He'd be luckier still, if Becca would get in that truck and drive herself to safety.

Instead, as he elbowed Parker hard in the face, he saw her begin to pick her way down the slope of the hill, *toward* them.

Dammit!

Lightning flashed, illuminating Parker's bared teeth as the man tried to grab Mitch's throat. And right then and there the world seemed to shift.

And for the oddest fraction of a second, Mitch was back in that alleyway in Wyatt City, looking into Casey Parker's eyes an instant before he fired the bullet that was to wipe clean Mitch's memory.

And in that oddest fraction of a second, everything, *everything* came rushing back.

Stolen plutonium. An unlikely lead in New Mexico. Admiral Jake Robinson's covert Gray Group.

He was not a criminal, not a hired killer on the run from the law! He was Lieutenant Mitchell Shaw of the U.S. Navy SEALs.

There was no jail term in his future. There was only hope and sweet possibility.

And Becca.

With a burst of renewed energy, Mitch fought even harder.

Becca couldn't find the gun.

She'd seen it fall near this tumble of rocks, but in the pouring rain, it would have been hard to find her own feet. And that would've been *without* the water starting to rise. In just a few seconds it had gone from a slow trickle to ankle deep, the current tugging at her as it rose even higher.

The rain began to let up as swiftly as it had started, but the gun was as good as gone, the water now up to her knees.

She could see Mitch, still struggling with Casey Parker, his shirt stained bright red with his own blood. He was in serious danger of bleeding to death—that is, if he didn't drown first.

Parker was tiring, but then so was Mitch. But at least Mitch was on top—or at least he was until a current of water tossed them, pushing them over and Mitch underneath.

Oh, God!

She could see Mitch struggling, fighting and splashing to get free, to get air. But Parker was so much bigger than he was. And Parker wasn't bleeding from a gunshot wound.

Becca charged toward them, splashing and stumbling through the water, stopping only to pick up a rock large enough to do some damage when it connected with Casey Parker's head.

But the water was still rising and before she reached them, she was knocked off balance. As she struggled to regain her footing, Parker was pulled under. With a swirl of bubbles, both men disappeared downstream.

Becca crawled to the side of the now swiftly flowing river, bedraggled and gasping for air, barely getting out of the way of a chunk of wood being tossed along by the water. She remembered the rainbow-colored bruise Mitch had received from what he'd called a "glancing blow."

As if Casey Parker and his gunshot wound weren't dangers enough, Becca knew that the river could kill Mitch, too.

She struggled out of the water, and ran toward her truck, water squooshing from her boots. She started the engine with a roar, and drove, following the bend in the riverbed, shading her eyes against the rapidly lightening sky, praying as she searched for any sign of Mitch in the raging current.

Underwater.

It was the great equalizer in a fight that Mitch had been afraid he was starting to lose.

But underwater, the advantage spun once more in his direction. As a SEAL, he was at home beneath the water. And Parker—judging from his current floundering—could barely even swim.

Mitch went with the force of the river, using it instead of fighting it. He could tell when Parker's air ran out. He could tell by the way the man was twitching that Mitch had to get him up to the surface, to air, quickly, or he'd die.

It wasn't easy pulling the heavier man out of the current and onto the rocky shore. And the water was still rising, so he had to pull him—with only one good arm—even farther up, away from the running arroyo.

Parker was breathing. But just barely.

He was out cold, thank the Lord. Mitch wasn't sure he had another fight left in him.

"Mitch!"

He turned to see Becca running toward him. Sweet Becca. With her angel's eyes…

"Thank God, thank God!" She scrambled down the hillside. "Where were you hit?"

"Just my arm. Only a nick." Lord, he was cold.

She was furious. "Only a…! Mitch, this is not *only a nick!*"

He'd lost a lot of blood. That would explain the cold.

"I'm all right," he told her. "Bec, I remembered. I'm a SEAL. A Navy SEAL. Parker has possession of stolen plutonium from a military lab. I've been working a covert op for months, trying to track it down. I'm one of the good guys.''

She took off her T-shirt, which confused him for a moment until he realized she was using it to tie around his upper arm in a tourniquet.

''Can you make it to the truck?'' she asked him, her voice sounding as if it were coming from a great distance.

Maybe he *had* lost too much blood. Mitch pushed himself up, forcing himself not to succumb to the blackness that was giving him tunnel vision. ''What about Parker?''

Becca told him in a very unladylike way exactly what Parker could do with himself. ''The sheriff can come back for him.''

Mitch shook his head. ''No. I've been after him for too long. Get the key from his pocket, Bec. At least let me tie him up.''

He could see from her eyes that she was scared for him.

''Rope,'' he said. ''Please. I've been after this guy for months. I can't risk losing him now.''

''And I can't risk losing *you* now,'' she told him hotly. ''You're it for me, Mitch. It's you or no one. If you die—''

''I'm not going to die.''

''Promise?''

In his line of work, it wasn't good luck to make a promise like that. In his line of work, any kind of promise was hard to keep. But Mitch wanted to promise her everything he possibly could. ''Marry me, Becca.''

He'd shocked her. She stood up. ''I'm getting that rope.''

She vanished from the narrowing scope of his vision, and he floated—he wasn't sure how long, seconds probably—until she returned.

As Mitch watched, she hog-tied Parker with knots that

would've made any sailor envious, then searched through the man's pockets for the key. She held it up for Mitch to see when she'd found it, then stuffed it into her own jeans pocket.

And then she was beside Mitch, hauling him up, nearly carrying him to the truck.

His arm was starting to hurt, and the pain sent him spinning as she did everything short of throw him into the cab of the truck. He felt her fasten a seat belt around him.

And then they were moving, bouncing, seemingly soaring across the rough land. His tunnel vision was getting worse, his world turning to shades of gray.

"Stay with me, Mitch," Becca said, her voice tight. "Talk to me. Tell me what you remember. Do you remember everything? Childhood? First kiss? Senior prom? Where you spent last summer's vacation?"

"I don't know," he said. "I think so, but..."

"Tell me what a SEAL is."

"We're good in the water." Lord, it was such a struggle even to speak. "We go away a lot. Away on missions all the time. Do things I could never tell you about. Leave again, too soon. Not sure—as your friend—I can recommend you marry me."

She laughed at that. "Do you come back?" she asked.

"Always," he told her. "For you, I'd come back not just from hell, but from heaven, too."

"I'm going to hold you to that. Dammit, don't you close your eyes!" She was crying. He hadn't meant to make her cry. "Mitch, we're almost there. I'm going to have the sheriff call for a medical chopper to take you into Santa Fe."

"Admiral Jake Robinson," Mitch managed to say. "Call him for me?"

"Admiral Jake Robinson," she repeated.

"He's—"

"I'll find him," she promised.

"Don't forget—"

"Parker?" she finished for him. "I won't."

"That I love you," he said.

Her laughter sounded more like a sob.

And there was shouting. Becca's voice, loud, calling for medical assistance. Hazel, shrill. The sheriff's deep bass.

And Mitch gave in to the darkness.

Becca raked her fingers through her hair as she hurried down the hospital corridor, trying to tame her curls.

There had been no room for her in the medevac chopper, and she'd driven halfway to Santa Fe. She'd left the sheriff standing in the driveway with Casey Parker in custody, changed her sodden and bloodstained clothes, grabbed her cell phone and headed into the city.

She'd connected with Mitch's Admiral Robinson on her first try. She'd actually called the Pentagon—it seemed like the best place to look for a U.S. Navy admiral. She'd been put on hold when she'd said she was trying to reach Robinson, put on hold again when she mentioned to the young but very efficient-sounding assistant who came on the line that she was calling on Mitch's behalf.

And ten seconds later another man had picked up the phone. She'd spoken to him for close to a minute before she realized she was speaking to the admiral himself.

She gave him the story in a nutshell—Mitch's gunshot wound to the head and the resulting amnesia. His search for his identity. Today's nearly fatal run-in with the real Casey Parker. She'd told him that Mitch had probably already arrived at the hospital in Santa Fe, that she was rushing over there now, via truck. She'd told him she was sorry, but she couldn't talk any longer, she had to call the hospital to make sure Mitch was all right, when he'd asked her the color of her truck and the route she was taking. He told her to watch the sky—he'd send an air force chopper to scoop her up ASAP..

The chopper had landed right in the middle of the state road. She'd locked her truck and gotten to Santa Fe in minutes.

The nurse in the E.R. hadn't given her any information on Mitch's condition over the phone and Becca was running by the time she reached his room and...

She stopped short.

The most gorgeous blond woman she'd ever seen was sitting on the edge of Mitch's bed and holding his hand.

The most gorgeous blonde, nine-months-pregnant woman...

Oh, God.

She started to back away, trying to move silently, and ran into a very solid wall of a man.

"Hey." He, too, was blond—although his hair was more sunstreaked—and nearly as gorgeous as the woman. He was one of the men who had been in the van outside the bus station in Wyatt City. "Are you Becca Keyes? Mitch's friend?"

Mitch's *friend*. Becca nodded, unable to speak. It seemed that his marriage proposal had been a little hasty. Apparently he hadn't remembered *everything*.

He held out his hand. "Lt. Luke O'Donlon, Alpha Squad. My friends call me Lucky. Although I may have to give the nickname back after the hell of the past few weeks, the fact that Zoe Robinson isn't hovering anxiously at *my* bedside, and the added injustice that I didn't manage to meet *you* first."

He pushed her toward the door to Mitch's room.

"Come on. We're all under strict orders to bring you right in if we see you."

"But—" Zoe *Robinson?*

"Ms. Rebecca Keyes," the man named Lucky announced loudly as if he were a very proper English butler.

"Thanks, Jeeves," Mitch said dryly. He was smiling at her from his hospital bed. He still looked pale, but his arm was bandaged and he had an IV tube hooked into his hand.

And as Becca watched, the pregnant blonde moved gracefully from the bed, crossing the room to stand beside a uniformed man who couldn't be anyone other than Admiral Robinson.

But then Becca didn't look at anyone but Mitch. She crossed to his bed. "Are you all right?"

He held out his hand for her, and she took it. He tugged her down, and then he had his good arm around her.

"I needed a transfusion," he told her. "And afterwards, I felt so much better—"

"He tried to talk me into taking him back to your ranch," the Admiral interjected. "I'm Jake R—"

"Introductions later," his wife interrupted. "Everybody out."

Mitch's hand was in her hair, and she knew from his eyes that he was only waiting for the door to close before he kissed her.

But she didn't want to wait. She kissed him and kissed him, sweetly at first, then harder, deeper, infused with the fire his kisses always sparked.

When she pulled back, he was breathing hard. "I have to stay here overnight," he told her as if that were a total tragedy.

"I can wait," she told him. "I'm good at waiting."

She wasn't talking about just one night, and he knew it.

"There are things you need to know about me," Mitch said. "It wasn't fair of me to ask you to marry me before you know—"

"I know what I need to know." She pushed his hair back from his face. "You love me and I love you. Everything else is inconsequential." Becca laughed. "I never thought I'd get married, but..." She shrugged. "That was before I met you and discovered maybe true love isn't a myth."

He smiled at that, but his smile quickly dimmed. "I don't want to make you unhappy." He was so quietly serious, so intense.

"Good," she said. "Because it would make me really unhappy *not* to marry you. You know when I walked in here and saw what's her name? Zoe? I thought she was your wife."

He shook his head at that. "I told you, I knew I wasn't married."

"Yeah, but you also told me that you were this terrible criminal, and you'd spent time in jail and—"

"I *did* spend time in jail." He smiled at the look on her face. "It was part of a sting operation. I was trying to get close to the brother of a survivalist group leader. I was inside for nearly a month." His smile faded again. "See, these are the kinds of things that I do."

"Think," she said, "what fun it would have been knowing that I was there, waiting for you when you got out."

Mitch laughed. "I'm not sure *fun* is quite the right word."

"Yes," she said, "it is."

She kissed him to prove her point.

"We can make this work," she murmured. "I know we can. I've got forever—how about you?"

Mitch surrendered and kissed her. It was *definitely* worth a try. Because he loved her and she loved him. And like the lady said, everything else was inconsequential.

* * * * * *

Don't miss Silhouette's newest cross-line promotion,

Four royal sisters find their own Prince Charmings as they embark on separate journeys to find their missing brother, the Crown Prince!

Royally Wed

The search begins in October 1999 and continues through February 2000:

On sale October 1999: **A ROYAL BABY ON THE WAY** by award-winning author **Susan Mallery** (Special Edition)

On sale November 1999: **UNDERCOVER PRINCESS** by bestselling author **Suzanne Brockmann** (Intimate Moments)

On sale December 1999: **THE PRINCESS'S WHITE KNIGHT** by popular author **Carla Cassidy** (Romance)

On sale January 2000: **THE PREGNANT PRINCESS** by rising star **Anne Marie Winston** (Desire)

On sale February 2000: **MAN...MERCENARY...MONARCH** by top-notch talent **Joan Elliott Pickart** (Special Edition)

ROYALLY WED
Only in—
SILHOUETTE BOOKS

Available at your favorite retail outlet.

Silhouette ®

Visit us at www.romance.net

SSERW

MONTANA MAVERICKS
Big Sky Brides

Legendary love comes to Whitehorn, Montana,
once more as beloved authors

Christine Rimmer, Jennifer Greene and Cheryl St.John

present three brand-new stories in this exciting anthology!

Meet the Brennan women:
SUZANNA, DIANA and ISABELLE

Strong-willed beauties who find unexpected
love in these irresistible marriage of
covnenience stories.

Don't miss
MONTANA MAVERICKS: BIG SKY BRIDES
On sale in February 2000,
only from Silhouette Books!

Available at your favorite retail outlet.

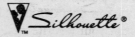

Start celebrating Silhouette's 20th anniversary
with these 4 special titles by
New York Times bestselling authors

Fire and Rain*
by Elizabeth Lowell

King of the Castle
by Heather Graham Pozzessere

State Secrets*
by Linda Lael Miller

Paint Me Rainbows*
by Fern Michaels

On sale in December 1999

Plus, a special free book offer inside each title!

Available at your favorite retail outlet
*Also available on audio from Brilliance.

Silhouette®
™ *Where love comes alive*™